Overwhelmed by passion

Giving himself no time to think, Max took what he'd wanted since arriving at Redrock. His lips crushed hers as he plundered her mouth.

For a long moment, Hope was too surprised to move, but as his tongue boldly entwined with hers, she sagged against him, relishing his kiss as if it were food and she were starving. She tried to pull away, but her body would not cooperate. It was reveling in sensations she'd experienced only in dreams.

Light flared deep in his blue eyes as he trailed kisses across her cheeks, brightening their color and blurring her pupils. Her chest tightened, spilling heat into her womb that weakened her knees. Her hands had somehow become entangled in his hair, combing the unexpectedly soft waves with sensual delight. . . .

The Beleaguered Earl

Allison Lane

A SIGNET BOOK

SIGNET
Published by New American Library, a division of
Penguin Putnam Inc., 375 Hudson Street,
New York, New York 10014, U.S.A.
Penguin Books Ltd, 27 Wrights Lane,
London W8 5TZ, England
Penguin Books Australia Ltd,
Ringwood, Victoria, Australia
Penguin Books Canada Ltd, 10 Alcorn Avenue,
Toronto, Ontario, Canada M4V 3B2
Penguin Books (N.Z.) Ltd, 182–190 Wairau Road,
Auckland 10, New Zealand

Penguin Books Ltd, Registered Offices:
Harmondsworth, Middlesex, England

First published by Signet, an imprint of New American Library,
a division of Penguin Putnam Inc.

First Printing, February 2000
10 9 8 7 6 5 4 3 2 1

PUBLISHER'S NOTE
This is a work of fiction. Names, characters, places, and incidents either are
the product of the author's imagination or are used fictitiously, and any resemblance to actual persons, living or dead, business establishments, events, or
locales is entirely coincidental.

BOOKS ARE AVAILABLE AT QUANTITY DISCOUNTS WHEN USED TO PROMOTE
PRODUCTS OR SERVICES. FOR INFORMATION PLEASE WRITE TO PREMIUM MAR-
KETING DIVISION, PENGUIN PUTNAM INC., 375 HUDSON STREET, NEW YORK, NEW
YORK 10014.

Chapter One

Abandoning the curb he'd held on his temper for the past two days, Maxwell Longford, Earl of Merimont, slammed his study door hard enough to rattle the wall. Emptying a glass of brandy in one long gulp, he poured another, then paced the floor.

Damn Montcalm! Why did he have to come the tyrant over everyone within reach? And damn himself for thinking his father might have mellowed. The Marquess of Montcalm would never mellow. He was a disapproving perfectionist who demanded instant obedience to even the stupidest orders.

"Never!" he spat, emptying and refilling his glass. How could he live with himself if he abandoned his hopes, his dreams—his very soul—to a hidebound fool?

You exaggerate.

"Balderdash!" He shook his head to dislodge his conscience.

The man hated independent thought and never missed an opportunity to prohibit pleasure—like that incident five years ago.

He knew better than to complain near his father, but conflicting invitations from two friends had irritated him into reckless grumbling. Montcalm had overheard, disparaged both gentlemen, then ordered him to remain at Widicomb Abbey for the rest of the summer.

That was when Max had moved permanently to London, a change he'd never regretted. Remaining at home would have locked him into perpetual childhood, for Montcalm refused to admit that he was capable of making his own decisions. If he'd stayed, he would have become an abject creature with no will or mind of his own.

And that would bode ill for the marquessate when it finally came into his hands.

Or so he had claimed at the time, for protecting his inheritance was a noble goal. The truth was less lofty. He'd been tired of his father's demands and the constant reminders of past blunders. The only way to find peace had been to leave.

He reached for the brandy decanter, then shook his head. Fogging his brain would solve nothing. Only clear thinking would extricate him from the bog tugging at his knees.

His latest trek home had been a disaster because of bad planning and worse execution. He should have known that his summer in Brighton would still be an issue. Montcalm hated Prinny, considering him disloyal to the king and a shocking influence on impressionable young men. He'd opposed the Regency bill last winter and dismissed Brighton as a den of iniquity because of Prinny's patronage. So he interpreted Max's visit as a personal insult.

But that wasn't his only mistake, he admitted, kicking aside a stool so he had more room to pace. Montcalm respected no opinions but his own. He even ridiculed friends who ignored his advice, so why would he treat his son any differently? Never mind that Max was thirty years old and considered intelligent and sensible by those who truly knew him. By now Montcalm was too set in his ways to change.

He cursed himself for not recognizing that truth earlier. He'd been so wrapped up in his own plans that he'd forgotten the nature of his opponent. So he'd made his request to a man already nursing a dozen grievances, had begun his argument in the middle instead of the beginning, then had allowed Montcalm to divert him into side issues that touched off new disputes.

Thus he was now in a worse position than before.

Yet approaching his father had been his only option, he admitted, dropping into a chair. If only he had kept his head and introduced his request differently! But his mind had ceased working the moment he'd crossed the Abbey's threshold.

"Idiot!" he murmured.

His father had been in the hall when he'd arrived, giving him no time even to wash away the dust of travel.

"So you finally came home," he'd growled. "Have you stopped toadeating that fat popinjay, or are you fleeing your creditors again? I will never forget the ignominy of having to haul you out of the River Tick."

The words had stung, as they'd been meant to. Only once had he overspent his allowance—ten years ago, and by a paltry ten guineas—but Montcalm never let him forget it, decrying his profligacy to everyone he knew. The complaints made him seem incompetent, though in truth his allowance was barely half of what his friends enjoyed.

"Of course not," he'd protested. "But I—"

"Then you are headed for another of your disgraceful hunting parties. Wasting the summer consorting with fools was bad enough, but this is beyond bearing. Have you no care for the family name?" With that, the man had launched his favorite tirade, decrying the calumny Max was heaping upon a name that had been respected for centuries. He interpreted every incident in the worst light, accepted exaggerated rumors as truth, and even believed that the latest parody of society's young bucks depicted Max instead of mixing his funniest scrapes with those of a dozen others. Montcalm conveniently ignored the very real scandals perpetrated by previous marquesses—such as his grandfather, who had fleeced more than one unsuspecting greenling, and a more distant ancestor, who had fled the country after killing a baron.

Max had been unwilling to endure an hour of the same old complaints, so he'd interrupted—another serious misjudgment, he admitted now. "I wish to run Dearborn," he'd said, naming the poorest of the family estates. "It could be—"

Montcalm's face had purpled. "Never!" he'd hissed. "I won't have you conducting your debaucheries on my land. I have put up with your nonsense long enough, Maxwell. You must settle down and prove that you are worthy of your breeding."

"Exactly. Dearborn could become far more producti—"

"You will obey your father! Cease your drunken rev-
els and your despicable raking. Remain at home where
I can prevent you from making a greater fool of yourself.
How can I hold my head up when I hear your name on
every tongue? It is long past time that you grew up."

Max rubbed his temples, trying to block Montcalm's
final tirade from his mind, but the charges echoed as
they had for two days—*profligate . . . fool . . . wastrel . . .
embarrassment to the noble family of Longford . . . wish
you had never been born. . . .*

He'd heard them a hundred times before, but this time
Montcalm had gone a step further. Instead of ordering
him to give up his London rooms and return to Widicomb—which he'd done at every meeting for five
years—he had canceled Max's allowance to force obedience. With the new quarter due in less than a month,
he must find another source of income if he was to remain free.

"I won't return to Widicomb," he swore, again pacing
the floor. He would flee the country before he'd give his
father that satisfaction. Living at home would land him
in Bedlam in a month. He couldn't tolerate constant
argument, abandoning his dreams, or listening to his father's outdated ideas. Reaching accommodation was impossible, for the man heeded no one and never changed
his mind.

Max's reputation was an example. He might be a little
rakish and indulge in occasional pranks, but so did his
friends, and he was welcomed everywhere. He was no
saint, but neither was he the profligate his father depicted. In truth, he was more serious than many heirs to
great titles.

Heirs were rarely allowed to do anything productive,
but he was becoming bored with idleness. He wanted to
practice estate management so he would be ready to
handle his inheritance—which was what had prompted
this latest trip home. He had meant to describe his interest in agriculture and ask to run Dearborn.

"I'll find another way," he swore, again pacing the
room.

He had to. Enduring another thirty years under his father's thumb would drive him to an early grave.

Donning what she hoped was a cheerful smile, Hope Ashburton carried a dinner tray into her mother's bedchamber. This chill was the latest in a long line of ailments that had attacked in recent years. The lady spent more time in bed than on her feet.

"Squire Foley brought you some lovely pork jelly," she announced, setting the tray on a table. "It should have you up in no time. Everyone swears by its restorative powers."

Her mother shrank into the pillows. "You should not have accepted it, Hope. It makes us beholden," she whispered. "Who knows what he will demand in return?"

"One jar of pork jelly hardly creates an obligation." She pulled her chair closer to the bed. "Helping one's neighbors in times of trouble is a friendly gesture that requires no recompense. Did you expect payment for visiting his son when he broke his leg last year? Billy might have remained abed far longer if your efforts had not kept him quiet, as his father knows quite well."

"It was nothing."

"Not according to the squire. He remains grateful."

"So he claims, but I saw how he looked at you the last time he called. Never trust men, Hope. Especially when they smile and bear gifts. They are scheming liars who always want something in return."

"Do not fret yourself into a megrim, Mama. He flirts with all the girls, for he needs a mother for his children. But I have no use for a marriage of convenience, as you well know. So we will accept this gift as recompense for entertaining Billy."

Her mother gasped for breath as she struggled to sit, raising new fears in Hope's heart. If illness had exhausted her this early in autumn, what would happen when winter descended?

"Eat, Mama," she urged gently. "You need to build your strength. I do not like the sound of your cough. Nor do I like your lethargy. If you don't make a firmer effort to recover, I must petition Uncle Edward to send us a London doctor."

"No!" The thin face paled alarmingly. "If he learns that I am ill, he might send one of his servants to help us—or come himself. How can you risk such persecution?" She suddenly blanched. "What if he locked me away, leaving you at his mercy? Don't ever ask a favor of him, Hope. He is evil and will turn any weakness against us." A coughing spasm cut off her voice.

"Then eat, Mother," urged Hope, already regretting her words. This was the worst attack yet. Mentioning her uncle had produced a dangerous amount of agitation. She would never petition him, of course, especially when illness made her mother vulnerable. But she had hoped to spark some interest in recovering.

And her empty threat had done some good, she decided half an hour later. Her mother had consumed more food than in the last three days combined.

Hope bit back a sigh, for their roles had reversed in recent years. Despondency made her mother timid and indecisive, forcing Hope to take charge of the house, nurse her through increasingly serious ailments, and handle Uncle Edward's calls.

She shivered.

Each new illness brought the end closer. One day there would be no recovery, and she would be on her own. Not that it would relieve her of other responsibilities, but she needed her mother's support to stifle her doubts and give her courage.

Could she continue alone? She was twenty-six years old. Despite reading widely, she knew little of the world beyond this small corner of Devonshire. Once her mother was gone, she would have no one who could discuss ideas, share a moment of beauty, or commiserate over defeats. The future loomed as a lonely road leading nowhere.

She shook her head. Such thoughts would lead to melancholy, making it harder to carry on. Fretting was pointless. She would adjust to whatever fate had in store, and at least her home was safe. Grandfather had protected them from most of Edward's malice.

Thoughts of her grandfather stirred ancient dreams, forcing a sigh from her lips. If he had lived another year, she would have married, for he'd planned to bring her out in London.

Stop wishing for the moon, demanded her conscience. His death was fate's way of protecting her from misery. Life was better here, full of purpose and reward. Her mother needed her. Even the tenants needed her, for she was all that stood between them and Uncle Edward's spite

Unless he forces you to wed . . .

That was the fear she had been trying to ignore, she admitted. Once her mother was gone, he would give her to the worst man he could find. And not just to remove any claim she might make on him. He wanted her miserable, under the thumb of someone who would treat her like an animal.

This time the shiver sank icy claws deep into her chest.

She had learned much about men in the ten years since death had revealed how dangerous her childhood fantasies had been. Men were bad enough when contentedly pursuing their own interests, as her neighbors demonstrated all too often. But when forced to act against their wills, they became intolerable—like Uncle Edward; like her father; like others her mother had once known. Men were violent creatures who could never be trusted. Rank added an arrogance that worsened their natural tendencies.

So she welcomed spinsterhood. It meant she would never suffer as her mother had done.

"Rest, Mama," she murmured. "I will return in an hour to read to you." Hoisting the tray, she slipped from the room.

"How is she?" asked Mrs. Tweed when Hope reached the kitchen.

"The same, though she ate most of the food this time."

"Wonderful!" The elderly housekeeper clasped her hands to her breast. "I knew it wasn't serious. You fret too much."

"It is early days for rejoicing." Sometimes Mrs.

Tweed's optimism irritated her. "Her cough has moved deeper into her chest. This may turn into something worse."

"But she will recover. She is still young." Tears shimmered in her eyes. "I will never forget the day she arrived here—so thin and weak I feared she would lose the babe. That man was a bad one, as I knew from the moment I saw his—"

"Enough, Mrs. Tweed. Those days are far behind us. We will do what we can to aid Mother's recovery, but the outcome is out of our hands." She bustled about, dishing up dinner for herself and her three-person staff and trying to forget the past. But it was difficult.

She was weary of Mrs. Tweed's tales, which had intruded into every conversation for ten years. She saw no reason to dwell on her father now. Besides, the story had a happy ending, for the babe had survived. It was he who had died.

Her childhood had been quiet, with only her grandfather's annual visits to vary the routine. But his death had changed everything. Not only had it brought her uncle into her life, but for ten years she had rued that their last meeting had ended in harsh words.

For years, she had foolishly woven dreams of what life would have been like if her father had not died so tragically young. But her grandfather's last visit had destroyed those fantasies. He'd bared her father's crimes, believing she was old enough to hear the truth. In a burst of disbelief, she'd cursed him for maligning his own son. So he'd left—and died of an apoplexy on the way home. Her guilt had increased when her mother verified every one of his claims.

She had left childhood that day. Never again would she accept people's facades as truth. Even her grandfather must have feigned his affection, for he could not have enjoyed those annual reminders of his son's perfidy. Thus his visits must have been an unwanted duty.

Stop this maudlin prattle!

Her life was good. She had a roof over her head, clothes on her back, food in her stomach, and friends nearby. If a meager income meant she must cook and clean, it was a small matter. The highest sticklers might consider her position humiliating, but it was hardly a serious breach of propriety. And who were they to judge? Was she supposed to turn Mrs. Tweed and Rose off because they were too old to do a full day's work? While it was true that Mrs. Tweed was growing forgetful and Rose's rheumatism made it difficult to negotiate stairs, they had nowhere else to go and no money with which to support themselves.

So she kept the house running and took the years one at a time. Brooding on things she could not change served no purpose.

If only her mother's spirits would revive . . .

Max stumbled into Brook's near dawn. He had two days to find the next quarter's rent or he would be out on the street. Montcalm had placed a notice in the *Times* declaring that he would no longer pay his son's debts, making Max an instant pariah. Families with well-dowered daughters shunned him, his mistress looked at him askance, and several tradesmen now refused him service. Longfords rarely died young, so it would be years before he inherited his father's fortune.

He had regretfully postponed any hope of running his own estate and turned to finding a steward's position. Implementing Coke's reforms on another man's land would not be as satisfying, but at least he would be doing something he enjoyed.

Or so he'd thought. Harvest was not the ideal time to look for a job, though his luck would have been out anyway, he admitted, handing his hat to the porter. Heirs of marquesses did not work—especially for others. He still prayed for success, but hope was dwindling fast.

He'd tried to stretch his purse by selling his horses, but they had brought less than he'd hoped. Though well trained, the team lacked speed, and their color had recently fallen out of favor. He could not bring himself to sell his books, and the proceeds would hardly pay his bills for long, anyway.

So he was penniless, or nearly so. His last ten guineas rested in his pocket. With two bottles of wine curling in his stomach, he no longer cared about tomorrow. Why not enjoy life while he could?

"That's enough for me," slurred Bainbridge, rising as Max entered the gaming room.

"And me," agreed Norton, collecting his winnings.

"Anyone else care for whist?" asked Ashburton, shuffling the deck.

Max shrugged, but took a seat. Brook's was noted for deep play. Ten guineas wouldn't last beyond a single game, and no one would accept his vowels after Montcalm's announcement. But he might as well go down fighting. A loss would change nothing, but a win . . .

As dawn filtered around the window draperies, he stared at the mound of vowels in front of him—five hundred guineas, which could stretch for two quarters, if he was careful.

Quit while you're ahead, whispered his conscience.

Lady Luck is with you tonight, answered Temptation. *Six months isn't much of a reprieve.*

It's better than nothing, countered his conscience. *By then you can convince someone to give you a chance.*

"One more game," he murmured in compromise.

He regretted his words almost immediately. Brandy was turning his thoughts to gibberish. The room brightened and dimmed, making it difficult to see. His ears roared, drowning most conversation.

"I'm for bed," announced Timmons, scribbling a vowel.

His voice pierced the fog shrouding Max's senses. He groped for consciousness, then wished he had not. At least an hour had passed. His winnings had dwindled to a single vowel for twenty guineas.

"I must cut my losses," said Peterson morosely. "Lady Luck has obviously deserted me tonight."

"A game of piquet, Merimont?" asked Ashburton.

"It's growing late," he murmured. *Later than ever,* he silently acknowledged, cursing himself. He'd just thrown away his reprieve.

"One hand," Ashburton insisted, nodding at the heap of vowels at his elbow. "I'll stake my winnings and Redrock House. No points. Winner take all."

Max stared.

Ashburton shrugged. "Don't you want a chance to recoup?"

"I've nothing to bet."

"I'll take a vowel."

"You know my father won't advance me a shilling."

Ashburton's gaze sharpened. "You could bring him round if you wanted to. I offered you a game, Merimont. Are you a man or a mealymouthed stripling?"

Don't do it!

What difference does it make? There must be a thousand guineas in that pile, and he's added an estate. If you walk out, you'll have to crawl home to Widicomb. Will groveling be any worse because of a debt? You might as well make Montcalm suffer for putting you in this position.

"Well?" demanded Ashburton.

Max glanced around the gaming room. Only a few men remained, and none was watching. Letting out a long breath, he scribbled a vowel for ten thousand guineas. "One game."

Dizziness attacked the moment he saw his hand. It would take a miracle to win with these cards. The image of facing his father with a ten-thousand-guinea debt churned his stomach until he feared he would cast up his accounts on the table.

Hope rekindled as they began the declarations. He scored, lost, scored again, won one trick, then two, lost the next . . .

Dizziness blurred his senses. He couldn't hear, couldn't see, couldn't think . . .

His head smacked onto the tabletop.

Ashburton laughed. "Damn! Worst hand I've had in my life."

Max pushed himself upright. Ashburton was shuffling cards.

"Who won?" asked Brummell as he and Alvanley sauntered over.

"Merimont." Ashburton shoved the vowels across the table and rose. "Well, I'm for home. Enjoy Redrock,

Merimont. She has great amenities." Laughing, he strolled toward the door.

Max stared at the vowels, hardly aware that Brummell and Alvanley remained behind him.

"Must have drained an extra bottle," murmured Brummell. "Not like him to laugh at defeat."

"It's even less like him to wager Redrock. You know how he feels about—"

Max ignored them, shakily counting markers. Ten thousand guineas above his own reckless note. An estate named Redrock. Peterson's team of matched bays. So Ashburton had been playing for high stakes all evening. No wonder Peterson had looked green when he quit; half of society coveted those horses.

Awareness filtered slowly through the haze still clouding his mind. He had no idea how, but he'd won.

He was free.

Chapter Two

Max was still reeling when he left Ashburton's solicitor. Redrock House was his. Twice the size of Dearborn, it included four tenant farms. Excitement nearly overwhelmed him. The harvest had just concluded, making it the ideal time to institute changes. He could study his new property at leisure before making decisions.

Study would be necessary, he admitted as he headed for a celebration at White's. Conditions varied from one place to another. Having never been to Devonshire, he did not know how it compared to Dearborn. Was the soil as fertile? What about wind, rain, and temperature? Perhaps the sheep that flourished there were a different breed than he knew.

But nothing could dull today's euphoria. Never again would he be at his father's mercy. Never again must he pinch pennies to maintain the image expected of a marquess's heir. Never again would he lie awake long after dawn, fearing that his father would break him.

Ten thousand guineas.

A productive estate.

He was free.

"Congratulations, Max."

He grinned at his closest friend, Blake Townsend, Earl of Rockhurst. "You heard?"

"With Brummell as witness, everyone in town has heard. You have the devil's own luck."

"Hardly. Devil's luck would have given me a reasonable father." Blake was the only one who knew the details of his battles.

"I must admit that I was surprised." Blake signaled a

waiter for more wine. "Deep gaming is not like you, Max."

"No." He exhaled in a long sigh as shock again rolled down his back. "I can only plead insanity. I should have quit after winning that five hundred guineas."

Blake raised his brow.

"I stayed in the game and lost nearly everything, then accepted an insane wager for another hand. I am not sure what happened, even now." He shrugged.

"Not sure?"

"Too much wine," he explained. "I all but passed out. Ashburton could have claimed victory and I wouldn't have known the difference," he added, seeing Blake's surprise.

"Living down to Montcalm's expectations?"

Max would have called out anyone else who made that insinuation, but this was Blake. And he remembered scrawling that vowel, so he nodded. "Not my greatest idea. My cards were marginal at best."

"The devil's own luck," repeated Blake.

"Hail the conquering hero," sang out Terrence Sanders, joining them. "Quite a change."

Max nodded. He had sat in this very room with these two only yesterday, lamenting the choice he faced—fleeing the country or surrendering his independence to his father's demands.

Other friends joined them. Wine flowed as they toasted his good fortune and laughed about other times when he had not been so lucky. But he ignored the jibes over embarrassing moments. Today was for celebration.

"So when will you inspect your new property?" asked Terrence.

"Soon." He stretched his legs toward the fireplace, basking in his newfound freedom. "The roads will be bad before much longer."

"Maybe we should come along," slurred Dornbras. "See what sort of place it is."

"Why not?" Max said, draining another glass as voices hummed around him.

"Rather a long jaunt."

"—least we can do is see if you won a pig in a poke."

"—warm my bed—"

"A little wine is hardly a celebration. Ought to do more."

"Capital suggestion, old boy. I've just the filly."

"You still keeping Annette?"

"I leave tomorrow for Leicestershire, so must regretfully decline."

"Say hello to your mother." Laughter followed Tuckleigh from the room.

Before Max realized what had happened, the plans were complete. Blake, Terrence, Dornbras, and Sir Reginald Dabney would join him at Redrock. Somehow, his mistress and four others had been included—he wasn't sure who was arranging that, though London was thin enough of company this time of year that plenty of courtesans would welcome a trip to the country.

His conscience poked him one last time, but he ignored it. He was starting a new life. Why not celebrate? He had never attended a bawdy house party, but this occasion required something special.

"I suppose you'll need a week or two to prepare and staff the house," said Dornbras.

"It shouldn't take that long. Ashburton's solicitor claims all is in readiness. I'll leave tomorrow. You can follow in a couple of days."

A week later, Max turned his curricle through Redrock's gates. The estate was nestled against a line of hills just north of Dartmoor. The land seemed wilder than Kent or Lincolnshire, stirring his senses and making him feel reckless.

He stifled the excitement that had been building since that night at Brook's. He could not afford more recklessness. It had already threatened his purse and affected his manners. He should have warned the caretaker that he was coming. He should also have written to his father.

The first oversight had been inadvertent. Between shock and an excess of wine, he hadn't remembered the formality until yesterday. By then there had been little point.

But ignoring his father had been deliberate. It would

be just like Montcalm to interpret the announcement as
an invitation to visit. Once here, he would take charge—
just as he'd done with Max's first team of horses. Dis-
trusting Max's judgment, he'd fired the groom who had
trained the team since their birth, then assigned their
care to his own trainer, who had promptly ruined their
mouths.

So he would deal with Montcalm later. At the moment, he had more urgent considerations. He'd outpaced
his baggage coach to make sure he arrived before his
friends, though with luck their journey was as plagued
with trouble as his had been—delaying rains, a lame
horse near Bath, a cracked wheel five miles later. But
they could arrive as early as this evening. He hoped the
staff was adequate.

He frowned as the drive entered a small wood. Several trees were dead or dying. Broken branches lit-
tered the ground, raising questions about the steward's
competence.

Other problems caught his eye as he emerged. By the
time he reached the house, he was furious. The park was
unkempt, with walls in disrepair and a drive so rutted it
would jolt teeth even in a well-sprung carriage. The
house was equally grim, its double wings tucked behind
a narrow facade boasting cracked windows and crumbling brick. Had Ashburton increased his profits by
allowing a house he never used to decay?

He hated men who raped the land to line their own
pockets. Landowners were caretakers for the future.
Even an unused house would eventually be pressed into
service for a relative or other dependent. How could
anyone justify such neglect?

But Ashburton might not be at fault, he admitted as
he climbed down from his curricle. If an owner never
visited, a dishonest steward could claim fictitious repairs,
appropriating the cost for himself.

He grimaced. If that were true, the house might be
unstaffed and in worse condition than it appeared. If
only he had been sober when the idea of a party had
come up. He might have been less willing to believe
another man's solicitor.

Frowning at the cracked paint on the door, he tried the latch. It was open.

The entrance hall seemed dark as a cave. But his eyes soon adjusted, bringing details into focus—satinwood paneling that showed signs of recent care, a marble floor, six-panel doors leading to rooms on either side, arched hallway openings just beyond, and a graceful stairway rising in the back.

Not until a gasp sounded in the shadows did he realize that a maid in a dark brown gown stood beneath the stairs, one hand clutching a feather duster, the other clasped to a generous bosom. She wore no cap. Auburn hair had come loose from a tight knot, framing her face in a nimbus of fire. Gray eyes held surprise and curiosity. His groin stirred.

"Who are—" she began, but he cut her off.

"What a charming picture, though it looks like you need help," he added, noting cobwebs near the ceiling.

Three steps brought him to her side, allowing light from the open door to turn her hair into a blazing inferno, driving all thought of cleaning from his mind. His arm circled her shoulders, holding her still while he studied that stunning face.

She gasped

Lust engulfed him, stronger than anything raised by Annette's most practiced tricks. "Lovely," he murmured. "A welcome addition to any staff. You would be an instant success at Covent Garden, sweetings. Gentlemen would overrun the greenroom to meet you."

Her head reached his eyes. She twisted away from his gaze, grazing his chin with an elegant ear. Surrendering to irresistible temptation, he nibbled it.

"Cad!" Her hand connected firmly with his cheek as she jerked out of his grip.

Only then did he realize that she'd been trying to escape. He clenched his fists against retaliating, for she had every right to protest his reckless assault. "My apo—"

She interrupted. "How dare you walk in without even knocking?"

"I own this house. Where is the caretaker?"

*   *   *

Hope stared at the stranger. He looked perfectly normal, if she ignored the fury seething in his eyes. Dark hair curled from under an elegant top hat, one strand escaping down his forehead to draw attention to brilliant blue eyes. A greatcoat broadened shoulders already wide enough to rival those of her most powerful tenant. But he was typical of the aristocracy—selfish, arrogant, and demanding. Might he become dangerous when she pointed out his error?

Fear choked her. He probably embodied every vice her mother had warned her against. His willingness to enter a strange house and accost the first female he met branded him a rakehell, and he was clearly contemplating how to avenge her slap.

She suppressed her dread of the power embodied in those shoulders, for displaying fear, or even nervousness, would be a mistake. Like any predator, he would pounce on the first sign of weakness. Backing another pace, she spoke slowly, as to a dull-witted child.

"Your driver has lost his way, sir, bringing you to the wrong estate. My mother and I lease this property from my uncle."

His brow furrowed. "Is this not Redrock House?"

"Yes."

"Then it is mine."

"You must have fallen victim to a charlatan. My uncle would never sell it."

"He did not sell it. He lost it in a card game."

Her knees nearly buckled. "You are sure?"

Sympathy flashed briefly in his eyes, surprising her. "My apologies for being the bearer of bad news, Miss—"

"Ashburton," she said when he paused.

"And I am Lord Merimont." He proffered a card. "Ashburton wagered Redrock House eight days ago. I won."

She cursed herself for flinching at the abrupt words. He was watching her like a hawk and would not have missed so telltale a reaction. When she refused to respond—she didn't trust her voice—he continued.

"You are in shock, Miss Ashburton. Not that I blame

you. Losing one's home is always upsetting. Why don't you summon your mother so we can sort out the next step?"

Losing one's home. The gall of the man! "Mother is ill." She motioned him toward the office.

Damn Uncle Edward for finding a new way to annoy her. It was just like him to hand over his despised relations to a man who would use them ill. She recognized Merimont's name. Only last summer the London papers had reported an incident at an unsavory brothel, and no one would ever forget his appalling behavior at the Horseley ball.

But she could not allow him to intimidate her. Redrock House was all they had. She should have expected something like this, for troubles never arrived singly. Her mother's chill had returned with a vengeance, sinking deep into her chest with wracking coughs that occasionally led to vomiting. She must deal with Merimont quickly, so her mother would not discover so dangerous a man under her roof.

She took the seat behind the desk, ignoring another flash of his fury. He had the most expressive eyes she had ever seen—odd for a man reputed to have no morals and no regrets.

"As I said," he continued, assuming his own chair. "I am sorry to bear bad news, but the estate is now mine. As I am in need of it, I must cancel your lease."

"Impossible."

His eyes widened. "You are misinformed. A contract with your uncle does not bind me. He can house you elsewhere."

"*You* are misinformed, my lord. If not for the lease, my uncle would have tossed us out ten years ago. It was established by my grandfather. Changes in ownership do not affect its terms. They remain in force until it expires— in another seventy-five years."

"What?" He sagged into his chair, his shock too overdone for sincerity. Everyone knew his father owned property in half the shires of England, so finding this house occupied was hardly a tragedy.

She forced calm into her voice. "It is a ninety-nine-year lease, my lord, and attaches to the estate itself, giving us free, unmolested use of the house and guaranteeing us half the estate income. Obviously you were unaware of its provisions, but winning an estate at the gaming table is no different from buying a pig in a poke. You have no cause to complain if it is less than you expected."

"But—"

"No buts, my lord. The lease cannot be broken. Believe me, my uncle tried everything, including a petition to the king, but he could not evict us. Nor can you. The White Heron in the village is simple but clean if you need accommodation. Or you might prefer the Spotted Pony in Oakhampton, which is larger and renowned hereabouts for its ale." Oakhampton was three miles away.

"Not so fast, Miss Ashburton. Where is this infamous lease?"

Pulling open a drawer, she extracted a sheaf of papers. "This is a copy, as is the one my solicitor holds. Another is on file at Somerset House in London, as part of my grandfather's will. Copies are also lodged in other places, so it would be nearly impossible to destroy evidence of its existence."

"If you were a man, I would call you out for such calumny," he growled.

She frowned, detecting real pain in his voice. "Then I beg your pardon. Uncle Edward burned two copies before he discovered that Grandfather had anticipated his reaction. I have no evidence that you are different. Not only are you Uncle's friend, but you have already proven yourself a lecherous gamester."

The new blast of fury from his eyes nearly made her falter, but she could not afford to show weakness. So she glared back until he dropped his eyes.

"I must look into this matter further," he finally said on a long sigh. "Who is your solicitor?"

"Mr. Fisk of Fisk and Farley in Oakhampton." Before he could raise new objections, she whisked him out the door and bolted it behind him.

Her mind swirled with uncertainties, for though she

rejoiced that Uncle Edward no longer owned Redrock, this man might be worse. What little she knew of him was not encouraging.

Lord Merimont was a frequent topic of conversation at Squire Porter's house. His daughter Agnes had met Merimont in London and been instantly smitten by his dark good looks and roguish reputation. Hope doubted that Merimont had even noticed the girl, but that didn't prevent Agnes from sighing over him—or from repeating every scrap of gossip about him.

He was heir to Lord Montcalm, passing his time in idleness and debauchery. Other tales suggested he was a drunkard and a prankster, the worst describing how he'd arrived at Lady Horseley's ball deep in his cups and emptied his stomach over the hostess and two of her most important guests. And now he'd admitted that he was a gamester.

She sighed. She would doubtless face more of these confrontations in the future. An estate won at the tables could be as easily lost—many times. And would be. Encumbered and derelict as it was, it was hardly an attractive property. Its only real use was as a wager.

And that would place her in danger. Men did not enjoy being crossed. To his credit, Merimont had kept a firm rein on his temper, but others might attack. Could she afford to hire a sturdy footman for protection?

The question raised a new dilemma. The lease paid them half the estate income or a thousand guineas a year, whichever was higher. If the estate failed to produce their thousand, the difference had to come from the owner's pocket. Could she collect? So far, she'd not had to try, but a series of owners could make identifying who was responsible a legal nightmare. And what would new ownership mean for the tenants?

"Later." With harvest complete, she had received this year's income. Rather than fret over the future, she needed to plan her next confrontation with the rakish Lord Merimont. She'd not seen the last of him.

But how was she to cope with so unpredictable an opponent? He'd walked in without even knocking and immediately accosted her.

Heat flooded her face. Her ear tingled where his teeth had nipped. The weight of his arm still warmed her shoulders. No man had ever caressed her so boldly. The shock of it had turned her stomach on end and weakened her knees. She'd had to inhale several times before she could slap him. Appalling man! He should be locked up to protect the ladies.

She hastily suppressed curiosity about what a real embrace might have felt like. "Scoundrel!" She stiffened her spine. He was dangerous, all right. Who but a rake would draw such a reaction from a mere touch? No one would be safe until he was gone.

Max clenched his fists as he strode out of Fisk's office. The situation was ridiculous, but Miss Ashburton had been right. The lease was unbreakable.

Leaping into his curricle, he headed back to Redrock. They must address two problems, though the first should cause no contention. She would surely welcome his plans for improving the estate, as she would benefit as much as he.

The realization that his work would support a snippy spinster made him grind his teeth, but he could not complain. Like the proverbial gift horse, Redrock came with drawbacks.

The second problem was more difficult—the imminent arrival of his friends. Greeting them with the news that Miss Ashburton had barred him from his property would make him a laughingstock. He had no illusions that the story would remain secret. It would join the other anecdotes his friends repeated when in their cups—he hated being held up to ridicule, even in fun. But worse, it would provide another embarrassment his father could throw in his face.

So he and Miss Ashburton must work together. If he held his irritation in check, surely she would cooperate.

Or would she? His greeting had been unacceptable even if she'd been the maid he'd thought her. The fact that she was a viscount's niece made it a serious blunder.

Rain clouds moved in as he reached the gates, providing the first good news of the day. With luck, mud would delay his friends.

The door was locked. He pounded for five minutes before she answered.

"You again?"

"Why don't you keep a butler?" he demanded, pushing his way into the hall before she could slam the door in his face.

"How I run my household is not your concern, my lord." But she shut the door and followed him to the office.

He took the same chair as before. "I discussed the lease with your solicitor, Miss Ashburton," he began, grateful that rain made the room gloomy enough to dull her hair. "As you so eloquently pointed out, it cannot be broken. However, nowhere does the document give you exclusive use of the house. As owner, I am responsible for overseeing the estate, common lands, and tenant farms. It is a duty I intend to assume. Your solicitor agrees that I can reside here while inspecting the property and meeting the steward."

Her face blanched. "You cannot be serious!"

"Deadly serious. I must remain here if I am to adequately carry out my responsibilities."

"Then move to the dower house."

He raised his brows. "Is it well maintained?"

"Nothing around here is maintained."

"Then I must begin by replacing the steward."

She clamped her mouth shut and breathed deeply several times before responding. Her effort to remain businesslike marked her as an unusual woman and allowed him to rein in his own temper.

"No honorable man would draw conclusions before learning the facts," she said deliberately. "So far you've seen nothing that is under the steward's control. Uncle Edward prohibited Watts from spending a shilling on the house or allowing estate workers onto the grounds."

"And he agreed?"

"Should he have argued and been turned off?"

"Of course not." His question had been stupid, but her claims were so astounding that he'd been unable to hide his surprise. "I take it Ashburton does not believe in compromise."

"Not in the least. Watts has been in an impossible situation since his arrival. Without a reference from my uncle, he could never find another position, so he is forced to carry out abhorrent orders. In his favor, he has done everything possible for the tenants, so they have not suffered as much as they might have."

"Meaning?"

She shrugged. "Uncle Edward deliberately ruined the estate. It is the tenants who were most affected, not that he cared."

"Your point?" he asked. She couldn't mean that literally.

"The orders prevent Watts from keeping the estate productive. Large areas now lie fallow. When Watts realized what Uncle Edward was doing, he abandoned the estate's own land, using his meager resources to keep the tenants from starving. He has done what he could to minimize the damage, but his hands are tied. Do not blame him for conditions."

"I will keep an open mind until I speak with him," he agreed. "But why would Ashburton issue such ridiculous orders? They must hurt him as well."

"It no longer matters, my lord. As the new owner, you will do whatever you want." She rose to escort him to the door, but this time he refused to budge.

Shifting his eyes to the silk-covered walls with their patterns of brightly colored birds—the room must have been a sitting room before it was converted to an office—he switched to the next order of business. "The house and grounds are under your care. Is there staff enough, or must I hire extra during my stay?"

"You really must move either to the dower house or to the inn," she said firmly. "Consider the situation. You are a well-known rake."

"Hardly. My proclivities are no different from what is usual for my class," he protested.

"That may be, but your reputation is otherwise and is well known locally. I may be long on the shelf, but many would look askance at you for remaining under this roof without a chaperon."

"Your mother is here."

"She is too ill to know who is in the house. You would be more comfortable at the White Heron."

"I doubt it."

She sighed, resuming her seat. "Then move into the dower house. It is not in pristine condition, but the main bedchamber is usable. A little work will restore the rest."

"In that case, you move there. I am expecting several friends."

"No."

"I assure you that my friends could arrive as early as today—certainly by tomorrow. If you do not wish to join us, you and your mother must move to the dower house."

"We cannot."

He glared.

"My lord," she began, pushing her fingers into her hair—which released additional wisps of fire, "my mother's illness is severe and growing worse. Moving would kill her. And how do I know we could return to our home? Once you are in sole possession, I am helpless."

"I would never do something so dastardly. No man of honor would," he swore hotly, ignoring the fact that he had proposed to displace her only a few hours ago. That was before he'd seen the lease.

She met his eyes. "Very well. I apologize. My experience with gentlemen says otherwise, but I will give you the benefit of the doubt." Her tone belied the concession.

"Thank you *so* much," he snapped sarcastically.

"Don't patronize me," she snapped back. "We should not even be holding this discussion without a chaperon. I agree that the dower house is too small for a crowd, but you cannot entertain them here. If the White Heron is too rustic for your fine London friends, then put them up in Oakhampton."

"No." He would not allow this chit to throw him out. They had come to inspect his new estate, and he would see that they did. "It is only for a fortnight. The staff can care for your mother, and you can visit friends."

"Hardly. My only friends live nearby. Not one would believe that I could leave Mother's sickbed. And they know that my staff cannot provide adequate care."

"Why not?"

"Mrs. Tweed often forgets what she is doing, and Rose suffers severely from rheumatism."

"What about the others?"

"Ned? He stays in the stables."

"That's all?"

"Why do you think you found me dusting the hallway, my lord?"

His face heated at the memory of his initial mistake. "Very well. You will have to stay. We will remain out of your way."

She laughed. "You are drawing conclusions without facts again. How large do you think Redrock House is?"

"Ashburton's solicitor described it as two wings off a central block—small as manors go, but that should be large enough for us to remain separate. I've only invited four friends." And five courtesans, he remembered, but it was too late to back out now. They could arrive any minute.

"Grandiose claims, my lord. Based on that description, the central block consists of the entrance hall."

He stared. That was it?

"Each *wing* contains five bedchambers. Only those used by myself and my mother are clean. The east side includes this office, a morning room, and the library. The drawing room, dining room, and music room are on the west side. If you insist on staying, you must hire your own staff. Mine is already overworked."

"Five bedchambers on each side?"

"Correct, though two from the east wing have been converted to sitting rooms. And you must keep the one next to Mother's vacant. She will go into a decline if she is disturbed. But that should not matter. There are only five of you."

"Ten," he choked.

"Ten? But you said—" She gasped, blanching—which made her auburn hair seem brighter even against gray skies. "My God! You cannot mean to bring—" She couldn't force the word out.

For the first time, her breeding smote him between the eyes. He should have paid attention to Fisk's ramblings. Miss Hope Ashburton's father had been the heir until his untimely death. She and her mother belonged in society, though neither had made their bows in town. He could not allow her to mix with his guests.

You should cancel, warned his conscience, but he ignored it. He had invited them here. His word was sacred. He never reneged on a vow. Honor forbade lying. He couldn't drag his friends all the way to Devonshire, then turn them away.

Yet he had to consider Miss Ashburton. Even if honor did not demand it, protecting women had long been a personal crusade. Now he had two genteel ladies under his wing. All he could do was make the best of it.

Miss Ashburton recovered her voice. "You cannot bring your mistress here. That is beyond even your reputation."

"I have no choice."

"Of course you have a choice. Move your party to Oakhampton. You should find the Spotted Pony entirely to your taste. The serving girls are very accommodating, by all accounts."

"Absolutely not!" he snapped, abandoning further attempts to persuade. "We will stay on my estate. By avoiding your wing, we will not disturb your mother."

"And how do you propose to do that?"

"Simple. Redrock is hereby divided into two establishments. You stay in the east wing; I'll take the west. No one will enter yours without permission."

"Do you take me for a fool, or do you still think me fair game?"

"That's not—" But he caught himself staring at her generous bosom, his hands itching to touch. Damn the woman for diverting his attention. "You will receive the respect you deserve, Miss Ashburton."

"Why does that not reassure me?"

"Enough!" He stood, looming over her desk. "A gentleman's word is binding. We will leave you alone. I trust you will return the favor."

"Gladly. I would be delighted to never see you again."
She also rose, glaring into his eyes. "And make sure
your *friends* stay away from my mother."

"We won't hurt her," he protested as she strode
toward the door.

"Really?" she countered stonily, her hand on the latch.
"You force your way into our home, fill it with libertines
and fallen women, then have the audacity to claim we will
be safe? Just what do you consider harmful?"

He could feel his face heat. "If I could change things,
I would."

"No, you wouldn't. You've already refused every
decent solution. And don't cite honor again," she continued as he opened his mouth. "Honor has nothing to do
with this. You are stubborn and arrogant, but since you
outweigh me, I have no recourse."

"You are overreacting."

She held up a hand to silence him. "Let us be done
with this farce, my lord. You will do whatever you
please, for you are a man." She made it sound like a
curse. "I will survive this siege, as I've survived others,
but if anything happens to Mother, you will pay for the
rest of your life—and that's a promise. If you have the
slightest doubt about your friends or about your ability
to control your other guests, now is the time to change
your mind. Mother is unaccustomed to vice, having
grown up in a vicarage."

"So be it." Fury suppressed second thoughts. Maxwell
Longford did not take orders from others, and certainly
not from a redheaded spinster with a blistering tongue.
"We will remain out of your way, and no one will enter
this wing. Where is the kitchen, by the way?"

She shook her head. "On your side. I will prepare our
meals in the stillroom."

"I will need servants."

"That, my lord, is *your* problem." Glaring at him, she
left. He was still debating whether he should follow her
when an ancient housekeeper shuffled in, a disapproving
frown on her face.

"Come along," she said. "I'm to show you the west
wing."

Chapter Three

Max cursed as he followed Mrs. Tweed. This would never work. The rooms were positively tiny.

The drawing room was really a cozy sitting room, with faded red walls and a threadbare carpet. The music room was little better, though its cornices and ceiling boasted Adam-style stuccatori, and the painted walls showed no signs of cracks. The dining room was pleasant but could seat no more than a dozen. He'd seen intimate family breakfast rooms that were larger.

Upstairs, the bedchambers were just as cramped. While his afforded room for pacing, the rest barely had space for basic furnishings.

Yet he had made a vow—several of them, in fact. Reneging would tarnish his image in the one way he could not tolerate. He had worked for years to prove that he was trustworthy. Only his father continued to view him as a recalcitrant child who must be watched every second.

So he must continue as he had started. Changing his mind would attract attention—not that bawdy parties were uncommon, but it was bad form to flaunt them. Montcalm would be irritated.

"That is the lot, my lord," said Mrs. Tweed, gesturing to the last bedchamber. It lacked a dressing room but overlooked a walled rose garden behind the house. He would assign it to Reggie, with Dornbras in its twin next door. Blake and Terrence could have the larger rooms across the hall. But where could he put the girls?

"Is there nothing upstairs?" he asked, calculations circling grimly through his head.

Five bedchambers.

Five gentlemen.

Five courtesans.

Annette could share his room, but the others lacked official protectors. How would they accommodate frequent changes? And how would his friends react to sharing quarters? Even he disliked the thought.

Mrs. Tweed plodded up another flight of steps. By the time she reached the top, she was gasping for breath. "The nursery, my lord."

He nearly groaned. No one had used the space in years. Dust lay thick on every surface; cobwebs festooned walls and ceilings. Only the governess's room contained a bed large enough for an adult, though it appeared Spartan and uncomfortable. The children's beds were impossible, as was the cradle. He glanced toward the east wing.

"The schoolroom is there," Mrs. Tweed informed him. "And storage, but that is part of Miss Hope's establishment." Her sarcasm was patent.

Five bedchambers.

Ten people.

Temptation urged him to flee, but he stiffened his spine. Dependability was the one aspect of his reputation he could point to with pride. Losing it would cost him far more than a little pique over cramped quarters. It made no difference that Ashburton had lied. Offering that excuse to cancel the party would make him an object of pity. *Poor Merimont. He can't do anything right. Even his estate is a ruin, and he let a pair of females turn his friends away. No backbone . . .*

Imagined laughter echoed through his ears. His father's voice drowned it out. *Stay home so I can keep you out of trouble. You are a hopeless bumbler, Maxwell. I won't tolerate another scandal . . .*

A quick shake of his head banished the voices, but they had hardened his resolve. His course was set.

"I need a staff," he said as they descended the stairs. "Cook, butler, maids, footmen—and at least two more stable boys."

"Can't be done." Not even her puffing disguised the implacable refusal.

"Of course it can. Just last month, Lady Bentley assembled a staff of twenty-seven overnight."

"In the city, mayhap that's true," she said, glaring at him. "But that many servants don't change positions around here in a year. The hiring fair was last week, so the few who might be interested won't be free until next quarter day. Those not already in service won't work for libertines and fallen women. Even Miss Hope's uncle never tried nothing this bad. The poor girl will be ruined."

He bit back a sarcastic response. He had forgotten that domestic contracts expired on the quarter days, particularly in the country. Trained servants would not be available again until Christmas. If he had more time he could order his valet to produce a staff—Wilkins often wrought seeming miracles—but Wilkins was with his baggage coach. His friends could arrive any minute.

He cringed, recalling the dustcovers hiding the furniture in his five bedchambers. "We must find someone. What about the tenants? With harvest over, they have little enough to do."

She muttered what might have been a curse. "No."

"No what? Are you saying the tenants are too busy?"

She shook her head. "No one who knows Miss Hope will work for you, and there's some as might call you out for harming her. Have you no decency? How can even a London lecher force his sins on an innocent girl?"

"It is not your place to judge, Mrs. Tweed," he reminded her through gritted teeth. "Your place is to obey orders. Anyone who wishes to protect her should welcome the chance to move in."

"I work for Miss Hope, not you," she said stubbornly. "And for Mrs. Ashburton. They don't need more grief. Haven't they suffered enough? Enduring twenty-five years of spite should entitle them to peace." Tears dripped down her cheeks.

"Just find me some servants." He ignored her tears as the tools of manipulation he knew them to be.

She cried harder.

"Enough!" he snapped, exasperation unraveling his temper. "I have no wish to harm Miss Ashburton or distress her mother. But my guests will arrive very soon. Without a staff, we are bound to disturb them. Where can I find servants?"

She sniffed into her handkerchief. "The nearest registry is in Exeter, but it takes them a week to respond and then it's only to say they'll keep you in mind. You would do better to send to London."

"Impossible, as you well know. Do not allow loyalty to blind you, Mrs. Tweed. Surely there are local girls who would work."

"No."

Taking a deep breath, he seated her in the drawing room, choosing the chair across from her for himself.

"Mrs. Tweed, we are speaking at cross-purposes. Miss Ashburton ordered you to help me. I own this house. I will be living here for the foreseeable future, and I intend to entertain my friends whenever I choose."

"And highly improper it is," declared the housekeeper, displaying not the slightest awe at his position. "How dare you corrupt Miss Hope's home?"

"This house now contains two homes."

She snorted.

"Dividing buildings is a common enough practice in London," he declared. "My guests and I will remain in the west wing. They needn't even know she is here."

"What will Mrs. Ashburton think?" she wailed, again breaking into tears. "Beset by the very beasts she was raised to avoid. Provoked beyond bearing by the tools of Satan. Held captive while evil men ravish her only daughter."

"That is more than enough," he snapped, his temper shattering. "Since you harbor such a low opinion of me, perhaps you will believe this: Either you find me the staff I need, or I will seduce Miss Ashburton, ruining her in truth. Is that clear?"

She gasped, recoiling from his glare. "M-my lord!"

"Do you understand?"

"Yes, my lord."

Max watched her march away, already hating himself for threatening her. Touching a well-bred innocent was the last thing he wanted to do, for it would tie him to the chit for life. Not that he had the slightest intention of carrying out his threat. He would turn his friends away first.

But Mrs. Tweed's implacable stubbornness could not be tolerated. Servants had to remember their place.

Shaking his head, he strode back upstairs. Intimidating servants was not something he could point to with pride. Nor was anything else he'd done today. But it was too late to turn back.

Grumbling, he jerked covers off the furniture, piling them in the hall. Then he threw open the windows, coughing to remove dust from his throat. These rooms had not been cleaned in years.

But beyond baring the furnishings, he was helpless. None of the beds were made up. He did not even know where the linens were kept, let alone what to do with them. Poking about his own room revealed other deficiencies. Where were the washbowls and chamber pots? What about pillows and towels? He threw himself into a chair, then spring back to his feet as something stabbed his backside.

Glaring at the broken chair, he considered the larger problem. How the devil was he to feed his guests without a cook? He hated confronting Miss Ashburton again, but that was preferable to another meeting with Mrs. Tweed.

He was beset with troubles, without a solution in sight.

"You should not have argued with him, Mrs. Tweed," said Hope when the housekeeper finished pouring out her woes. "He owns the estate, which means he can stay here."

"It's not right," insisted the woman.

"Perhaps not, but he is within his rights to increase the staff. We can only hope that he honors his vow to remain in the west wing. Did you find servants?"

She nodded—reluctantly. "But the girls won't stay in the house at night."

"I cannot ask them to. Nor can he. Whom did you find?"

"The Prices," she said, naming the neediest tenants. "Mrs. Price will cook, though it will be cottage fare, and the girls will clean. Henry Oats will double as butler and footman."

"It will do. If the service is less than they prefer, they can take themselves elsewhere." It was her fondest hope, and might yet come to pass. Two maids and a fourteen-year-old butler would hardly manage the work generated by ten people. But using tenants would protect her. They were so grateful for her past help that they would say nothing to damage her reputation.

"He's an odd one," said Mrs. Tweed, relaxing for the first time since returning from the Prices'.

"How so?"

"You'd have thought him the most arrogant lord on earth when he was threatening me, yet when I sought him out to introduce the Prices, he was trying to open the bedchambers by himself."

"Really?" Definitely odd.

"He'd piled the dustcovers in the hall. Of course, he'd taken no care to fold the dust inside." She laughed. "They'll be sneezing for a week on what he dumped on the beds alone."

Hope chuckled. "I wonder if he knows that none of the beds are made up."

"He can't have missed it. Half of the coverlets are mixed with the dustcovers."

"The poor man." He'd been waited on since birth, so he would be helpless on his own. Yet he deserved credit for trying.

"Don't you go feeling sorry for him," warned Mrs. Tweed. "He brought this on himself. 'Tis you I fear for. You'll pay dearly before this is done. Mark my words. When I think what your mother—"

"I haven't forgotten," said Hope, hastily interrupting. "But this is one situation I can't control. Have the Prices taken over the cleaning?"

"Most of it." Her eyes lit up. "We found him under a bed, trying to reach a chamber pot. He was relieved to hear that his luggage had arrived, for he was head to toe cobwebs and dust."

Hope grinned. The arrogant Lord Merimont covered

in the dust rolls that collected under disused beds was a sight she wished she'd seen.

But she had her own preparations to make. Sending Mrs. Tweed to help the Prices, she resumed moving pots, dishes, and cutlery into the stillroom. Its fireplace contained the chimney crane and spits she needed. Now she had to prevent anyone from wandering into it.

The ground floor was a maze of rooms leading into one another. The kitchen, laundry, and servants' hall were in the west end, with the stillroom, dairy, and apartments for the housekeeper and butler in the east. The door connecting the laundry and the stillroom was the only way between them, but it had no lock.

The Prices knew she remained, of course, but visiting servants would dine with Merimont's staff. It would not do for these intruders to guess she was here.

It was later than she'd thought, she realized, catching sight of the kitchen clock. Postponing the job of sealing the door, she built a fire and prepared a simple meal. An hour later, she carried a tray to her mother's room.

"She's said nothing for hours, Miss Hope," said Rose, rising stiffly from the chair near the bed. "I believe her fever is worse."

The scarlet patches on those pale cheeks confirmed the diagnosis. "Send Ned for more willow bark. Dinner is in the morning room, then I need you to watch Mother while I speak to Lord Merimont."

His guests had not yet arrived. She hoped they had been delayed by the afternoon's storm, for there were details she must discuss with him.

She should not have fled their last meeting, but frustration had threatened her with tears. Breaking down in his presence would reveal a weakness that he would exploit.

Rose was right about her mother, she realized as she tried to coax food into the lady. The chill had clearly worsened. Dr. Jenkins employed none of the time-tested remedies Dr. Willit had favored. Unfortunately, Willit had died three years ago. As her mother's health failed, she had to question the new doctor's competence.

Which added to her fears. Like her uncle, Merimont might force her into marriage the moment her mother

was gone. She didn't know why, but he wanted this
house, and not just for his party. He would do whatever
was necessary to gain control. A rake would not bother
with scruples. His easiest recourse would be paying
someone to wed her—by force, if she objected.

"Stop looking for new trouble," she muttered as the
last of the tea trickled down her mother's throat. She
had more immediate problems, like setting up rules for
managing this dual household. Since that would require
cooperation, she must ignore the fact that Merimont was
her enemy.

He was in the office, sprawled negligently across a
wing chair near the fire—which he had lit, though she
could not afford coal so early in the season. Between
her mother's room and the kitchen, she was already
burning too much.

Biting back a protest, she reminded herself that they
needed to work together.

"Allow me to apologize for losing my temper this afternoon," she said, taking the other chair.

"If you will forgive my own lapse. This predicament
caught us both by surprise."

"Very well." He must also have realized that they had
decisions to make. "We will start over. I presume you
want control of the central block?"

"Of course." But a sudden frown creased his brow.
His voice lacked his usual arrogance when he continued.
"Are there other stairs you can use?"

She nodded. "We also need to separate my house
from yours. Imaginary lines will not be enough. I cannot
allow others to infringe upon my wing."

"I already vowed that we would not."

"Yet here you are." She gestured to the room and fire.
"Lounging in my office, burning coal I can ill afford."

"But—" He stopped, running his hands through his hair.
Without a hat, it was luxuriously wavy. "I didn't think."

"Not surprising. In my experience, gentlemen rarely
think except in their own self-interest."

"Harsh words, Miss Ashburton." His voice revealed
the control he was exerting to be pleasant, reminding
her that he could destroy her. There wasn't a soul who

could help if he chose to ravish her. "A gentleman's word is his bond. I take that seriously."

"So your threat to seduce me was a promise." She should not be goading him, but neither could she expose her fear—which was growing as she recognized a new danger. Her hands had wanted to follow his fingers through that wavy mass of hair, petting him as she would a cat. But this was no harmless tabby. He was an unconscionable rake who proved his prowess by inciting appalling ideas she had never dreamed she could entertain.

He flushed. "I must apologize for that remark," he admitted. "I would never consider actually doing so, but spoke in the heat of the moment. The woman's intransigence bested my temper."

"She has a name," she reminded him. "Mrs. Tweed may have overstepped her place, but she was trying to protect us. Even you cannot deny that this situation is highly irregular."

"We will remain out of your way."

"So you said, yet here you are," she repeated.

"I— You are right. I did not think." He sounded harried.

"Which will happen often in the days ahead. Redrock would be small for a house party even if you had full use of it. As it is, you will long to escape the crowd, as will your friends. How am I to avoid encroachment? How can Mother remain undisturbed? Even if your friends scrupulously follow your lead, can you say the same for your other guests? They will occasionally seek privacy, for they cannot wish to remain in a gentleman's company every moment of the day. Or are they all official mistresses?"

He shook his head, his cheeks suspiciously pink.

She continued relentlessly. "Then there are your personal servants, who will fill the attics of both wings. How will you confine them to your own servants' stairs when it will frequently be more convenient to use mine? And how will you hide my presence when I must be in and out of rooms all day?"

He took a turn around the room. Several minutes passed before he resumed his seat.

"The house is falling apart," he announced. "Portions of it are too dangerous to enter until I can make repairs. A water leak rotted floors and ceilings. I will block the hallways with wardrobes, obstructing the view."

She reluctantly nodded. "I suppose that will work, though I am not sure we have enough wardrobes to do the job. There is one in the attic that I removed from my sitting room. And there is another in the governess's room. Miss Ellis thought it almost decadent to have a real wardrobe instead of pegs on the wall." She smiled, recalling her governess's pleasure. The girl had shared a bed at the vicarage with three sisters.

"We need only block two halls."

"But the wardrobes are narrow and together will barely fill the hall upstairs. You will have to devise something else for this floor. We also need to block the door between the laundry and the stillroom. This door locks." She pointed to the one leading to the entrance hall. "As does the dressing room door that leads from my spare room into the central block."

"More problems," he muttered, sounding as beleaguered as a general surrounded by enemy troops.

"But you will contrive." The words surprised her, for she could hardly trust him. Again he was affecting her strangely. She rose. "I must see to Mother."

He also rose.

"How is she?"

"Worse. As the fever climbs, she grows increasingly restless. And her breathing is more labored."

"My sympathy, and another apology for creating trouble when you have problems enough already. I regret placing you in this position more than I can say, Miss Ashburton. If there is anything I can do—order medications, summon a doctor, whatever—please ask."

"Thank you." He seemed sincere. On the other hand, taking his party elsewhere was the best help he could offer, but he refused to consider it.

"And keep her warm." He glanced at the fire. "Do not fret about coal. I like comfort and will lay in a good supply. Make use of it. Do not scrimp on anything she might need, Miss Ashburton. I intend to restore Red-rock, so next year's income will be higher."

This time shock left her speechless.

"May we meet briefly in the morning? I would like to know as much as possible about the estate before meeting Watts." He smiled.

"Very well. I must go now. Rose needs rest, or I will have another invalid on my hands." She was babbling, trying to ignore the effect of that smile.

Danger, warned a voice in her head. No wonder Agnes had fallen top over tail for the man. That smile was a formidable weapon.

He bade her good night and left, apparently not seeing her sudden confusion. Locking the door behind him, she slipped out the other door and up the servants' stairs.

His words echoed in her mind as she kept vigil at her mother's bedside. He intrigued her, infuriated her, and terrified her. She would do well to remember her mother's warnings. *London gentlemen are evil sinners,* she would say, repeating tales she'd heard in her youth. *Selfish. Arrogant. Liars. Cheats. They will drive you down a path to perdition. Stay safe, Hope. Never allow one to approach you.*

But she had. And his eyes spoke volumes, none of it bad. Could she trust him? He vowed to keep his word. And while his reputation terrified her, when she faced him, she was more afraid of herself than of him.

Already you are in danger, warned her conscience. *You are befriending him. Have you forgotten what happens to those who believe a rake?*

The reminder was necessary. Look at her poor mother. Seduction and betrayal. Men were practiced at it. Even those who swore by honor would do anything in pursuit of pleasure. Rakehells were worse. Like Millhouse. Only last summer he'd ruined the innkeeper's daughter, then denied responsibility for her child.

Agnes reported that Merimont was little different. Hope could only pray that he would tire of this remote estate and accompany his friends back to town.

Soon.

In person, he could make her forget the harshest lessons.

Chapter Four

Max grunted as he and Henry wrestled a sideboard across the hallway, blocking access to the east wing. A heavy cabinet would sit on top to hide the view, though sound could still carry through a gap near the ceiling. The same was true upstairs, though he had barricaded the hall with a pair of wardrobes. Miss Ashburton would have to keep her doors shut tight and remain quiet if she wished to remain undetected. Only in the stillroom would she have more freedom. He had rigged a bar across the door. The guest servants were unlikely to spend much time in the laundry—or so he hoped.

"I don't like lockin' her in," mumbled Henry as they fought to lift the cabinet into position. "What if a fire breaks out?"

The words raised the hair on Max's arms, triggering a memory of the fire that had swept part of Seven Dials last year. A dozen people had burned to death because they had no escape.

But that was not true here. "There are other exits," he said soothingly. In addition to the servants' stairs, she could reach the main staircase through her extra bedchamber. Here, the office opened into the entrance hall. She could unbar the laundry door to reach the kitchen or go directly outdoors through the dairy.

Yet his conscience pricked him. It was all very well to declare this wing uninhabitable. Blocking the halls would keep the households separate. But it wasn't enough. Hiding her protected her reputation, but he should also protect her modesty. Sound would pass the barrier in both directions. Would she understand what she was hearing?

Having grown up in a vicarage . . .

He shivered. What sensibilities did the mother possess? Were they even more rigid than the daughter's?

But that raised another question. Miss Ashburton confused him. One minute she was as prissily disapproving as the most ardent spinster. The next, she pragmatically accepted suggestions he almost blushed to make, and revealed considerable understanding about the party's purpose.

And her face was as open as any he'd seen. He couldn't blame her for the distrust that often clouded her eyes. Mrs. Tweed's outburst had hinted that the Ashburton ladies had a low opinion of men, which explained her eagerness to escape his touch yesterday. She had no way of knowing that he rarely even treated maids as he'd treated her—in fact, he had a hard time explaining why he'd done it.

Touching her had been more than a social *faux pas,* he admitted, swearing. He couldn't forget the feel of her. It had awakened something better left dormant, leaving him decidedly uncomfortable and in great need of Annette's attentions.

Thrusting the memory aside, he concentrated on the manor's limited space. Closing off the hallways made the house seem even smaller. At best, his friends would be disgruntled. He was even less happy about it than yesterday. While he enjoyed Annette's skills, her inane prattle was annoying. How was he to live with her for two weeks, not only sharing a bed, but sharing the only private space he had? He preferred sleeping alone, as did most men. If only he could think of an alternative.

But he couldn't, and the others would arrive soon. At least the neglected grounds and threadbare furnishings would make his claims about the east wing seem reasonable—it was structurally unsound and could not be safely entered.

It was time for his meeting with Miss Ashburton. He rapped on the office door.

"Enter," she called.

When he pushed it open, she was already seated behind the desk, a ledger open before her. Brisk. Efficient.

Businesslike. It was yet another image, at odds with the others he'd seen—the delectable maid he had accosted on arrival, the fierce protector of her mother and home, the anxious woman trying to handle a job too large for her. And her appearance offered other contrasts—the lush bosom molded by her thin gown, the spectacles perched on her nose as she studied the accounts, the wisps of hair blazing in a shaft of sunlight.

His senses stirred.

"How is your mother today?" He closed the door, forcing his mind onto business.

"The fever is no higher, but neither is it lower." She bit her lip, drawing his attention to its sensual fullness.

Annoyed, he frowned. "Have you called in a doctor?"

"Of course, but he claims it is yet another chill that must run its course. He refuses to bleed her, and won't even blister her when she slides into delirium. I don't know what to do. She has grown frailer in the three years he has treated her. This is her fourth serious illness this year alone, with several lesser maladies. Yet Dr. Jenkins does nothing. He swears that all we can do is pray. Either she heals or she doesn't. It is out of his hands. What sort of doctor says that?"

Her outburst surprised him, though he could understand it. She had no one in whom to confide, for she did all the work. Those in charge could not reveal their fears to those who depended on them.

"Do not doubt his judgment," he said soothingly, relieved that he could perform this one service. "I have a friend who was trained in Scottish medicine. His patients are remarkably robust, recovering from ailments that kill those treated by others. He swears that bleeding is rarely a cure and often makes illnesses worse."

"Really?" She frowned. "Why? Doctors have sworn by it for centuries. It releases the evil humors of disease."

"Perhaps, but the Scots insist on testing all treatments. When they compared patients who were bled to those who were not, they discovered that those not bled were much healthier. So they concluded that bleeding was

harmful. The test of blisters found no difference in recovery, but those being blistered suffered more pain."

"Goodness!"

"Exactly. I suspect that your doctor is well trained
and quite competent. You are fortunate."

"Thank you." She smoothed the anxiety from her
face. "You asked about the estate. What do you wish
to know?"

"Everything you can tell me. Ashburton described the
place as lucrative, yet you say he deliberately destroyed
it. How?"

She paused, clearly disturbed at mention of her uncle.
When she spoke, she chose her words with care. "The
estate was reasonably profitable in my grandfather's day.
Our half of the income averaged five thousand guineas
a year."

He straightened, for that was good indeed. It could
earn even more if his experiments worked. "What is the
current income?"

"We settled the annual accounts after the harvest last
week. My thousand guineas plus Watts's salary as steward exhausted all proceeds."

"What happened to produce such a loss?"

"Destruction is quite easy. The year Grandfather died,
Uncle Edward demanded every shilling of the profits,
allowing no repairs and turning off most estate workers.
Believing the orders were a mistake that would soon
be rectified, Bellows—who was steward at the time—
borrowed operating funds from us, repaying them out of
the next year's profits. It cost him his job, though the
loan did not come to Uncle's attention until after it had
been repaid."

He gasped.

She continued. "Watts has specific instructions, one of
which is eschewing loans, and even gifts, especially from
us. The only benefit the tenants enjoy is that he is not
allowed to raise rents, but the lack of maintenance and
Uncle's other orders more than cancel that advantage.
Watts hates the situation, but he has no choice."

"Why is Ashburton so determined? I know men who
strip estates to line their pockets, but I've never heard

of anyone throwing away his inheritance. That is little better than shooting oneself."

Her eyes dropped to her hands, watching them twist a handkerchief into knots. "It does not matter why. Your concern is learning what happened so you can address the resulting problems."

She was right, though admitting that hardly satisfied his curiosity. He did not know Ashburton well, but he would have heard rumors if the viscount was this negligent with all his properties. So this must be something personal.

He shivered. The man had thrown away five thousand guineas a year for nearly ten years. Pique over his inability to evict his brother's family could hardly explain such insanity. So why had he done it?

But he could not ask. "What is the current situation?"

She relaxed. "Several fields have not been planted in years. Others were converted to unsuitable crops. Inbreeding has weakened our sheep, resulting in less wool and fewer lambs. We no longer raise cattle or dairy cows. The pottery that used to supplement the tenants' incomes is closed. Timber cutting ceased five years ago, despite the increased demand for wood—that is one place in which you can produce immediate income, by the way. The wood needs cutting. While the willow may be too overgrown to bring much, the hornbeam should more than compensate."

"What about buildings, fences, and lanes?" Fury made his voice harsh. How could Ashburton be so stupid?

Her mouth curled into a smile that showed no sign of humor. "Without maintenance, what do you think?"

"Roofs leaking, hedgerows overgrown, walls crumbling," he muttered.

"Exactly. One lane is impassable, even on foot. Its hedgerow is so overgrown that you will likely destroy it trying to cut it back. The estate outbuildings all need work. The tenant farms are less derelict, for the tenants have done their own maintenance." She frowned. "I wonder if Watts warned Uncle that future income would fall below the estate obligations unless he changed his orders. That might explain him risking its loss."

She's right. An idea that had been lurking in the back of his mind suddenly bloomed. Words he had not heeded echoed. *Laugh at defeat . . . wager Redrock . . . you know how he feels.* He had no recollection of playing out the hand. Had Ashburton taken advantage of his dizziness to concede without showing his cards? His own had been inauspicious. To win, all eight cards in the stock pile must have been face cards.

But he'd discarded five losers.

He swallowed the sudden dryness in his mouth. Ashburton had deliberately conceded.

His father's announcement had told the world that Maxwell Longford needed a home. Everyone knew that the last place he wanted to live was Widicomb. Thus he would personally take possession of any property he acquired.

Trepidation crawled down his back. This business seemed havey-cavey even beyond the questionable card game. For some reason, Ashburton wanted him at Redrock. If the man knew how ill the mother was, he would know that occupying the house could create a scandal demanding marriage. Was he scheming to trap a marquess's heir? They were virtual strangers, so the viscount would not know that Max's rakish reputation was exaggerated.

But that was for later. Right now, he was safe enough. They had physically divided the house so that contact was impossible—he ignored the fact that they were alone together for the fourth time in two days. She held the keys to all exits. They shared nothing, not even servants. To be doubly safe, he would block the nursery floor and check the lock between Miss Ashburton's stairs and the attic. Once his guests left, he would repair to the dower house.

In the meantime, they would discuss business. Her grasp of agriculture had already surprised him.

"Can Watts really serve me well as steward? Surely the tenants despise him."

"No, for they know where the blame lies. If you are serious about returning Redrock to prosperity, Watts will rejoice, and the tenants with him."

"I wish to experiment with new ideas and techniques, so I need a steward who will accept machines."

"He will be comfortable with that. As will the tenants. They are quite intelligent." This time her smile was almost sly.

"What are you hiding?"

"Watts oversees a small property I own. I have encouraged him to try anything that might make it more productive."

Glancing around the dilapidated room, he shook his head. "It would not appear that he has been successful."

"Do you always judge without facts, my lord?"

He raised his brows.

"I could not allow the tenants to suffer. Our current income may be less than it used to be, but it *is* guaranteed. The same cannot be said for the tenants, who are at the mercy of Redrock's owner. After Bellows left, I realized that the estate was doomed. But I could not abandon the families who had served my grandfather, so I bought land they could work jointly—they've time enough, for even with Watts's help, half of their own land lies fallow."

His mouth was hanging open. Never had he met anyone who would consider such an arrangement. "Where did you find the money?" he finally asked.

"Most came from the repayment of my loan to Redrock. The rest was our profit that year. Our needs are simple and can be met by our guaranteed income. The project has cost me nothing beyond the land itself. The tenants split the profits. Watts donates his time—probably to assuage his guilt."

"So that is how the tenants maintain their own homes."

She nodded. "I believe you will find Watts knowledgeable about the latest agricultural theories."

"Undoubtedly," he agreed, chuckling. "Does your property include a house?"

"Would you use it?"

"Of course not!" he snapped, abandoning the intimacy that had crept into their exchange.

"I thought not." She shook her head, sadness dulling

her gray eyes. "Had one existed, I would have suggested it yesterday, but I bought only land."

He was distracted by her sensuous lips, nearly missing the rest of her admission.

"If I'd known then how bad things would become, I would have bought a full estate and left. We could have lived more comfortably and the tenants would not be in such straits. But I considered only land that would be convenient to Redrock. None of those parcels held homes."

He straightened. "So he destroyed Redrock to hurt you?"

She shrugged. "It no longer matters."

"But it does," he insisted. "If Ashburton hates you, he might trap me into some new plot against you. I need to understand the dangers, so I can avoid them."

Terror blossomed in her eyes. "Then you had best leave. Believe me, if he decides to use you, he will make your life a living hell. Nothing ever stops him—not honor, not decency, not even sanity. If only I had understood sooner, but I didn't. Don't fall into the same trap."

It was clear that she feared her uncle, seeing him as an omnipotent demon. "I can care for myself, and I assure you that I will never treat you like that," he said firmly.

"We shall see. In my experience, men do whatever they wish according to the desire of the moment."

"Men are not all alike, Miss Ashburton."

"So you say, but I would rather err on the side of safety," she snapped, turning away.

The subject was closed. They spent the next hour discussing Redrock. When he left, his head reeled with questions, but few of them concerned estate matters. Why the devil had Ashburton involved him? And why had the man wasted ten years and nearly fifty thousand guineas persecuting two women? Some men would kill for a fortune that large.

Then there was Mrs. Ashburton's own family. They should have stepped in to protect her. Was she an orphan, or did her father lack power? Perhaps she'd married above her station.

Yet that still failed to explain Ashburton's behavior. Even men who despised cits would hardly waste a fortune on one who posed no threat. As near as he could tell, neither Miss Ashburton nor her mother had made any effort to enter society.

This did explain the lease, however. Ashburton's father had expected this battle, which meant the grievance had roots long in the past and must be aimed at the mother.

But the real victim was Miss Ashburton. She should not be shut away in the country, nursing a sick mother and scheming to help needy tenants. Most ladies her age had long since produced the requisite heir and a spare and were now enjoying life. Her father had been a viscount's heir. Helping her take her rightful place in the world could solve both their problems. She would marry and join society, and he would gain full use of his property. Mrs. Ashburton could either live with her daughter or move to the dower house.

He was reviewing names of eligible gentlemen when carriages approached along the drive. He opened the front door. Acting as his own butler would signal the hardships that awaited his friends. He could find Miss Ashburton a suitable match after everyone departed.

Hope sighed as she locked the door behind Lord Merimont. He was not at all what she had expected of a disreputable rakehell. How did he know so much about agriculture? Even Squire Porter—who willingly answered all her questions and followed Coke's experiments with fanatical interest—knew less than Merimont. He must have studied the subject, though such concern did not fit his reputation.

Even when he was not staring at her with heat in his eyes—she had to admit that such evidence of debauchery was flattering, for he made no move to force her—his wit made him the most attractive man she'd ever met. If this was typical of rakes, she must forgive her mother for becoming ensnared by one. Only constant reminders of the danger he represented had kept her eyes off his broad shoulders and twinkling blue eyes.

He had surprised her so often in the last hour that she hardly knew what to think. His fury when she'd described Uncle Edward's orders had clenched her stomach. He cared for the land as much as she did, despite never seeing it before. From his questions and comments, she was sure that the tenants would enjoy a better future than they'd ever dreamed.

If he followed through. She had no proof that he actually meant to restore Redrock. Perhaps he was toying with her, using her loyalty to her dependents to gain her trust so he could seduce her. And he had won Redrock in a card game. Uncle would never have risked losing it to a man who would treat them well.

But it was difficult to fit him into her image of other lords. He seemed almost reasonable, someone she could work with in the future.

Danger.

Her conscience was right, she admitted. She must not allow his charm to blind her. He was a libertine every bit as bad as her father, a man who frequented the most debased brothels in London. He was a friend of her uncle, participating in card games in which fortunes changed hands. His exploits shocked all of society. He might be protecting her from his guests, but only because allowing her to mix with them would restrain their enjoyment.

A sound drew her attention to the drive. His friends had arrived.

She ought to relieve Rose at her mother's bedside, but curiosity drew her to the window. She had to see what fallen women looked like.

Standing well to one side so she could peer through a crack in the draperies without being noticed, she watched the line of carriages disgorge Merimont's guests.

She wasn't sure what she'd expected, but this wasn't it. Like Merimont, his friends were impeccably dressed and could have stepped into any Devonshire drawing room without attracting criticism. She could have passed any of the ladies on the village street without pause. Each wore a cloak or pelisse in deference to the autumn chill, but no paint covered their faces, and their hair was arranged in the current mode.

But while their appearance was bland, their behavior was shocking. A petite blonde snuggled into a redheaded gentleman's embrace. His hand reached down to pat her backside in a most intimate way, inciting giggles and a lewd comment loud enough to penetrate the window.

Hope's face burned.

A black-haired lady boldly threw her arms around her escort's neck when he lifted her from the carriage, wiggling deliciously as she slid down his front. Hope snatched her gaze from the lascivious kiss they exchanged.

The next carriage disgorged a dark gentleman of medium height and a stately brunette. When he turned to survey the house, Hope gasped. His gaze brushed past her window, turning her stomach icy. Never had she seen such malevolence. He embodied everything she feared, and more.

She shook off the fancy. He was merely tired from a long journey and disappointed at the size of the house. She could not blame him for grimacing in a direction none of his companions would see.

Turning her gaze to the last carriage, she watched another gentleman assist a laughing redhead to the ground. Then Merimont stepped forward to lift down his own companion. Blonde ringlets caught the breeze, dancing about the girl's face. His mistress, Hope decided, for the blonde's eyes lit with pleasure as he bent to whisper something into her ear that drew a flirtatious giggle. He wrapped an arm about her waist and headed for the door.

Cursing herself for watching, even as she stifled an unexpected memory of that same arm across her own shoulders, Hope strode away. Voices carried from the hall.

"Too gothic for words," drawled a man, accompanied by a feminine giggle.

"Place is falling apart," grumbled another.

"Too true," said Merimont, "though the west wing is sound enough. I can't say the same for the rest. More than one ceiling is down, and the library floor contains a hole large enough to swallow a carriage. It will be months before all the repairs are complete."

"Good idea to block it off," said someone matter-of-factly. "We wouldn't want any accidents."

Feminine squeals hinted that the women were using the danger to their own advantage.

"The doors are marked if you wish to examine your rooms," Merimont continued, a wealth of suggestion in his tone. "We'll sort out luggage and ladies later."

"Just find me something soft to lie on," said another gentleman. "A carriage ride with this tease leaves me in need of a bed."

Hope fled the laughter that followed his quip. Foot-steps clattered upstairs. She knew their voices would fill that hall as well, so instead of relieving Rose, she scurried down to the stillroom, where she splashed cold water on her face.

Why had she listened to them? They were rakehells, debauchers, purveyors of every evil in the world.

Again she felt Merimont's arm on her shoulders and his teeth on her ear. Scowling, she resumed splashing, but nothing could relieve the embarrassment.

Chapter Five

Max shook his head as he entered the music room. Dornbras, Reggie, and Terrence had gone upstairs, but Blake had demanded a private word. He hadn't expected trouble from that quarter.

Nor had he expected Annette to start pouting. Granted, his greeting had been restrained, but he was nervous about reactions to the sleeping arrangements, and he could not forget that a lady might be watching this very public arrival. He'd felt eyes on the back of his neck as he'd lifted Annette down from the carriage—which was why he'd kept his welcome almost platonic.

Not that it mattered. He could have ravished Annette on the drive without reducing Miss Ashburton's regard. But golden curls seemed insipid after watching the light play across auburn tresses. Their morning discussion had left him straining at the bit to begin work on Redrock, making the next fortnight's frivolity seem intrusive. Why had he ever agreed to this party?

Cursing himself, he shut the door and faced Blake. Annette and Missy were in the drawing room, probably disparaging his house. "How was the trip?"

Blake was staring over the garden. "Too easy. Dornbras is in a very odd mood."

"Odd?"

"For him." Blake paced to the fireplace and back. "He's been congenial, even when Terrence's carriage slid into a ditch, costing us half a day digging it out—he *would* have to land in a bog."

Max laughed. "That spot near Bury St. Michael?"

Blake nodded.

"How the devil did he lose control there? That road is wide, with hardly a rut in sight."

"I suspect the coachman was listening to Terrence and Flo instead of watching the horses."

Max laughed even louder.

"Humorous in retrospect," agreed Blake. "But Dornbras should have been furious at having to soil his hands. Instead he said nothing. He's stayed with Francine since leaving London and ignored every serving wench who tried to catch his eye."

Max shrugged. "Why should he hire a tavern maid when he has Francine?"

"He's easily bored, Max. And he is a blackguard. Pitting a London courtesan against a country charmer would appeal to him. I wish you hadn't included him in this gathering."

"You sound like my father."

"Occasionally your father is right."

Max sucked in a deep breath, gritting his teeth to hold his temper. He allowed few people to criticize him, but Blake was his closest friend.

"When are you going to admit that Dornbras is using you?" asked Blake softly. "The only reason hostesses tolerate him is because of you. But his reputation is sinking fast. Soon even you won't keep him afloat. At least a dozen sticklers already prefer the ire of a future marquess to allowing Dornbras into their drawing rooms. If you persist, you'll sink with him."

"Blake—"

"No, I won't let it drop this time," he said, ignoring the warning tone. "Dornbras is dangerous. The moment your power no longer protects him, he will turn on you."

"Don't exaggerate. I know you don't like him, but give me a little credit. Most of his bluster is an act. You know he enjoys shocking people—especially sticklers like Lady Horseley and Mrs. Drummond-Burrell. I've shocked them more than once myself, for they remind me too much of Father. I suspect that Dornbras feels the same way. His father is worse than mine."

"Perhaps, but don't put Dornbras in your shoes. They don't fit."

"You're wrong. He occasionally goes too far, but beneath his careless facade, he is little different from anyone else."

"I doubt Madame LaFleur would agree with you. One of her girls suffered a broken arm last month."

"Meg. But that was an accident," insisted Max.

Blake raised a skeptical brow.

"Meg told me herself that it was an accident—she wanted out of the business, so I helped her." While he enjoyed the attentions of willing courtesans, he hated to see girls, particularly young ones, forced into brothels. So if one wanted out, he helped her establish a respectable life. Most needed assistance, because few had any money. And the brothel owners hated losing their merchandise. "Meg's story matches his. They tumbled off the bed, landing awkwardly with him on top. Her arm broke."

"No other injuries?"

"Not that I know of. It was an accident, Blake."

"Very well. It was an accident. But I've heard too many rumors of brutality to dismiss him as harmless. I wish he was not here."

Max shrugged. He and Blake would never agree about Dornbras. His two friends had raised each other's hackles since school. "You needn't fret. Dornbras is relaxed because there is no one nearby he cares to annoy. He is a different man away from society. And there will be enough here to keep him occupied."

"Perhaps, though that is another subject we must discuss. You and Annette are the only ones who will be comfortable sharing rooms. This arrangement cannot work."

"Room shuffling is inevitable," he agreed with a sigh. "But I have no choice. The east wing is falling to bits. Ashburton's solicitor must have confused Redrock with some other property. Not only did he claim the manor was well maintained, but he described it as being three times this size."

"You could have warned us."

"Hardly. You aren't the only one who had a regrettable journey. I ran into a spot of trouble south of Bath and arrived only yesterday. The staff consisted of an elderly housekeeper who should have been pensioned off years ago. I spent today finding temporary help. I've not even met the steward."

"Then the situation is worse than I feared," said Blake, running his hand over the harpsichord.

The motion drew Max's eyes to a Broadwood pianoforte in the corner, clearly Miss Ashburton's. How could he explain an instrument from a fifteen-year-old company in a derelict, unoccupied house? He didn't play well enough to justify buying it, and he could hardly have acquired it in a single day, anyway.

Pulling his mind back to the discussion, he faced Blake. "What is wrong with the situation?"

"You know that Dornbras demands the best. He is as rich as Golden Ball and as arrogant as the most exacting duke."

Max chuckled, for the description was apt—the contrast explained why even innocuous pranks had made such an impact when he'd first come to London. Now that people knew him, he had to use more extreme pranks to achieve the same effect.

"Did you know that Prinny is dangling a knighthood in front of him, hoping for a loan?" asked Blake.

"Dornbras mentioned it. He's holding out for a title, but he won't get it. Even Prinny's debts aren't that bad just now. Parliament paid most of them when they appointed him regent."

"True, but Dornbras refuses to admit that. I hope I am nowhere nearby when he does."

"What is your point?"

"Dornbras never shares quarters. Isn't there a corner where one of the girls can sleep and where they can all keep their belongings?"

"I wish there were. Even one extra room would make life simpler." He ran his fingers through his hair in frustration. "I've been butting my head against the math since I arrived. There are only five bedchambers that are safe to enter. This floor contains only the drawing room, dining room, and music room. The nursery is falling to bits and has no furnishings worth mentioning. The attics are full of personal servants, even if I find no staff—the few helpers I located this morning live elsewhere. Where would you suggest I put the girls? Your dressing room? It is the only one that opens onto the hallway. But that would leave you without even a wardrobe in which to store your clothes."

He did not mention the dressing room that mirrored Blake's, which also opened onto the hall. It was attached to the unused bedchamber in the east wing, and he could not allow anyone that close to Miss Ashburton. Besides, she had the only key.

"There is nothing on the nursery floor?"

"A cradle and a cot. But even the governess's room contains only a peg on which to hang clothes. And there must be years of dirt up there. Can you imagine how much the girls would track down here? I haven't the staff to clean another floor."

"Then I will sacrifice my dressing room," said Blake grimly. "Perhaps that will keep Dornbras from losing his temper."

Max shrugged. If Blake wanted to give up his comfort rather than admit that his prejudices were unjustified, who was he to argue? And it would simplify matters immensely if the girls kept their luggage out of the men's rooms.

"If you wish. I will have Henry bring down that cot. One of the girls can sleep in there, though I hate giving special treatment to Dornbras."

"We will understand."

Maybe. Max wasn't sure he understood his capitulation himself. But it was done. "Anyone else who is unhappy with the arrangements is welcome to leave," he muttered.

He was feeling harassed again. Everyone had been thwarting him lately—his father, Miss Ashburton, Blake. Annette would undoubtedly be next. He should have dismissed her in London, as he'd planned to do before agreeing to this party. She'd grown petulant, increasing her demands even when she knew he'd suffered financial reverses. Perhaps he should cut her loose and sample some of the others. Missy looked enticing with her mop of red hair. Of course, hers was not nearly as magnificent as Miss Ashburton's.

Suppressing a wave of unwanted heat, he poured two glasses of wine, handing the second to Blake.

"I checked your rooms before leaving," Blake said. "This had just arrived." He pulled out a letter.

Max grimaced, recognizing his father's hand. As expected, it was a new rant demanding that he return home immediately. "He has heard rumors that I am playing deeply every night," he said lightly, hiding his pain that Montcalm would rather believe exaggerated gossip than discover the truth for himself.

"He was bound to hear."

"But he didn't have to— It doesn't matter. He will never change." Exhaling sharply, he turned the subject. "What new rumors arose after I left town?"

"Reggie surrendered to his mother's pressure and agreed to wed next Season."

"I thought he looked a bit strained." He shook his head. "Another good man caught in parson's mousetrap."

"Worse. He fears his mother will maneuver him into taking on a martinet. His revelry these past days contains a note of desperation, as if he fears that he will have to stay home and become respectable."

"He will come about. A monkey says he will propose to the most conformable pea-goose in society before the Season is a fortnight old. Such a one will turn a blind eye to his adventures."

"I'll have to pass on this one, for I entirely agree. Like Devereaux, Reggie will always be a rake—unlike you. If you find the right lady, you will never stray."

"I could say the same for you, but I have no plans to wed any time soon. Only after Father admits that I am no longer a child will I look to the succession." The letter had also contained that demand.

"But he—never mind." He obeyed Max's scowl and changed the subject. "Ashburton may regret losing that game. Society is now watching him."

"Why would he care?"

"I'm not sure, but a rather garbled story turned up the morning we left. Something about his wife locking herself in the cellar to escape his son's threats over some missing jewelry."

Max frowned. "*Garbled* is right."

"Ashburton left town, so no one can confirm or deny it. Some claim the tale is a hum and that he is pursuing a long-standing enemy."

A shiver touched Max's shoulders. It made little sense, yet it might explain that card game. Had Ashburton dragged him into an elaborate plot? He must be careful to stay away from the fellow.

Blake drained his wine. "Perhaps he is merely playing hard to find. He must know that you would discover his lies about Redrock. How bad is it?"

"I would have no legitimate complaint, even if the estate were worse, for it cost me nothing. But it has potential. In his father's day, it brought in ten thousand a year. I believe it could do even better with the proper management."

"But it will take time and money to rescue it." It was not a question. Blake knew as much about Coke's experiments as Max did.

"I have both. What else am I to do with them? I have no intention of going home."

They discussed agriculture for nearly an hour. Max described the problems Miss Ashburton had revealed. More than once he nearly slipped and named her. Thus he rejoiced when Terrence and Jeanette came downstairs. Changing the subject would guard his tongue.

Two evenings later Hope paused outside her mother's room. Shrieks echoed from the west wing. Footsteps pounded up the stairs.

"Caught you," growled a male voice.

"So you did." The girl giggled. "What will you do with me?"

"Take you right here." Something slammed against the wardrobe.

Hope tried to ignore the sounds that followed. She needed to relieve Rose at her mother's bedside, but she dared not open the door. What if her mother was awake?

A throaty giggle ended in a breathless suggestion.

Hope clasped her hands over her ears as a rhythmic thumping echoed along the hall, raising the memory of the dogs she had once seen copulating. She ought to shoot Merimont for subjecting her to this.

Harsh panting finally ended in a long moan. Only then did Hope realize that one hand had loosened as she strained to hear.

The man made another lewd suggestion as he led his partner of the moment away.

Heat washed over Hope's face. How could she have listened to such debauchery? Even curiosity should have bounds. Society was right to shelter innocents. The sounds from the west wing made her uncomfortable in ways she couldn't explain.

Taking a deep breath, she picked up her tray and opened the door.

Rose seemed as composed as ever. Either her hearing was worse or the heavy door had muffled the noise. But as she sent Rose down for dinner, an insidious little voice wondered how many similar incidents she had missed. Did Merimont also enjoy servicing his mistress against a wall where anyone might see them?

This time the heat engulfed her entire body.

She should have realized the real danger of allowing him to hold his party here. His preparations protected her from physical assault, but they did nothing to dull her imagination. Though this incident had been the most blatant, it was far from the first.

Chasing seemed common, complete with squeals, giggles, and mock threats. At least one man had ripped off a gown. And she could only be grateful that she did not understand some of the words that floated over the barricades—though her imagination tried. Banishing such thoughts did not prevent them from creeping into her dreams.

She shivered, for the dreams seemed far too real, tormenting her nights with stroking hands, with teeth that slid deliciously around ears and lips, with—

Stop this!

She was worse than Merimont's guests. Her mind concocted outrageous images out of snatches of conversation, but such fantasies were dangerous. They assigned pleasure to debauchery when everyone knew ladies derived no enjoyment from that activity. Her mother had once described it as disgusting and painful—which accounted for the bloodcurdling scream she'd heard last night.

If only Merimont would leave. She'd been restless ever since his arrival, fearful of what he might do, terrified that her mother might die, yet equally terrified that she would recover enough to realize who was in the house. Merimont had even invaded her sleep last night, adding a face to the hands that prevented her much-needed rest.

Why had he arrived when she was already beset by fear for her mother? At any other time, she could have kept him out—out of her house and out of her dreams. Instead, he was insidiously seducing her without even trying. The cad!

He and his friends had taken a picnic to the woods yesterday, the ladies giggling like ninnies as they hung on the gentlemen's arms and snuggled against gentlemen's chests, squealing in delight at wanton caresses.

She blushed to recall how she'd watched through her mother's window. Perhaps her uncle was right to complain that her behavior was not up to snuff. No lady would stare at a covey of courtesans. And she had no business entertaining regrets that she could not join them, especially after seeing their clothes. Even the unseasonably warm temperatures had not prepared her for so many scandalous necklines. Not one girl had a stitch on beneath her thin muslin gown, as anyone could tell in the sun.

Had her father boldly taken what he wanted as Merimont had done that first day? Had he seduced her mother into giggles and squeals like the fallen women at Redrock, or had he forced her with determined brutality?

Probably force, she concluded grimly. She'd seen no evidence that rakes respected anyone, regardless of background. Even Merimont had not protected her, de-

spite his soothing promises. She must try harder to shut
them out. Nothing good could come of listening.

Her mother moaned, returning her attention to business. Dipping the cloth in cool water, she bathed her
face and neck. But her puny efforts had little effect on
the fever raging through that frail body.

Hope slipped into the walled rose garden before
dawn, praying that the worst was over. Her mother's
fever had risen until she'd feared that convulsions were
inevitable, but an hour ago it had finally broken, soaking
the bed in perspiration. Hope had struggled to change
the linens without awakening Rose or Mrs. Tweed, then
fixed another cup of willow tea to prevent the fever's
return. Now her mother was sleeping soundly for the
first time in days.

With relief had come exhaustion. Her back hurt from
constant sponging. Dizziness reminded her that she'd
eaten little since breakfast yesterday—or had it been the
day before?

She needed sleep, yet she was too tired and too
restless.

But at least her mother's improvement kept her safe.
When she had described the lease to Merimont, she had
implied that he could not touch Redrock for seventy-
five years, but that was not strictly true. Her mother
retained her rights until death, but her own ended when
she married. Thus this recovery would remove any in-
centive to force her into marriage and would give him
time to grow bored and leave.

She completed a circuit of the garden and started another, listening to the silence. Most of the birds had left
for the winter. Yesterday's unseasonable warmth was
gone, leaving a thin coating of frost on the ground. A
phalanx of geese crossed the moon's face as they headed
for warmer climes, teasing the silence with distant
honking.

She ought to seek her bed, she admitted as her feet
moved quietly across the grass. But she was still beset
by restlessness and other odd sensations. And there was

no need to rush. Morning was usually quiet in the west
wing. Everyone would be asleep.

"An angel, come to earth to greet the dawn. Or are
you rosy-fingered Eos herself?" asked a male voice.

She spun around. A man stood just behind her. The
dark one whose grimace had disturbed her on arrival.
His words may have been poetic, but his voice grated
like a hinge in need of oil.

"No wonder dear Max hides the maids. Does he hope
to keep you to himself?" His smile seemed more preda-
tory than friendly. One hand reached out to caress the
side of her neck.

"No!" She stepped out of reach.

"Don't be coy, my dear. Max needn't know a thing."

"I don't know what you're talking about, sir," she
tried, panicking when she realized that her retreat had
cornered her in a thicket of roses.

He slid an arm around her shoulders, reviving images
of Merimont's arrival. But this touch was cold, making
her skin crawl.

"Leave me alone," she begged, twisting to escape.

"Forget Max. His mistress is here—and a delightful
young filly she is," he added, licking his lips. "I'll double
the usual fee." He named a figure that would support a
laborer for months.

"I'm not interested. Go back to the house."

"You don't mean that." His face turned ugly. "Don't
hold out for *carte blanche,* girl. This is my best offer. No
whore is worth more." His hand slid over her bosom.

Fighting off nausea, she screamed, then swung wildly,
managing to connect with his nose.

He caught her arms and twisted them behind her
back. Blood dripped onto his cravat.

"The chit isn't interested, Dornbras." The drawl from
near the gate silenced her attacker's snarl. "It's not
worth bedding a screamer—and bad form to force your
host's servants."

Dornbras froze, then stepped back—reluctantly, if his
eyes were any indication. With deliberate moves he
pulled out a handkerchief and wiped the blood from
his face.

Hope cringed against a rosebush. Thorns tore into her arm as she hugged herself to control her shaking.

"You are out early this morning," grumbled Dornbras. "Did Flo throw you out of bed?"

"No earlier than you," said the newcomer calmly, adding, "Missy was looking for you."

"I doubt it. The girl has no stamina. I used her hard enough that she'll sleep 'til noon."

"Shall I check her for bruises?"

"Why? So you can carry tales to our host?"

"Tale-bearing would be worth it if it would open his eyes to what you are." A definite threat underlay the words.

"He already knows." Dornbras grinned without a hint of pleasure. "Now get you gone so I can conclude my business."

"No."

The looks they exchanged could have sliced steel. For a moment, Hope feared they would come to blows. She wanted to run, but that would have meant touching the man called Dornbras. She stayed where she was, cowering into a rosebush.

Dornbras finally shrugged. "She's probably got the pox anyway."

"Then you are lucky she declined your offer."

Relief washed over her as Dornbras strode away, but she ignored it, turning her attention to her rescuer. Would he also attack? Like his friend, he was a libertine, though at least he did not radiate evil. But he was enjoying this party as much as the others.

He stepped back, turning half away from her. "You need not fear me. I never make unwanted advances," he said softly. "But don't tarry here again. Report to work promptly. Dornbras is growing bored, and he welcomes challenge. Avoid him."

Holding her breath, Hope slipped past him, snagging her cloak on a thorn in an effort to remain as far away as possible. But he made no move to touch her. She relaxed.

"Thank you, sir." Her voice shook. "For both the rescue and the advice."

Without waiting for a response, she fled toward the gate. *I'll kill him for this,* she muttered, cursing herself for allowing Merimont to move in. Why had she listened to him? His first touch should have told her where it would lead. *Lord Merimont, indeed. Lord Rakehell is more appropriate. Lord Scoundrel. Lord Blackguard. Can I not even enjoy a moment at dawn in my own garden?*

She should have sworn to expose him to the world if he didn't leave. To cry rape or accuse him publicly of every dishonorable act known to man. Maybe then he would have taken himself and his friends somewhere else.

"What did you say?" A hand grasped her shoulder, halting her in her tracks.

"Nothing." She shook off his touch, furious to realize she'd spoken aloud.

"The truth."

She glared into his amber eyes. Another man bent on his own desires. And he now stood between her and the gate, though he made no further move to touch her.

"Well? Who the hell are you?" Anger was growing in his eyes.

She shrugged. "I thought you did not assault unwilling females."

"I am not assaulting you. I am trying to find out what is going on."

"Nothing, though I fear your friend might be lying in wait for me. I doubt he accepts defeat gracefully."

"He does not, but that is not what you said in your very genteel voice. You mentioned Merimont."

"Someone taking my name in vain?" Merimont pushed open the gate and froze. "Miss Ashburton!" He sounded appalled.

"I take it you are acquainted." His friend sounded even more furious. Violence crackled through the air.

Hope shook her head, forcing her terror aside. Somehow, she must relieve the tension before these rakehells unleashed their anger on her. "What is this?" she demanded lightly. "The fashionable hour at Hyde Park? I thought gentlemen slept the mornings away."

"What the devil are you doing here?" demanded Merimont, glaring as he loomed over her.

"Would you believe sleepwalking?"

He snorted.

"I didn't think so. In truth, I hoped a turn about the garden would relax me. I hardly expected to meet anyone."

Merimont sighed. Turning his back on his friend, he squeezed her hand. "Forgive me. We never discussed the grounds, did we?"

The words revived her other grievances. "We neglected to discuss a great number of things, starting with how noisy you people are. If Mother hears you, the shock will kill her."

Merimont's face darkened. The hand that gripped hers tightened.

"What the devil is going on?" demanded the other man.

She jumped, shrinking against Merimont's side. The moment he'd touched her, she'd forgotten his friend. Fool!

Merimont inhaled sharply. "Miss Ashburton, may I present Lord Rockhurst. Blake, this is Miss Hope Ashburton. She and her mother lease Redrock House."

Chapter Six

Max wished the ground would swallow him. He'd never been so embarrassed in his life. Yet he did not feel the slightest irritation with Miss Ashburton for placing him in this position. In fact, her hand was still clutched in his own, and she stood close enough that he could smell lavender.

But her willingness to seek his protection proved that the situation was worse than he'd feared. Finding her with Blake was unfortunate, though Blake would never hurt her. But Dornbras had stomped into the house only minutes ago. Had she met him?

The jagged flash of fear that accompanied the question did more to remove the scales from his eyes than all of Blake's warnings. Miss Ashburton was not safe with Dornbras, who would welcome the chance to ravish an innocent. If she protested, Dornbras would derive even more pleasure from the encounter.

He groaned. How could he have been so blind? Dornbras's father might be more rigid than his own, but he was trying to rein in a son who was racing toward disaster.

But that was a problem for later. If Blake's glare was any indication, he was in for a tongue-lashing. This wasn't something Blake would ignore. And rightly so.

"Ashburton?" repeated Blake, his quiet voice hiding the fury Max knew was raging.

"My uncle is Lord Ashburton, former owner of Redrock." She flashed a look of pure malevolence at Max and dropped his hand.

Her sudden antagonism was another problem he could address later, though he suspected she was thinking of the noise she'd mentioned a moment ago. Clearly she still believed all men were alike. "I only discovered her existence upon arrival," he said in excuse.

"I did not know that Ashburton had siblings."

Miss Ashburton shrugged. "My father died shortly after my birth."

Max drew her aside. "We can discuss your connections later. How is your mother?"

She smiled. "Her fever finally broke, thank heaven. Forgive me for intruding on your guests, my lord. I did not expect anyone to be about."

"I am at fault, Miss Ashburton. I should have anticipated a great many more things, I see."

Her smile faded, leaving her face pale and lifeless. "I will not make that mistake again."

Her vow made him feel smaller than the hedgehog nosing about under the roses. She was the only innocent at Redrock. "You are not at fault. It should have been perfectly safe. I cannot believe that any of us is awake at this hour." He realized he was babbling, trying to restore the sparkle to her gray eyes. He sighed. "We must talk. May I join you in the office once I explain to Blake? He is my closest friend and will not harm you. Nor will he mention this to others."

"The library would be more convenient—and more private, as voices would carry less." She nodded toward a door opening onto the end of the terrace, obviously her exit from the east wing.

He cringed at this latest jibe, just as he had cringed at every suggestive sound for three days. Never before had he realized how noisy people could be when they set propriety aside. No one heeded convention, bouncing enthusiastically about and abandoning every shred of modesty. Reggie had pulled Francine under the table during dinner last night, and he'd heard Terrence and Jeanette in the hall a short time later.

But this was no time to recall such things, he reminded himself through a new wave of embarrassment. Lifting Miss Ashburton's hand to his lips, he smiled. "The library it is. I will join you shortly."

He watched to make sure she reached the house without incident, then turned back to Blake.

Blake watched with growing amusement as Max soothed the girl's anger and sent her toward the supposedly uninhabitable wing of the manor. That touch of tenderness went far beyond the concern he had shown when rescuing females in the past.

Which was just as well. If this situation was as bad as it looked, those two would be spending a lifetime together. A touch of tenderness might well make it bearable.

But neither observation was one he could mention. Max's most glaring fault was stubbornness. Once he made up his mind, he never changed it—just like his father, though that was another observation Blake had been careful to keep to himself. He'd learned that lesson the hard way by disparaging Dornbras when Max was smarting from one of Montcalm's tirades and determined to show the world that he could make his own decisions. Society had been plagued by the man ever since.

So he could not let Max claim disinterest in Miss Ashburton or deny that he'd compromised the girl.

Max turned back to the garden, glaring.

Blake held up a hand. "You needn't call me out. I'm not the one putting that girl's reputation in jeopardy."

"How dare you accuse me of ruining her. I've done everything possible to protect her."

"You don't have to fight me, Max. I'm not your father. Nor did I accuse you of ruining her. But being here puts her in jeopardy."

Max shook his head, all anger draining from his eyes. "What happened?" he asked wearily.

Blake shrugged. "I came outside for some air. Flo had fallen asleep in my bed. You know I dislike sharing."

"Don't we all?" Max muttered.

Blake nearly smiled. It had been obvious for days that Max was bored with Annette. Now he had to wonder if Max was more enamored of Miss Ashburton than he'd appeared. "I walked down to the stream and back. As

I was approaching the terrace, I heard Dornbras assaulting someone."

"Dear God."

"It hadn't progressed very far. In fact, she drew blood planting him a facer as I reached the gate. Obviously she does not know that he abandons all scruples in pursuit of revenge," he added daringly. "If I had not happened along, she would now be ruined in truth. I feared I would have to pull him away as it was."

"She's a lady!"

Progress. Max did not protest the attack, merely the class of the victim. He made his voice as dispassionate as possible, though he longed to shake the truth into his friend's thick head. "Dornbras attacks anyone who rebuffs him, Max. Open your eyes. The man is an unscrupulous scoundrel. But even scruples would not have mattered this time. He thought she was one of the maids. I suspect he was lying in wait for them—he was muttering about the lack of variety last night. He still thinks she is a servant, for I had that impression myself until you introduced her. That gown is hardly the dress one expects of a lady."

"She's been nursing a sick mother." He sighed. "I must apologize to her."

Blake shook his head. "You had better do more than apologize. Your only choice is to send us all packing before something worse happens. What possessed you to set up this party?"

"It wasn't my doing," Max protested again. "Ashburton said nothing about the house being leased when he signed over the estate. Nor did his solicitor."

"Start at the beginning," he begged, then was shocked when Max did.

"So you must admit that she is all right," Max said. "She lives in a separate household, protected by her mother and her own staff."

"Two elderly servants, a mother abed with a raving fever, and a shared roof over her head. She may be safe from the gossips—though the technicality may escape some—but I would hardly call her protected." He waved at the rose garden. "If I hadn't been nearby when she screamed, she would have been ruined—and not gently. How dare you introduce five courtesans and a predator like Dornbras into a genteel household? Quit hiding behind excuses and look at yourself. You should have moved into an inn on arrival and sent us packing."

"I will have to work harder to protect her," Max said doggedly.

"You need to send us back to London," insisted Blake, pacing restlessly about the garden.

"On what pretext? You are just as blind as you think me—as I was, for you are right about Dornbras. He should not be here."

Blake stumbled and nearly fell. If the attack on Miss Ashburton had brought this change, then Max was serious, indeed, though he would undoubtedly deny it.

"But he *is* here," continued Max. "If we ask him to leave, or even cancel the party so we all leave, he will rightly conclude that this incident is to blame. Temper will force him to avenge the insult by tracking down the girl. What will he do when he discovers Miss Ashburton's station and residence?"

"Ruin her reputation by denouncing her to society," Blake said wearily. "Then cry compromise in an attempt to ruin you as well."

"Exactly. He will feel the same grievance toward me for tossing him out as he would toward her for precipitating the action. So we must stay at least a week. By then, the cramped quarters will be excuse enough to leave."

"Does that mean that Miss Ashburton must remain indoors?"

"We will discuss that shortly, but I cannot risk her running into anyone else. Nor can I risk Dornbras exploring the east wing—if he is truly bored, he might enjoy flirting with its supposed dangers. Why the devil did I not see through him earlier?"

"Do you really want to know?"

Max nodded.

Blake drew a deep breath and laid his friendship on the line. "I made the mistake of criticizing him when you were smarting so badly from Montcalm's orders that you automatically denied any suggestion."

Max's fists clenched, but he said nothing. Several minutes passed in silence.

"That's it?" he finally asked. "That's stupid."

Blake breathed again. "Probably, but—" He stopped, unwilling to push his luck a second time.

"But what?" Max demanded.

Did he dare?

"Don't coddle me, Blake. If you can't tell me the truth, who can?"

Who, indeed? "Once you lodge an idea in your head, you rarely let it go."

"Good God." The sun slipped above the horizon, illuminating his white face. "That's what my father does."

Blake nodded.

"I'm turning into my father?"

"I didn't say that, Max. You share one trait with him, but you needn't keep it. Now that you are aware of the tendency, you can let it go."

Max shook his head. "I need to think. But first I must safeguard Miss Ashburton. The provisions I made earlier won't work with Dornbras, but I can block the most easily penetrated access by moving into the dressing room attached to her wing."

"What?"

"I should have considered it earlier. The two wings mirror each other, so the empty bedchamber in the east wing is like yours, with a dressing room that opens onto the central hall. I can position a bed in there so it blocks the bedchamber door. It will increase her safety."

"And how will you explain moving into a dressing room when you have a perfectly good room of your own?"

He shrugged. "I'm through with Annette anyway. Her pouting is annoying enough that I needn't mention she has the brain of a hen."

"So why not turn her loose under the same rules as the other girls?"

Max frowned. "It is not fair that you gave up your dressing room. Now that I am unencumbered, I can play the perfect host by taking the room we all know is dangerous, giving the largest room to the girls. They can sleep there, making all of us happier."

"And reducing the urgency of terminating this party for lack of space."

"Do you have a better suggestion?" snapped Max.

"Only that you keep the girls out of your new room. This situation is already too close to being compromising."

"True, though her mother is recovering. And that dressing room is the only real way anyone can enter. The wardrobes take two hefty men to shift, and my presence will prevent anyone from experimenting with keys. She will be safer than before."

"Very well. But I will be watching. If any harm comes to her, I'll hold you responsible."

Max watched his friend stride away, astonished at the threat—which echoed the similar one Miss Ashburton had made the day he'd arrived. Hers he could understand, but what was Blake's interest? Had he formed a *tendre* for the girl? It seemed unlikely, but so did his interest in a stranger's welfare.

The sun was barely up, yet he'd already suffered more shocks today than in years. The worst was that doubler Blake had landed. Was he really as stubborn and close-minded as his father? Granted, he had supported Dornbras long after he should have seen the truth, but some of that had arisen from manipulation. If he were honest, he had to admit that Dornbras flattered him often. After enduring his father's complaints for so many years, he had welcomed the adulation—ignoring evidence of the man's true nature.

He wasn't sure he completely understood that nature even now. It would take time to sort out the facts from his long-standing impressions. But that was for later.

Tension had infested the party from the beginning. He had assumed that his imagination was to blame, for he knew that every sound could be heard in the east wing, but now he had to wonder what else was going on. Maybe Dornbras was the source of it, though he hoped not. With luck, freeing Annette would inject new interest. And allowing everyone to sleep better should also help.

He would soon find out. Glancing at the windows to make sure he was not seen, he rapped on the library door. He had a full morning ahead. First he must deal with Miss Ashburton, then give Annette her congé and move his things to the spare bedchamber—he would not sleep in the dressing room, though Blake need not know that. Once that was done, he could settle the girls in their own room.

Hope pulled a book of poetry from a shelf, praying that it would calm her shattered nerves. The morning had brought so many shocks she could hardly think.

Her mother's improvement was good news, though recovery was a long way off. Yet it had led her into trouble, for she would not have ventured outdoors if the fever had remained. Now she faced a new danger. Merimont's eyes had nearly scorched her with their fury.

And he was right. If she had stayed out of sight as he'd asked, Dornbras would not have cornered her. His assault had shaken her badly—far worse than Merimont's own attack. If Lord Rockhurst had not heard her screams for help . . .

The thought pulled her up short. She had always believed that all gentlemen were alike—unscrupulous, arrogant libertines who never looked beyond the desire of the moment and cared nothing for others. The description fit her father, her uncle, and Lord Millhouse, whose estate abutted Redrock.

Now she had to admit that honorable gentlemen also existed. Rockhurst had forced Dornbras to leave, then made no move to take her for himself. And once he'd discovered her breeding and residence, he had been furious at Merimont.

Had she taken her mother's admonitions too seriously? Though the aristocracy was small, it was large enough to encompass variety—just as other classes did. The local gentry included the very silly Mr. Croman, stuffy Major Baldwin, kind Dr. Jenkins, hunting-mad Squire Foley, and lecherous Sir Virgil.

Even Merimont had tried to protect her, though his reputation was quite sordid. And she had let him. How could she have pressed against him, allowing the heat of his body to thaw her fear?

She shivered, praying that he would attribute the action to shock. If he discovered her lascivious dreams, he might yet turn on her. Prudence demanded that she stay away from him. He made it difficult to think. And prudence also demanded that she remain wary of his friends. Rockhurst clearly hated Dornbras. His interference might have sought only to annoy an enemy.

A rap on the window interrupted her thoughts. Merimont stepped inside, then stopped, staring. "This room is huge."

"It occupies half of the wing." There was little point in mentioning that it had originally been the dining room. She had converted it, with her grandfather's assistance, when she was thirteen and had run out of space in her sitting room. Now tall shelves lined the walls, crowded with leather-bound volumes. Lower shelves surrounded study tables, a comfortable couch where she could relax while reading, and a corner where she and her grandfather had debated ideas. She'd not seen another room arranged this way, but he had agreed to every request, for the library was her personal refuge. Even her mother never used it.

Merimont wandered along the wall, pulling out an occasional volume to riffle its pages.

"I've rarely seen such an extensive collection, Miss Ashburton," he murmured at last. "Quite a find."

"But they are not yours, my lord. Only that shelf belongs to the estate." She pointed to a dozen volumes of collected sermons. "The rest are mine."

"Do you claim to have read all of these?" he demanded incredulously, waving a copy of Homer's *Odyssey* in the original Greek.

"You need not sound so shocked," she snapped in that language before returning to English. "Grandfather encouraged me to study anything of interest. I could not attend school, for Mother needed my help even before he died, but he provided anything I requested—probably to make up for keeping us here rather than at Ashburton Park, as was Mother's right. I have continued to add new titles whenever finances allowed it. Books are my window to the world."

She stopped talking. Gentlemen did not care for educated women, she remembered too late. She certainly should not brag about it, though she had read every volume at least once. Many were favorites that she reread often. Reading was her one indulgence. She knew well that she would never leave Redrock House, never have a family of her own, never experience life in London, let alone in other lands. But giving him a new reason to despise her could only lead to trouble.

He made no comment, replacing Homer, then thumbing through a volume on agriculture that had arrived only a month earlier. "I've not seen this one yet—not that I could have afforded it if I had." he muttered.

"It only cost five guineas. You probably lose more than that at cards of a night."

He stiffened. "You can hardly claim to know me."

"I read the London papers." She hid her instinctive recoil at his displeasure. She could not let him intimidate her.

He slammed the book back onto the shelf. "But you don't understand them. Gossip columns carry titillating stories, but they are usually exaggerated and sometimes false. One should never form an opinion of a stranger based solely on gossip."

"I stand corrected." She tried a conciliatory smile. "I suppose drawing room conversation is equally bad."

He was also fighting to control his tongue. Circles under his eyes proclaimed that he had not yet been to bed. "If anything, it is worse. I have been credited with the deeds of others and had my own youthful excesses built into full-fledged scandal."

"Then you can hardly blame me for fearing the worst after listening to tales of reckless debauchery and descriptions of how you disrupted Lady Horseley's ball. Your recent behavior confirms those impressions. You admitted that you won Redrock at the tables, then immediately arranged a house party that society would shun."

"Yes, well—" His face flushed, surprising her. "Those tales are prime examples of how gossip twists truth. Lady Horseley's ball was a youthful mistake that I deeply regret, though it was not I who shot the cat that night. I merely passed out."

"Then what really happened?"

He shrugged. "Three of us slipped away from school to visit London. My memory of the affair is rather hazy, for we consumed far too much brandy before calling on Lady Horseley—she is a deplorable widgeon, but a high stickler, for all that."

She chuckled.

He flashed a charming smile. "I've no idea what happened, for I'd barely staggered into the ballroom when I passed out most theatrically on the floor." He demonstrated. "But I am certain it was not I who soiled her ladyship. I have no recollection of seeing her, and I was most vilely ill when I awakened in an antechamber two hours later. My friends had disappeared like will-o'-the-wisps, leaving me as the only one Lady Horseley could identify. So the bagwig sent me down for the rest of that term. Of course, I amply avenged myself," he added, jumping nimbly to his feet. "My friends had to serve as my squires for months once I returned."

Hope laughed. "I'm sorry," she said, wiping her eyes. "It must have been mortifying, but you do make it sound humorous."

He grinned. "I'm glad I can amuse you. Most gossip is exaggerated one way or another. As for this house party—which is a legitimate complaint—I will terminate it as soon as possible, though I must wait a few days if your reputation is to survive. I am deeply chagrined at this morning's unfortunate encounter."

"I know that you would have preferred that I meet none of your friends, but—"

"I am not referring to Blake, Miss Ashburton. He is a fine fellow who would never cause you a moment of grief. Unfortunately, I cannot say the same for Dornbras. I should never have invited him and should have sent him packing the moment I realized that you would be here. No man of sense would condone his actions today. Even had you been the servant he thought you, he should not have pressed once you made your disinterest plain."

"But why should he believe my protests?" she asked with a sigh. "He thinks himself irresistible—understandably, I suppose. Paying girls as much as he offered me must elicit praise for his prowess."

Merimont frowned. "An odd way of seeing things."

"Why? He is willing to pay for whatever he wants. If he wants to feel like the greatest man on earth, I'm sure he can buy that opinion." This time she made no attempt to conceal her loathing.

"At least he did not succeed in compromising you," said Merimont soothingly. "You would not have enjoyed marrying him."

"I would have refused," she said shortly.

"You couldn't. Society would ostracize you."

"Better that than marriage," she countered.

"I agree that wedding him would be unpleasant— though he's enormously wealthy—but you must wed someone. All ladies need husbands."

"Fustian! You won't drive me out that easily," she swore, glaring now that he'd confirmed her suspicions. "Some marriages might be pleasing, but most are contracts with the devil. Men lie and cheat, striking out at any who oppose them. Even wives in desired unions must remain wary lest they incite violence."

"What do you know of marriage, Miss Ashburton?"

"I need look no further than my parents." Or her uncle, for that matter. "Men are selfish creatures to begin with. Forcing them to wed someone they don't want creates a grievance that turns them into monsters."

"An interesting point of view—not that I agree. Honor does play a role in the world. You should look beyond your parents, Miss Ashburton, for men are not all alike. Consider Blake and Dornbras. But we have moved far afield. I will terminate this gathering as soon as it is feasible. In the meantime, I will strengthen your protection."

"Oh?" She didn't know whether to laugh or rant. "Is there a new threat?"

He hesitated. "As you pointed out, Dornbras is accustomed to having his own way. He will never forgive you for laying a hand on him. I fear he may ignore my claims and try to explore this wing, as a cure for boredom if for no other reason. To prevent that, I must move into your spare bedchamber, so he cannot enter through the dressing room." He must have seen her eyes widen in shock because he hurried on. "I will keep the hallway door locked—in fact, you may keep the key if you wish. And no one will share that room with me."

"I see." Though she did not. But the thought of Dornbras slipping through that dressing room to accost her in her own bed made any alternative attractive. "Very well, though it seems easier to simply send your friends away."

"Soon, I promise. But if Dornbras connects an early departure with meeting you, your reputation would be in danger."

"That hardly matters. My neighbors know me well enough to discount claims by a London wastrels."

"I am not talking about words but deeds, Miss Ashburton. He would stay in the area until he found the servant who struck him, then deal with her."

"Yet you claim him as a friend?" she demanded, her skin crawling at the image he painted.

"No longer. I had not realized how far he was willing to go. I cannot condone force."

"Nor I." His words warmed her heart, but she stifled the softening. No matter what face he put on his past, he was hardly harmless. "It grows late, and I was up all night with Mother. I will leave the keys in your dressing room. If we need to talk, slip a note into my hall." She motioned him toward the terrace, covering a yawn.

He yawned in return, then took a civil leave.

Locking the door, she made sure the draperies were firmly closed, then headed upstairs.

Max glanced around the table at dinner that night. In three days the character of the party had changed. The first night, they had gathered around Terrence at the pianoforte to sing bawdy tunes. The next evening they'd played a lascivious game of charades that had most of them laughing by the time it concluded.

Now he was so tense he feared he would shatter. The morning's revelations had kept him from sleep. Blake's claims were bad enough, but Miss Ashburton's notion that Dornbras used the flattery of hired companions to feed his arrogance had struck even closer to the bone. Was he also guilty of using insincere words to confirm his worth? Not sexually, but his position invited toadying. Dornbras was the most obvious example, trading praise for support, but there might be others.

Having to reevaluate long-standing friendships was one reason he felt nervous tonight. The other was Dornbras. Did he suspect whom he had accosted that morning? He had become more petulant as the day progressed, popping in and out of rooms, obviously looking for the mysterious servant. Max had finally drawn him aside, ignoring the slight swelling around the man's nose.

"She quit," he'd said firmly. "I had to hire tenants and villagers to help with this party, but they are not of the servant class. I promised that we would leave them alone, so please keep your hands off the others, or we will have no staff at all. One more incident and they will leave en masse. Most are related."

Dornbras had blustered, swearing that the girl had misunderstood.

"Your intentions don't matter," Max had finally said soothingly. "She was flustered enough to leave. Since no one else is available, I must ask all of you to ignore the remaining staff."

Now Blake frowned in disgust as Dornbras caressed Missy. Reggie also looked irritated, for Dornbras had grown too overt for even rakish tastes. But with luck the man would find a new interest by morning.

His eyes moved on to Annette. She had not been surprised when he'd dismissed her. He'd avoided her for two days, too concerned with protecting the east wing to enjoy her attentions. It hadn't taken her long to line up a new protector. Terrence had already taken her under his wing, becoming oblivious to both Dornbras and the growing tension.

It had not diminished. And it wasn't imagination. Blake also felt it, his eyes appearing troubled as he examined the guests. But he made no comment on Dornbras's increasingly explicit remarks.

Dinner finally ended. Dornbras and Missy headed upstairs, to no one's regret. Max followed, eschewing a second evening of music. Yet three hours later, he remained wide awake, standing at the window as he stared into the distance. A feeling of doom was growing.

Chapter Seven

Dawn crept through a crack in the draperies, waking Hope. Her neck was stiff from sleeping in the chair.

She had not meant to spend the night here. With the fever gone, it was no longer necessary to keep constant watch. But she had remained to make sure that no hint of the west wing revelries penetrated the door.

They had not, which had actually disturbed her, for she'd hoped that her mother's latest delirium had been triggered by voices.

It was not the first time illness had produced a rambling monologue, of course. The incidents had started several years ago, about the same time her melancholy had noticeably deepened. The first one had merely recalled Uncle Edward's most recent visit.

Hope had been appalled to realize how terrified her mother was to be alone with Uncle Edward, though the monologue itself had made little impression. Even the realization that her mother recalled nothing of her revelations once she recovered seemed unimportant. Hope took steps to see that her mother was always accompanied during his visits and put the incident behind her.

But the same thing had happened during the next illness, and the next. More than a year passed before she realized that each monologue relived a memory that preceded the last, reversing through every fearful event in her mother's life. Yesterday she had reached her ruination by Arnold Ashburton. The fever had flared at dusk, sending her into another memory.

"Call me Arnold, my love," she had murmured, after disjointed phrases that hinted she had slipped away more than once to meet him in the woods. Hope had bitten her lip as her mother continued quoting his blandishments. "So beautiful, love. Fresh as the fairest flower of spring. Must have a taste. Just one taste."

"No." Her mother had thrashed briefly, but whether she had protested to him or was trying to warn her younger self of danger, Hope didn't know. She soothed the brow with cool water as words tumbled from those dry lips—words that cajoled, words that flattered, words that pleaded for just one more touch or one last kiss, and words that subtly threatened if she refused.

"Sinful," shouted her mother. "Blasphemous." Her hand jerked to her throat. "But you know your father will never accept me, love. The only way we can be together is to force his hand."

Hope had listened in growing fury as her mother relived every moment of that encounter—her uncertainty that she was choosing the right course, the short-lived excitement that changed to bewilderment and pain, and finally to terror when he disappeared without a word the next day.

Tears had streamed down Hope's face, mirroring those flowing from her mother's eyes.

"Mortal sin . . . damnation . . ." her mother had murmured before sliding into a deeper sleep. Again the fever had broken, as it so often did following one of these spells.

Hope had stayed, pondering the revelations, straining to hear any sound from Merimont's room or the west wing, and finally falling asleep. Now she massaged the soreness from her neck as she watched her mother.

The lady's eyes remained closed, but her breathing seemed more labored. The fever was back. Yesterday's improvement might have slowed her decline, but she was not yet on the road to recovery.

Hope's fears returned, more debilitating than ever. Being alone would make her vulnerable. Only now did she fully understand her mother's warnings against rakes. They would do and say anything to achieve their goals—and sound sincere in the process. How else had her father persuaded her mother to abandon a lifetime of propriety and violate her own convictions to lie with him? One mistake, one moment of temptation, and her life had been ruined.

She would never fall into that trap. Once her mother recovered, she would eject Merimont from the house and keep him out. He might be better at hiding his true nature than most, but she would not allow him to pull the wool over her eyes.

She headed downstairs to make breakfast. The house felt even eerier than it had yesterday, when Dornbras's eyes had seemed to bore into her back wherever she'd gone. Imagination, of course. But she could not forget them—scanning the house on arrival, glaring daggers at her when she'd struck him, promising retribution in that last black gaze before he'd left the rose garden.

Her governess had once claimed Hope had a touch of the sight, for she knew too much about others. Hope had rejected the notion, claiming that she was merely more observant than poor Miss Ellis. But it was true that she could read eyes. Dornbras's were evil, hard and black, devoid of emotion, offering no glimpse of a soul.

Rockhurst's were cautious, though it was difficult to draw conclusions since she'd seen him only when he was suffused with anger. Merimont's were different yet— brilliant blue, amazingly expressive, and capable of great warmth.

It's a trick, swore her conscience. *He's trying to steal Redrock just as your father stole your mother's virginity. Beneath that charm lies a heart as cold as any other man's.*

She shivered, suddenly remembering the muffled shout she'd heard as she'd started to leave her mother's room last night. That was why she'd fallen asleep in there. Quickly shutting the door, she'd decided to wait until all was quiet. The shout had been male, though she'd not recognized the voice.

Reaching the ground floor, she entered the stillroom, then froze as a whimper escaped from the laundry.

"Who is there?" The eeriness was back, stronger than ever. Even the Prices should not be here this early.

Silence.

"Anyone there?"

Nothing.

Shrugging, she turned away, but the clatter of metal striking the stone floor jerked her back. Forcing the bar aside, she threw open the door and gasped.

"Dear Lord!"

A girl huddled under a bloody sheet. Hope's candle picked up red glints in the matted hair, though bruising around the eyes made identification difficult. A kitchen knife lay on the floor, bloodstains on the handle showing how the girl had gripped it.

"You are one of Lord Merimont's guests," Hope said, lighting the lamp on the table.

The girl nodded. Fear blazed in her eyes. One hand formed a peasant sign against evil.

"I am no ghost," said Hope quietly. "I live in the east wing."

A line appeared on the girl's forehead as though she was trying to puzzle out the words, but she said nothing. As she pulled the sheet closer, pain exploded through her eyes.

"How badly are you hurt?" Maintaining the calm tone was difficult, for the girl's recoil had bared one thigh, revealing cuts and bruises.

"I—I am fine." The sound barely carried across the six feet that separated them.

"You are not fine."

The contradiction increased the fear in those green eyes.

Hope sighed, taking a seat several feet away. "I am not angry with you. Nor will I do anything to hurt you further. But I must tend your injuries and find you a better place to recuperate. You'll catch your death lying on cold stone. Do you need a doctor?"

"No!"

"Can you walk?"

The girl nodded.

"Then let us move into the next room, where I can build up the fire and heat water."

She collected clean sheets and a nightgown from the linen press, then helped the girl to her feet.

Relieved that nothing seemed broken, Hope led her

into the stillroom. Warm water removed dried blood, exposing cuts and bruising on every part of her body. Up close, the girl seemed older than she had on arrival, at least ten years older than her own twenty-six.

"Do you have a name?" she asked as she tied off bandages.

"Missy."

"You may call me Hope." She turned toward the broth simmering on the fire. Missy had wrapped a clean sheet around her, hiding the heavy cotton nightgown. Since a courtesan would hardly feel modest, she must be seeking protection—or anonymity. The gesture seemed oddly youthful.

"How old are you, Missy?" she asked, setting a bowl on the table, then turning her back as she sliced bread.

"Four-and-twenty."

Hope glanced over her shoulder, unable to hide her shock.

" 'Tis a hard life," Missy murmured.

"How long have you pursued it?" Her curiosity often got her into trouble, but she could not remain silent.

"Da sold me to Madame when I were twelve."

"Twelve?"

Missy shrugged, then winced. "He needed my space." Her tone stopped further questions.

Hope set the softest slice of bread where Missy could reach it, then forced her mind back to business. "Who beat you, Missy?"

"I fell."

"Do not take me for a fool. I've nursed tenants and villagers for eight years and helped my mother for years before that. I've seen riding accidents, a fall from the stable roof, a shoulder full of birdshot, a tenant's leg sliced by a wayward scythe, severed fingers, victims of a drunken brawl at the White Heron . . ." She paused for breath. "You were beaten. Was it Lord Merimont?"

"No."

The relief that swept her was shockingly powerful. "Then who?"

Missy picked at a seam in the sheet, ignoring her.

"Missy. I know what fists do when they connect with

flesh. The marks on your neck can only have come from fingers, and there is a handprint on your back. I cannot protect you unless I know the culprit. Either tell me or tell Lord Merimont."

Missy met her gaze. Her lip trembled. Nearly a minute passed before she mumbled an answer.

"I did not catch the name."

"Do—"

"Dornbras?"

Missy nodded.

"I should have known. The man is an arrogant cad who does whatever he pleases." She shuddered, remembering their encounter. Drawing blood had been a mistake, though she'd had no other choice. She should have known he would turn on someone else when he couldn't find her. Why hadn't she demanded that Merimont check that angry voice?

Because you feared it was his.

Stifling guilt over allowing the attack to continue and fear that Merimont's charm was eroding her sense, she watched Missy eat as she arranged her mother's tray. By the time they both finished, she knew what she had to do.

"You need sleep and warmth. Estelle's old room will suit," she said, naming her mother's former maid, who had slept on the nursery floor. "It is tiny, but you will be safe there. And it has an adequate grate."

"He'll look for me." Her eyes again filled with fear. "I slipped out while he was asleep. That man is evil."

"I agree, but he cannot pass the barricades. The room itself is difficult to spot if one is unfamiliar with the house, for it is tucked behind a storage room. And I will keep your door locked. Lord Merimont will wish to speak with you, but no one else will learn of your presence."

Her face twisted, revealing her turmoil, but she finally nodded.

Hope settled her, forced broth into her mother, then rapped sharply on Merimont's door. He must pack up his friends and go.

*   *   *

Pounding reverberated through Max's head. It took a minute to realize that it did not arise from too much wine.

He had stumbled to the door before he awakened enough to recall that it led to the east wing. Why would Miss Ashburton be demanding admittance?

Donning a dressing gown, he jerked the door open. "What?"

"You are despicable!"

He blinked. Fury snapped in her eyes. Color flooded her cheeks. She looked magnificent with her red hair flying about her face. An Amazon. Or Boadicea poised to defend her people. Lust exploded through his groin.

But her next words doused his ardor.

"How dare you keep that monster in this house?" she demanded, striding into the room.

"Who?" Not that the question was necessary, but he needed a moment to order his thoughts. He was still half asleep.

"Dornbras."

"Did you run into him again?"

"No. I found Missy huddled in the laundry this morning. He beat her nearly senseless last night."

"Dear God!" Blake was right. Dornbras was more dangerous than he had believed. Had Meg's broken arm been deliberate after all? Threats might have induced her to lie. "How badly is she hurt?"

She glared as if he were responsible. "She is head-to-toe bruises and covered in blood. Four teeth are loose. At least two ribs are cracked. I don't think her nose is broken, though it is so swollen that she has difficulty breathing. The marks on her neck show that someone tried to choke her. Shall I go on?"

He could feel the blood draining from his face. What the devil had Missy done to incite such fury? "Did she say why?"

"What does that matter? The man is a monster, undeserving of forgiveness. Make him leave before something else happens. You should all leave."

"It is not that easy." Nothing had changed since yesterday. If anything, the situation was worse. "I can speak to him, but that might do more harm than good. Are you sure her injuries are that bad?"

"You can check for yourself if you don't believe me, but I'd rather you didn't. She spent hours huddled on a stone floor, gripping an inadequate knife for defense. She only now feels safe enough to sleep." Her eyes bored into his, seeming to see too much. "I won't allow you to blame her for this attack. Dornbras is an arrogant, spoiled fool who believes that his every whim should be instantly gratified. He was furious that I escaped yesterday, so he took his frustrations out on her. After all, she makes a convenient scapegoat as her position hardly commands respect."

"Is that what she said?"

"I didn't ask, but have you a better explanation?"

He paced the room, knuckling sleep from his eyes as he turned the facts over in his mind. She was right. Dornbras had been irritated to learn that the supposed maid would not return to Redrock. His own warning would have increased that irritation, for the man still wanted his patronage. So he'd turned on Missy, the quietest of the girls and the one least capable of fighting back.

He'd often heard tales from the courtesans he'd helped. Men used feeble excuses to explain their abuse— a wayward touch, silence, talking, a gasp of pain from rough handling—but in truth, they were usually angry before they ever arrived at the brothels. Yet no one had named Dornbras as a man with a penchant for violence.

He squeezed his eyes shut, wondering if his own blindness had condemned Dornbras's victims to repeated attacks. Were they unwilling to seek help because he had excused the man's other crimes?

"You are right," he finally said on a long sigh, looking her in the eye. "But I cannot ask him to leave, or even charge him with assaulting Missy. Whatever we think of his behavior, he's done nothing illegal. Holding him up to public ridicule would give him a new grievance. What do you think he would do?"

"Repeat the beating, then come after us," she said wearily. "His eyes are evil."

"They are black," he protested.

"Color has nothing to do with it. Tommy Price has black eyes, but his are warm and full of curiosity and mischief. Dornbras's are cold and empty, save for a flame of evil."

"Flame?" She wasn't making sense, but her voice raised goose bumps nonetheless. He stooped to add coal to his fire.

"A cold spark deep inside. It kindled when I struck him, then grew when he vowed I would pay for the insult."

"Blake said nothing of that."

"He used no words, but the vow was clear. We must drive him away from Redrock."

"I will terminate this gathering in another three days, but unless he chooses to leave early, that is the soonest we can be rid of him. In the meantime, I must keep everyone occupied. Have you any suggestions?"

"Would your guests enjoy the usual diversions, or are you looking for new places to practice your debaucheries?"

He swallowed his shock. "That is hardly a suitable subject for a lady," he protested.

"How am I to offer suggestions without knowing your preferences?"

She had tried to sound matter-of-fact, but he could hear a note of fear. Obviously her distrust had returned. But who could blame her? After finding Missy, her own confrontation with Dornbras must loom even larger. "I seek the usual diversions, nothing more," he said quietly. "Preferably an excursion or two."

"How about a drive to Exeter? Their theater cannot compare to London, but the current company is reputed to be good, and I can recommend the White Hart Inn for dinner. If the weather warms enough for picnicking, you can drive to Brent Tor, which offers spectacular views. Or visit Dartmoor Prison. They offer a weekly market with exquisite crafts." She nodded toward a model of Exeter cathedral sitting on a stand. The room also contained two paintings and other personal touches lacking in the unused west wing.

"That should keep us busy. Trust me, Miss Ashburton," he added, hoping to erase that elusive shadow from her eyes. "I will do everything possible to protect you."

"I'm sure you will try—as long as doing so serves your own interests," she added so softly he nearly missed the words.

"You have a low opinion of gentlemen."

"Can you blame me?" she demanded bitterly. "Uncle Edward plagued us for years. He would rather toss me to a pack of wolves than exchange a kind word." Her look indicated that he'd done just that. "And other gentlemen are no better. The property adjoining Redrock is owned by Lord Millhouse. Do you know him?"

He grimaced, for he did indeed know the man. Devereaux's rival in the art of seduction, he had entertained every courtesan in London, and at least half of the matrons. Well-born innocents were safe, but he considered every other female fair game.

"I see that you do," she continued. "He's probably another of your good friends. I'm surprised he isn't part of this gathering."

"I rarely see him, and only in passing. He must be ten years my senior."

"But he entertains in the same way. Wise parents lock away their daughters when Millhouse and his friends descend. Between your own behavior and that of your guests, can you blame me for having doubts?"

"Men are not all alike. One day you will recognize the truth of that statement. In the meantime, I will do everything possible to protect you, beginning with taking everyone to Exeter today. By the time we return, they should be tired enough for a peaceful night."

"Very well, my lord."

"Let me know if Missy's condition changes. I will see that she suffers no further harm."

He watched her leave, his heart heavy at the blows to his pride. He had failed in so many ways of late—subjecting Miss Ashburton to insult; leading girls under his protection into danger, for how could he be sure that Dornbras would not injure someone else; and exposing society to a man who should have long since been ostracized. Perhaps she was right to distrust him. Disaster followed in his wake.

Yet her suspicions had started long before he had arrived. And Millhouse would never harm her. Was it her uncle who had kindled that original fear?

He still did not know why Ashburton had destroyed Redrock. Nor did he understand that card game. Did Ashburton's absence from London mean that more danger threatened?

Chapter Eight

Max hastily donned a shirt and pantaloons, then let himself into the central block, locking the dressing room door behind him. The house was quiet, as if holding its breath against some new outrage.

Shaking his head over entertaining such a fanciful notion, he slipped into Blake's room and shook his friend awake.

"Wha—"

"Shh," hissed Max as Blake bolted upright. "Meet me in the drawing room. We need to talk."

They could not do so here, for Dornbras was across the hall. He would take no chance of being overheard until they had decided on a plan, which precluded using the music room as well. It was beneath Dornbras's room. Sound often traveled through shared chimneys.

When Blake nodded, Max retreated downstairs. But he'd hardly finished a second circuit of the room before Blake joined him, wearing only a shirt and pantaloons, his chin shadowed and his hair sticking up.

"What did Dornbras do now?" he demanded, keeping his voice low despite the closed door.

"He beat Missy."

Blake cursed. Like Max, he hated anyone who used force against a weaker opponent. "We have to send him away before he does something worse."

"I know, but ordering him out would be even more precarious now. I can live with his attempts to discredit me—few would accept his word over mine—but he would also turn on Miss Ashburton and might do worse to Missy."

"How is she?"

"Sleeping. We need to encourage him to leave, but he has to think it is his own idea."

"The rest of us could leave after raising a fuss about space and the lack of entertainment. If you demand that Dornbras stay to keep you company, he would be the first out the door."

"No. It would never work."

"Why?" Blake settled into a chair. "You know he never takes orders. If you tell him to go, he'll stay, so if you demand that he stay, he should go."

"With most people that is true," agreed Max, pacing to the fireplace and back. "But he wants something from me. God knows what, but he's been cultivating me lately. So he would agree with my request, leaving me with only him in residence. How many hours would pass before boredom prompted him to explore the east wing? Besides, I would rather not involve Terrence or Reggie."

"Then perhaps it is time to withdraw your favor."

"I will, and very publicly, but if I do it while he is here, he could find any number of ways to avenge the insult. And citing Missy as my excuse to cut him will draw reprisals onto her head, so I must find another reason."

Blake rubbed his temple. "How badly did he hurt her?"

"No breaks beyond cracked ribs and loose teeth, but she is head-to-toe bruises, according to Miss Ashburton."

Blake growled. "Damnation, Max! How could you involve her? If anyone learns that she is caring for a courtesan, her reputation will be in shreds."

"How could I involve her?" he repeated incredulously. "Why do you think I am up? She is the one who found Missy. She has her stashed in the east wing and won't even let me speak with her—not that I doubt her word. Her description was too realistic to have arisen in the imagination of a country spinster."

Blake paled. "Damn. He was shouting last night, but I didn't think it was serious."

"Nor did I. Maybe Miss Ashburton is right to distrust gentlemen."

Blake raised a brow.

"She read me a scold because men like us don't respect girls like Missy. I've been trying to convince her that men are not all alike, but this incident makes that difficult."

"Did you describe your crusade against forcing girls into brothels?"

"She was in no mood to listen, and who can blame her? Do you know who owns the next estate?" He paused while Blake shook his head.

"Millhouse."

"The devil!"

"Exactly." Setting aside Miss Ashburton's sensibilities, he returned to business. "We need to make Dornbras's life unpleasant, but without making it obvious. I will disband the party in three days, no matter what, but I'd like him to leave sooner. In the meantime, we will stay as busy as possible and as far away as I can contrive."

"Excursions?"

"Daily."

"But it's raining." He gestured toward the window.

"Not heavily. We will attend the theater in Exeter today. And Miss Ashburton has other suggestions for tomorrow."

"I don't like pretending that nothing happened. Dornbras should pay."

"He will," promised Max grimly. "I'll not let him get away with this, but my hands are tied until I can go after him without hurting others. I just wish there was some way to proceed legally. If Missy had struck him, she would be transported for life."

"Or hung. Miss Ashburton is right. We should not be able to do anything we want with impunity."

"He won't escape." Rising to end the discussion, he added, "Help me keep an eye on him. I want no one else injured before I can be rid of him."

"Of course. I should have checked last night."

"Why? A gentleman never interferes with another's pleasure. I only wish Dornbras did not abuse that privilege."

He let Blake precede him upstairs. What a mess. He'd repaid others for abusing women—a word here, a warning there, a collapsed deal coupled with a suggestion to control the temper, a coveted invitation suddenly withdrawn. It wasn't public, nor had his own name appeared, but most had become more careful.

This time he must make a public issue of Dornbras's failings. Like many younger sons, Dornbras had nothing to do. His father was an earl, but so many brothers stood ahead of him that he would never inherit the title. His mother had spoiled him badly before he left for school, and inheriting a fortune had worsened his arrogance. With no need to work and no responsibilities looming in the future, he was bored, weary, and ripe for trouble.

Yet even that did not fully explain Dornbras. Something wasn't quite right about him, for he lacked any trace of a conscience.

He is evil, Miss Ashburton's voice echoed.

Perhaps. Or perhaps he was merely twisted in the same way Sir Francis Dashwood had been half a century ago. In founding the Hellfire Club, Sir Francis had sought new ways to titillate his jaded senses. Eventually even orgies and Satanism had paled, sending the members scurrying for increasingly sordid—and ultimately vicious—ways to stimulate excitement. Dornbras had not yet involved other gentlemen in his exploits, but Max feared he was headed in that direction.

It must stop.

Shaking his head, he returned to his room, staring out at the rain as he pondered ideas for bringing Dornbras to ground. But none seemed right. Exposing this incident to society would do little beyond banning Dornbras from the better drawing rooms, and even that would happen only because they wanted an excuse to cut him.

So he must launch an investigation that would—he hoped—turn up evidence of an actual crime. Unless Dornbras was transported, he would strike back at his accusers.

Sighing, he turned to the estate books. An hour passed before footsteps announced that someone was looking for breakfast. He reached the entrance hall to find Dornbras jiggling a key in the office door, half a dozen others clutched in one hand.

"That wing is dangerous," Max reminded him. "I will not be responsible for injuring my friends." He nearly choked on the last word, but Dornbras didn't seem to notice.

"I was looking for Missy." He managed to look worried as he glanced at the rain spattering against the fanlight above the front door. "She isn't in the house. I hope she didn't try to explore and find herself in trouble."

"She's gone. Cook sent her to the doctor after she slipped on the stairs."

"You didn't talk to her?"

He shrugged. "I was asleep. It didn't seem bad enough to wake me. One of the grooms gave her a ride to town." He didn't address why she would seek out a doctor for an injury not serious enough to wake her host. Country physicians were chancy to deal with. Any injury severe enough to consult with one would make it risky to move.

But Dornbras accepted his offhand comments, dismissing the subject. He may have threatened Missy with reprisals if she revealed the truth. "Has this rain upset any plans?"

"No. We will drive to Exeter today for theater and a decent meal. I am heartily sick of cottage fare."

"What do you have in mind?" He started to slip the keys into his pocket, but handed them over when Max held out a peremptory hand.

"The White Hart offers good food, and if the weather worsens, we can stay the night. This place feels smaller every day. We will have to return to town soon to preserve our sanity. Do you think anyone will mind? It can't be pleasant tripping over each other every time we turn around."

"True. This old ruin doesn't even run to a billiard table. Maybe we should call on Ewston. His hunting box could house fifty with no trouble, and it offers other amenities."

Since it was located in the heart of Quorn country, that was no surprise. Ewston also kept it stocked with

the best London courtesans during the hunting season—
not that he would welcome Dornbras.

"That sounds interesting," he said lightly, hiding his
revulsion. Even with his patronage Dornbras could never
join one of Ewston's famed parties, but this was not the
time to mention it. When the others left, he would remain here. Perhaps Dornbras would be stupid enough
to go to Ewston's on his own. Being refused admittance
would turn his fury on Ewston, who would not hesitate
to retaliate. The resulting feud would provide ample excuse to cut the connection without endangering anyone
at Redrock.

It might even solve the larger problem. Ewston was
not a man to forgive and forget. If Dornbras attacked
Ewston or damaged his property, he would find himself
in Botany Bay.

He accompanied Dornbras to the dining room, announced the excursion to those already eating, then
withdrew, ostensibly to make preparations.

He needed to talk to Miss Ashburton, both to allay
her concerns and to share his explanation for Missy's
absence. He also wanted a clearer understanding of
Missy's injuries.

But he could not slip into the office. Too many people
were awake. Even if he entered secretly, someone was
bound to see him leave. Braving the wind and rain to
approach the library door was out of the question. He
did not have its key, and Miss Ashburton was probably upstairs.

Sighing, he returned to his bedchamber, took a deep
breath, and unlocked the door leading to the east wing
hallway.

"What are you doing here?" hissed Hope as Merimont emerged from his room. "You promised not to
bother me."

"We need to talk, but I cannot risk unlocking the
office. Someone is bound to see. Shall I meet you in
the library?"

She ought to refuse, for he was frustrated, making him
dangerous. Yet his eyes remained clear. Even when he

was angry, they bore no hint of evil. She wanted to believe him, wanted the protection he offered, wanted—

Him, supplied her heart when she refused to complete
the thought.

Dangerous, indeed. Plague take his charm, and her
own weakness for it. Never had she suspected she might
be vulnerable to a man's smile. Learning otherwise
added a new fear. "Rose is cleaning the library. Go
down to the office. I will join you after I look in on
Mother."

"How is she?"

"Not good." Her voice shook. Fever again ravaged
that frail body, harsh enough to hold even the ancient
memories at bay.

"Please accept my sympathy. I will await you in the
office." He looked around, then frowned.

"Through here, my lord." She opened the inconspicu-
ous door leading to a spiral servants' stair. "Be careful.
The steps are quite steep."

His nose wrinkled, but he plunged onto the staircase.

Hope peeked in on her mother, then followed Merimont. She should have handled their earlier confrontation differently, but she had allowed her fury with
Dornbras to overcome her sense. What had possessed
her to accost a man in his bedchamber when she knew
he was asleep? She was lucky he had not taken advantage of the situation.. He'd left her with too many disturbing images as it was. That hastily donned dressing
gown proved that his broad shoulders owed nothing to
artifice. Sleep tugging at his eyelids made him seem ap-
proachable, comforting, even trustwor—

Inhaling sharply, she diverted her thoughts. She would
never trust him. If he weren't so stubborn, they wouldn't
be in this fix.

Exhaling in an attempt to relax, she pushed open the
door. Merimont was standing at the window watching
the rain.

"Have you found a way to expel Dornbras?" she
asked, taking a seat by the fire.

"Blake has no ideas beyond what we discussed earlier.
I've been reviewing gossip and my own observations,

and can only conclude that Dornbras is worse than even you thought. He is also unpredictable."

"Why did you not discern his nature earlier?"

He wandered over to stare into the fire. "I allowed him to pull the wool over my eyes," he said at length, resting an elbow on the mantel. "He flatters me because my patronage keeps him in society."

"So he will do anything to remain in your good graces—such as leaving if you asked it?" Excitement stirred.

"I wish that were true." He took a chair facing her. "Think about it. Asking him to leave would proclaim that I no longer favor him. He is a vindictive man who would turn on Missy for carrying tales. Then he would settle with me. Even a cursory investigation would lead to you, giving him a new target."

"So we have no choice."

"Exactly. Even Blake agrees that there is nothing we can do just now. Ultimately Dornbras must pay, but not until we are sure he cannot retaliate. In the meantime, we will watch him closely. I found him trying keys on the office door this morning, so I will rig a bar as I did in the stillroom. And you can relax soon."

She raised her brows.

"Rain won't hamper a trip to the theater, though if it softens the roads too much, we may spend the night in Exeter."

"I must pray for more rain," she murmured.

He laughed, lightening his expression. "Please don't. Your other suggestions require dry weather."

"True."

"In three days, they will all leave." He paused as if unsure of himself. "Can you tell me more about Missy's injuries?"

"Not really. I peeked in on her an hour ago, but she was asleep. Why?"

"Dornbras was looking for her—at least that was his excuse for trying to enter here. I told him that Cook sent her to the doctor because she'd fallen on the stairs."

"And he believed that?"

"Of course. Why would he not?"

She compressed her lips lest she call him a fool. "I wish I could have seen his eyes," she muttered at last.

"Why? He would have questioned me if the tale seemed suspicious."

"Of course he wouldn't." She glared at him. "He knows what he did, but he can hardly deny your claim without admitting his guilt. On the other hand, he may think that you are stupid enough to believe such nonsense."

"I am not stupid."

"I did not say you were, but since he's been using you for so long, he may well believe it."

He turned another protest into a decent imitation of a cough.

"How did that come about?" she asked, seeking to understand him a little better. No matter how hard she tried, she could not feel threatened by him.

"I've known him since school." He leaned forward to stare into the fire. "Heirs to great titles are plagued by toadeaters, even as schoolboys. One learns to question the motives of nearly everyone. But Dornbras's father is powerful in his own right. And both of our fathers are disapproving, autocratic martinets who criticize everything we do and make impossible demands."

"Such as?" She hardly breathed the words.

"Cut all friends and stay at home so he can supervise every minute of my life."

"So you had a bond," she said when he fell silent.

He nodded. "I did not see him for several years after Eton, for he went to Cambridge, while I attended Oxford. Nor did he come to London until three years ago— at least not to respectable parts of London. I now suspect he was very familiar with its less reputable sections. But he called one day, asking me to introduce him to society, flattering me and expressing gratitude for how I'd helped him endure his father's animosity."

"So you took him under your wing."

He shrugged. "Blake warned me against it, but I ignored him, for they have never liked each other. In retrospect, I was especially receptive to puffery, for I'd just had a nasty row with my father." He cursed himself.

"Blind, as Blake has often claimed. I did not even consider the significance of being the only one Dornbras would obey. I thought we were friends."

"But why pick you? Surely your reputation makes your recommendations suspect."

He smiled, rather grimly. "That is innocence speaking, Miss Ashburton. Even if that exaggerated reputation were true—which it is not—expectations count for much, and mine are among the best. Eventually I will control the power and wealth of the Montcalm title. In the meantime, few willingly court my disdain. I would have to do far worse than Dornbras to draw any serious antagonism. Society teases me by exaggerating my foibles into lurid tales, but the tenor is what one would use on a favorite scapegrace nephew. While I admit to any number of youthful pranks, I have never lied, never cheated, and never harmed another of any class—at least not knowingly," he added in an undertone.

"So if you demand acceptance for Dornbras, you will receive it."

"In most places." Clenching his fists, he rose to pace the floor. "Damn me for a fool," he muttered. "I should have seen his purpose."

"Why? You said yourself that his birth is high enough that he shouldn't need you."

"Not for the usual things, but the other side of power is responsibility. I should have stopped him before he harmed others. But I didn't think. Perhaps Father is right. I am no fit heir to the marquessate," he added so softly that she barely heard.

"No one is perfect," she murmured. "And now that you know the truth, you will rectify any damage." The words surprised her as much as him. She did not like having her instincts so at odds with her training, but perhaps he could explain how her thinking had gone awry. "You puzzle me, my lord. You claim that gentlemen should not hurt others, yet they do so every day. Uncle Edward has conspired against us for years. Millhouse ruined the innkeeper's daughter with impunity, and she was far from his first. Sir Virgil's tenants suffer from exorbitant rents. And Dornbras must have a long history of black deeds. Do you not consider those harmful?"

"You are correct." He resumed his chair. "Selfish, greedy men have always used their positions unwisely, but that does not make it right. Even my father, who has long preached responsibility for one's dependents, is not immune. He is so stubborn that once he makes a decision, he never changes course. The steward urged him to redirect the stream last year so it flowed behind the village rather than through it. He refused. His great-grandfather had put that stream there and no one was going to change it."

"It overflowed?"

He smiled. "Exactly. It flooded half the village, sweeping a dozen people into trees and many more downstream. No one died, thank God, but we found Mrs. Haskell sharing her bed with a pig."

"A pig?" She burst into laughter.

"It must have been looking for shelter. A cupboard had tipped over, trapping her. The pig was happily munching the turnips that had spilled out."

A rap on the window froze her response. Merimont had not closed the draperies when she'd arrived.

"Damnation," he muttered, stalking across to throw open the window. "What the devil are you doing, Terrence? You are supposed to be changing for the theater."

"I heard voices." He obeyed Merimont's gesture and climbed through the window.

"Curiosity killed the cat," growled Merimont.

"Not unless he is unreasonable." Hope smiled at the blond gentleman who had alighted from the second carriage. He appeared younger than Merimont, and more carefree. But his eyes were honest.

"No wonder you released Annette," Terrence murmured, quizzing her with his glass. "Very nice. She makes a refreshing change, Max."

Merimont flushed. "Terrence, may I present Miss Hope Ashburton, niece of Lord Ashburton. This is Terrence Sanders, one of my better—and more discreet—

friends. Miss Ashburton and her mother lease the east wing," he added.

Hope smiled as horror burst through Terrence's eyes.

He murmured a conventional greeting, then turned to Merimont. "How could you put her in this position, Max?" he hissed. "You've compromised her beyond redemption."

"Hardly," murmured Merimont in reply. "Our establishments are completely separate, and she is well chaperoned."

"Then why are you here alone?"

"A small matter of business," he said shortly.

"You should never have invited us."

"I did not know of this arrangement until I arrived."

"No need to whisper." Hope was enjoying herself vastly. There was something very satisfying about watching Merimont being scolded by his friend. For all his protestations—to say nothing of the high rank he had boasted of only a short time ago—he was plainly in the wrong. "I am well aware of the situation, and am sure that Lord Merimont is doing whatever he can to maintain propriety."

"Hardly. This may be on the right side of the line—though you are skirting very close, Max—but it will raise more than a few eyebrows. We should all be packing."

"Even Dornbras?" asked Merimont. "Demanding that everyone leave will arouse his curiosity. What do you think he will do then?"

"Crucify anyone he can identify," Sanders said, glancing at Hope. "Though I am surprised to hear you say it. You usually turn a blind eye to his antics."

"I had not spent time with him outside of society gatherings."

Even to Hope's ears, the excuse sounded feeble. Sanders shook his head, but his expression darkened as Merimont explained Missy's fate.

"He is worse than I thought," murmured Sanders.

Merimont nodded. "Miss Ashburton is innocent, as you pointed out. To keep her reputation intact, we must end this party naturally, with no hint that the east wing is not an empty ruin."

"I can see why you must follow that course, but I

cannot stay. Sound carries. My conscience balks at introducing courtesans into a genteel household, no matter how divided."

"If that is your choice. All I ask is that you keep your reasons private."

"Of course." He frowned. "My aunt has been ill for some time, though not seriously. I believe she has gone into a decline. I must hurry home."

"Of course. She dotes on you."

"I will escort Annette as far as London," he continued. "She would be bored here alone."

"We will miss you, but I understand your concerns."

Terrence smiled at Hope. "Farewell, fair lady. Perhaps we will one day meet under more favorable circumstances."

"I will look forward to it, sir." She smiled, then murmured, "The Spotted Pony in Oakhampton is useful when roads turn to quagmires."

His eyes twinkled. Without another word, he climbed back out the window.

"Forgive me, Miss Ashburton," Merimont said, drawing the curtains tight. "This is yet another reason to keep everyone occupied." He glanced at the mantel clock. "We have spoken longer than I intended. I will have to bar this door after we return."

"And we must not meet in here again. What if it had been Dornbras who heard us talking?"

He nodded, dropping his voice to a whisper as his friend loudly greeted Sir Reginald in the hallway. "At least you can trust Terrence. I have placed you in an untenable position. Though the arrangement is proper enough, a malicious tongue could make it seem that I had set you up as my mistress—please forgive my plain speaking," he added. "But we must be clear on the danger."

"Then let us pray that you can truly trust your friends. Too many people know I am here."

"I would trust those two with my life—which I am doing, in a manner of speaking. I regret this situation more than I can say."

"Very well. Have a pleasant journey to Exeter. If I learn anything new from Missy, I will leave you a note."

Chapter Nine

Hope peeked through the library doorway, scanning the terrace and garden in case any of Merimont's guests were taking the air.

Yesterday had been the most relaxed since Merimont had walked into her house. There had been no need to scurry from place to place, fearful of making a sound or hearing lewd encounters. Her imagination had not attributed every squeak and thump to Merimont, painting lurid pictures of what he might be doing. And though her mother had remained critical, the situation had not seemed as terrifying.

His party had returned well after midnight, though she suspected that the delay was due to high spirits rather than bad weather. Terrence's departure seemed to bother no one. The girls were giggling and the men appropriately coarse, but she detected no signs of tension. Even Dornbras had sounded relaxed.

She regretted listening to their return, though, for it had triggered new speculation. If she understood Terrence's accusation, Merimont had released his mistress. Was he sharing the other girls with his friends, or had he satisfied his own cravings in Exeter?

The answer was important, for a rake in need was more likely to turn on her. But the question embarrassed her. And last night's dreams had been more disturbing than ever.

Relieved to see no one outside, she strode briskly toward the village. Her problems were multiplying, she admitted as she plunged into the woods. Missy's hours huddled on a cold stone floor had brought on a fever. Thrashing about had worsened her pain.

Hope had dosed her with every remedy she knew, which had eventually induced sleep. But her supplies were now dangerously low. She must visit the apothecary.

"What are you doing here, Miss Ashburton?"

She screamed.

"I did not mean to startle you." Lord Rockhurst's face twisted in chagrin as he stepped onto the path.

"I had not thought anyone was about." Though the sun had cleared the trees, barely five hours had passed since everyone had returned.

"You should not take the air until we leave," he said quietly. "If your identity comes out, you are bound to suffer."

"I've an errand that cannot wait."

"Which is?"

"I must visit the apothecary."

"Why not send a servant?"

She shrugged. "Rose is sitting with Mother—her fever has returned. Mrs. Tweed is watching Missy. That night on the laundry floor did her little good, I fear. Neither can walk this far, and Ned can hardly harness the gig for someone the other grooms know is not part of Merimont's staff. Besides, Mrs. Tweed's tongue often works faster than her mind. It would prefer not to raise questions."

"I will gladly fetch whatever you need."

She stared at him, surprised by the offer. But it would not do. "I doubt you could explain why you require healing herbs without raising the very suspicions you claim will harm me. Mr. Winters is accustomed to my visits."

"But he is bound to ask questions," he said, falling into step beside her. "Everyone must know that Redrock has a new owner, and they will have heard of his house party."

"In which case my reputation will be in shreds anyway, so nothing I do can make it worse." She kept her voice light, though a chill ripped through her chest. With her other troubles, she had not considered the very real curiosity that must be sweeping the neighborhood. Her tenants might be keeping mum, but others would have seen the carriages arrive. Only recognition that his party was little better than Millhouse's could account for the lack of callers.

"You do not know that. Why would everyone assume that you remained in the house, considering the company Max invited?"

"Because they know I have a lease and have nowhere else to go."

She could hear the despair in her voice. She was ruined. Never mind her twenty-six years of exemplary living. Most people welcomed scandal, for it enlivened their staid lives. And this was the biggest scandal since the innkeeper's daughter, she admitted grimly. If only she had learned feminine wiles in her youth. Surely throwing hysterics or fainting or *something* could have prevented this mess.

Or perhaps not. Merimont was exceedingly stubborn. Her mother could not move. And she could not leave Redrock for even one night.

"Is there nowhere on the estate that you could have moved for a week or two?" Rockhurst was clearly surprised.

"The dower house is tiny and in poor repair. Mother is too ill to move." She clamped control on her temper. "Why am I discussing this with someone I barely know?"

"Because you recognize that you have a problem," he said calmly. "And because you know you can trust me."

Startled, she stopped to stare into his eyes. "I suppose I do."

He nodded, taking her arm to assist her, for the path was rough and slippery with mud. "You must have an explanation ready for Mr. Winters if you wish to protect your reputation. How bad is the dower house?"

"I offered it to Lord Merimont, but he refused."

Rockhurst grinned. "I detect an interesting battle of wills behind that statement. That would explain why you two are sharing a house. Max does not take direction well."

"True. He is the most stubborn man of my acquaintance."

"He comes by it honestly. His father is worse."

"So I gathered. Is that why he is so determined to live at Redrock? I have trouble accepting that he needs it, for his father has many estates."

"But none that Max can oversee."

The path twisted downhill toward the footbridge, narrowing so they could no longer walk side by side.

"Consider my curiosity piqued," she said over her shoulder. "What has that to do with Redrock?"

"The Marquess of Montcalm hates London, shuns local society, passes his time alone, and refuses to admit that Max does not share his interests. His wife died when Max was a child, and his few friends are just like him. He and Max have fought for years."

"I take it he is master of all he surveys, and likes it that way." Many lords had that failing, especially those who achieved their titles late in life. After waiting so long for power to fall into their hands, they had to exercise it at every opportunity.

"Precisely, though the conflict with Max goes beyond the usual pattern of demanding parent and rebellious child. Montcalm hates embarrassment. Even mentioning Max's name infuriates him, whether the comment is good or bad, for it is proof that Max is making himself a topic of conversation."

"Even praise? He must embarrass easily. Most people are proud of their children's accomplishments."

"So is Montcalm, but he would rather keep Max locked away under his parental eye to avoid the least hint of scandal."

"That sounds far-fetched even for an autocratic lord."

"Life is rarely simple, Miss Ashburton. And you should be careful of judging without all the facts."

"True." She blushed, for she had accused Merimont of that very failing more than once. "So what would make a sensible lord behave so irrationally?"

"Lady Montcalm's death was an accident, but the circumstances were confused, so people talked. They embellished. They speculated."

"And they undoubtedly accused him of doing away with her," she concluded.

"Among other suggestions—suicide, an accident as he tried to kill her lover, self-defense when she tried to kill him."

"Heavens!"

"He withdrew into the Abbey and refused to see anyone for nearly a year."

"I suppose that increased the talk."

"Greatly. It has been twenty years, but people still believe he is hiding the truth. Thus he hates gossip. He hates rumor. And he hates hearing his son's name on anyone's tongue."

She shook her head. "Stubborn fools, both of them. So how did Lord Montcalm try to obtain obedience?"

"He canceled Max's allowance to force him home."

"So winning Redrock offered him a reprieve." Despite his success, she could not condone gaming as a solution to financial problems.

Rockhurst must have heard her disapproval, for he held up a placating hand. "Not really. Acquiring Redrock was an accident. He was actually looking for a steward's position."

"Why?"

"He wanted to experiment with his agricultural theories. He has followed Coke's successes closely and believes that even greater triumphs are possible."

"So why not work with his father's steward? He must know that no one of sense would hire a lord's heir. Even if he is competent, he could be called away without warning to assume his father's position."

"He tried. It was his request to run Montcalm's smallest estate that led to the latest argument. Montcalm feared he would use the place for illicit purposes."

"Can you blame him?" she asked bitterly, gesturing toward the manor that sheltered so many courtesans.

"He does not usually engage in such parties," he swore. "Nor do Terrence and I."

"So he needs Redrock because he has nowhere else to go?" she asked, returning to the original subject.

"Without an allowance, he cannot remain in London— Montcalm always kept him too short to save anything. So his choices are to live here or return home."

"Which means he will stay whether I want him to or not." She glowered, though the idea was not as infuriating as it ought to be. At least Rockhurst had confirmed that Merimont really did intend to restore Redrock.

"For a time. Montcalm always rescinds his worst edicts in the end. I remember the summer he ordered Max to stay on the property—he meant the Abbey grounds, but Max took him literally. He stayed on Montcalm's property—taking Montcalm's coach from one estate to the next, alighting only in villages owned by his father, consorting only with employees and dependents, including several se—" He snapped his mouth closed.

"You needn't censor your tongue, sir. I can hardly claim ignorance after the last few days. I presume he entertained himself with all manner of serving girls from estate villages."

"I should not be disclosing such information," he said stiffly. "Montcalm sent a messenger after us, rescinding the order, but since Max wanted to know how much ground he could cover before he had to break the ban, it took two months for the fellow to catch up with us."

They reached the edge of the woods, bringing the village into view. And just as well. She did not want to be charmed by Merimont's escapades. "I will leave you here, my lord. I can hardly explain your escort."

"What will you say about Max?"

"As little as possible. Admitting that we share the house can only create trouble. I will have to claim that I moved Mother into the dower house. Two rooms are still habitable, though the roof leaks badly. People will accept a temporary move." At least she hoped so. Anyone who had actually seen the dower house would look askance at such a claim.

But Rockhurst merely nodded. "I will wait for you."

"That isn't necessary."

"I disagree. Unless I escort you back, Dornbras may accost you again."

She could think of no argument that might deter him. Nor did she want to. Leaving him in the forest, she headed for the village.

The encounter with Mr. Winters went better than she

had expected. He kept his curiosity under control as he
measured out the willow bark and other herbs she
needed, but could not ignore the topic entirely.

"I hear the estate changed hands."

"Lord Merimont now owns it, thank heavens. Watts
tells me he plans to restore it to full prosperity. All of
us will benefit."

He grunted agreement, but his eyes gleamed. "Does
he have guests?"

She nodded. "Who can blame him for celebrating his
good fortune? And unlike Lord Millhouse, he is not
bothering the rest of us. He hadn't expected to find the
manor occupied, of course, but given the size of the
party, it seemed reasonable to allow him use of it for a
week or so."

"Some think you will leave Devonshire."

She shook her head. "A new owner does not affect
our lease."

There was much more, but she escaped without actually lying, though she left the impression that she had
moved out of the house. Rockhurst awaited her in the
woods.

"Max mentioned that Ashburton deliberately destroyed Redrock," he said when she rejoined him. "Forgive me for asking a personal question, but I cannot help
but wonder what his reason was."

"He hates my mother and me, by extension."

"Why?"

She glanced over her shoulder. The question was im-
pertinent, but his face seemed genuinely puzzled. She
felt compelled to answer, in part because he'd answered
her questions.

"It started with his brother," she said, sighing.

"Your father?"

She nodded. "Uncle Edward idolized Arnold, emulating him whenever possible. He was away on his Grand
Tour when Arnold met Mother and wed her. So he
blamed us for Arnold's death."

"Why?"

"Who knows? He has never explained his reasoning.
He also blames us because Grandfather recalled him

from his Grand Tour and forced him to wed. His wife
is not the easiest person to live with."

"Has he never changed?"

"That would require admitting he'd been wrong.
Grandfather finally gave up making him see reason and
set up our lease."

"Ah. Ashburton couldn't evict you, but he managed
to make life as miserable as possible."

"Exactly. But now that the estate is too derelict for
him to inflict further damage, he's passed the job to
someone else."

"Max will treat you better," he vowed. "He has long
aided the weak against the strong. He's even been
known to rescue birds from marauding cats."

"I doubt he would want that fact bandied about society," she said with a chuckle.

"Assuredly not. Or the puppies he pulled from the
river while we were at Oxford. He managed to keep
them hidden in his rooms for nearly a week before they
escaped. Unfortunately, they invaded the bagwig's office,
chewing papers, leaving calling cards where they were
most likely to be stepped on, and smashing a decanter
of French brandy."

She laughed. "How many pups?"

"Four, and quite fond of tug-of-war, particularly with
a pair of new boots."

She smothered another laugh with one hand as they
paused at the edge of the wood. No one was out, so
they headed for the terrace. She was turning to thank
Lord Rockhurst for his escort when the library door
opened.

"Where have you been?" demanded Merimont.

"That is hardly your concern, my lord," she said
coldly, feeling her cheeks heat when she realized the
impropriety of discussing him with his friend. "A better
question is what you are doing in my rooms—again."

Max inhaled deeply, shocked at his own reaction.
There was no reason to shout at Miss Ashburton.

He had awakened an hour ago. When he'd returned
last night after a frustrating day of being the odd man

in a group of couples, he'd been relieved to find no sign of notes. Only this morning did it occur to him that a crisis might have prevented her from writing one. So he had come to check on her patients—merely as a duty, he had assured himself; Missy was his guest. But Miss Ashburton had been gone. Rose claimed that she had left hours ago to fetch some herbs from the village.

Memories of the last time she had ventured out had stabbed fear into his soul. Dornbras did not accept defeat easily. A quick search of the house had increased his concern. Reggie was snoring loudly enough to wake the dead, but not a sound escaped Dornbras's room.

Then he'd found Blake's room empty. New images had surfaced—Blake finding Dornbras gone and following him to prevent any mischief; Dornbras escaping Blake's scrutiny long enough to force himself on Miss Ashburton; Blake arriving to discover Miss Ashburton's beaten body.

But nothing had prepared him for the sight of Blake and Miss Ashburton sauntering across the grounds, laughing as if they hadn't a care in the world. Finding her all right made him furious. And the guilt staining her face made it worse.

"You should know better than to venture out," he said, glaring.

"Missy is feverish. I had to visit the apothecary."

"So you risked running into Dornbras instead of asking me to send someone?"

"I was adequately protected," she snapped, nodding toward Blake. "And how can one of your servants run my errands without informing the entire world that we are sharing a roof?"

"She's right," drawled Blake.

"You stay out of this." He glared at his best friend.

"If that's what you want." He stepped forward, murmuring, "Don't be an ass, Max," as he passed. Then he gripped Miss Ashburton's hand. "It has been a pleasure, my dear."

She smiled warmly. "Thank you for the escort, my lord."

Bestowing a smile on her, he left them standing on the terrace.

She waited until Blake was gone, then stepped into the library, removing both her bonnet and her smile.

"When did you invite him along?" he demanded, drawing the draperies.

"He invited himself, though I am grateful. I had forgotten that the villagers would know about your guests."

"What is that supposed to mean?"

"Surely you are aware of how gossip spreads in the country, my lord. The identities of your companions are difficult to hide. If you truly wish to stay at Redrock, you need to cultivate a more conventional image."

"Gossiping behind my back," he grumbled.

"Putting an acceptable face on despicable conduct," she countered.

He snorted.

"What is wrong with you this morning?" she demanded sharply. "It is not your concern where I go or what I do. Yet here you are, in a place you swore would be mine alone, snapping at me like a furious terrier because I was not where you wanted me to be. You're as bad as your father. You aren't satisfied unless everyone is under your watchful eye."

"That wasn't—" The look in her eye stopped him, for she was not in a mood to listen. And she had a point. His fury was illogical. He couldn't blame her for responding in kind.

He walked to the front window, peered at a distant copse of trees, then returned. "It is not that I was upset over your going about your business, but I have no idea where Dornbras is, so finding you missing was a shock."

"You feared I'd fallen foul of him?"

He nodded.

The irritation drained from her face. "I've seen no sign of him. I met Lord Rockhurst in the woods, but he'd seen no one either."

He would check on Dornbras later. "So what did you tell the local gossips?"

"I only spoke with the apothecary, though he has the fastest tongue in town."

"A rattle?"

"Worse. Everything that goes in his ears comes out his mouth. So I pointed out that your party was not as disruptive as Millhouse's and posed no threat to the village maidens, then extolled your plans for rebuilding the estate."

"Does he know you remain here?"

"I stepped around that point, while implying that I did not. He expects you to take possession of the dower house when your friends leave."

"You said it was a ruin." But he knew she was right. One of them would have to move, and she had a lease for the manor.

"It is, though you can fix it easily enough. If you wish to remain at Redrock, you must have your own residence."

"Something else to deal with," he said on a long sigh. "We will drive out to Brent Tor this afternoon. Tomorrow, I will cite limited space and a mountain of work, then send the others to Dartmoor while I remain behind to deal with an emergency. Everyone will be gone by the next day."

She nodded, absently rearranging a pile of books. "So why were you looking for me?"

"How are your mother and Missy?"

"Not well. Both are suffering fever, though Missy shows no signs of delirium. Mother is worse again." Fear flickered in her eyes, but she suppressed it.

"I am sorry. Is there any way I can help?"

"Not while your guests remain. You are spending too much time in this wing already."

"I had only intended to ask about your patients, Miss Ashburton," he snapped. "But Rose claimed that you had left hours ago. Given what happened the last time you ventured forth, I was concerned about your safety."

"Rose's sense of time is distorted." She shrugged. "I was gone little more than an hour. Must I serve notice next time I have errands, or are you willing to accept that I've run this household long enough to make my own decisions?"

"I overreacted."

The admission triggered a brilliant smile. "Perhaps there is hope for you yet," she said, turning toward the hallway. "I must look in on Mother. Which way will you leave?"

"The same way I entered."

He mounted the twisting stairs just behind her, then had to endure her swaying bottom directly before his eyes all the way up. He should not find her this delectable.

Chapter Ten

Max locked the door to Miss Ashburton's hallway, then paced his room. He should not have lost his temper. What was wrong with him lately? It felt as if a stranger had crawled into his skin—betting money he didn't have, organizing this party, becoming so wrapped up in stubborn arrogance that he couldn't think straight, insisting that Miss Ashburton behave as *he* wanted.

Dear God. Another trait that mirrored his father. His hands gripped his head lest it explode. Had Montcalm won after all, tricking him into adopting his worst traits?

"No!" he vowed as his feet picked up speed. This wasn't the same thing at all. He'd demanded that Miss Ashburton obey only to protect her. It was a temporary measure made necessary because he had placed her in danger. Once Dornbras left, she could do whatever she wanted.

He was *not* turning into his father.

He reviewed all the ways he was different—genuine concern for the helpless, personally handling his responsibilities, eagerly trying new ideas, wanting to help his dependents. None of that was true of Montcalm. The marquess cared only for himself, placing the operation of his estates in the hands of others, then withdrawing into a brooding silence broken only by periodic exhortations to his son.

Max relaxed. He was not like that. When problems arose, he faced them head-on. So maybe he was a little stubborn, and maybe he was a little irritated when people who ought to know better did something stupid. He could fix that. All he had to do was think twice before opening his mouth.

He stopped at the window, again looking over the empty drive. He would be better off deciding how to end this party. He had promised to make the announcement tomorrow, but so far he had not come up with reasons that sounded legitimate. Yes, the house was small, but they were now reduced to seven people spread over six bedchambers—hardly inconvenient.

He did have work that he needed to do, but it was no more pressing than it had been last week, and it could easily be postponed until later. The food was simple, yet it was both tasty and filling. And while the service was primitive, it was tolerable for a little longer. So what could he say that would allay Dornbras's suspicions?

Every time he thought of Dornbras, he cringed. The man was a more poisonous snake than the one that had infested Eden, particularly since his ultimate goal was no longer clear. In retrospect, acceptance into society's ballrooms and drawing rooms seemed an inadequate reason to court favor. Dornbras's own family could have provided such entry. Had they quietly disowned him?

He shook his head, for word would have leaked out. London's gossips were too good at unearthing every last scrap of scandal. And Dornbras must have known that no one person could counter his drawbacks forever. Even Brummell lacked the power to keep Dornbras acceptable once people discovered his true nature. So why had he been cultivating the Montcalm heir?

It was an unanswerable question that he wished he'd never asked. It couldn't be for money; Dornbras had plenty, while Maxwell Longford did not. Power also seemed odd. And they had never argued, so revenge was unlikely. Perhaps Miss Ashburton could think of a reason. She saw a great deal more than most people.

But recalling Miss Ashburton diverted his thoughts. She was the most infuriating female he'd ever encountered—and the most startling. He never knew what to expect. She was accommodating when she ought to be angry, curious to a fault, upset by suggestions that were perfectly reasonable, and as stubborn as the most intransigent mule. Yet she had flashes of perspicacity that astounded him.

She was also creeping into his dreams, damn her witch's eyes and the red hair he could barely keep from touching. And that bosom . . .

His heart sped up until it was pounding uncomfortably in his chest. He should have taken advantage of his trip to Exeter to rid himself of lust, which would have made these meetings with Miss Ashburton easier. She was not suitable for dalliance. He must find some way to banish her from his head before he did something stupid.

You've compromised her. The voice belonged to Terrence.

"Not really," he muttered, trying to convince himself. And even Terrence agreed that she was technically safe—if he discounted all the tête-à-têtes.

He would keep it that way. He was not ready for marriage, and certainly not with a country spinster who did not understand society. She had no concept of honor, as shown by her acceptance of his own admitted dishonor. Most ladies would remove to a hovel rather than share a roof with the company he had assembled, and none would have acknowledged Missy's existence, let alone nursed her with their own hands. Yet he had to applaud her efforts.

He sighed. Instead of accompanying his guests to Brent Tor today, he would remain behind. Not only would it bolster tomorrow's claim of needing to work, but it would allow him to tour the dower house and order repairs.

So far he'd been lucky. His unsuitable guests kept anyone from calling, and no one would seek out Miss Ashburton while her mother was so ill. But that would change shortly. He would need the goodwill of his neighbors, which meant he must move to the dower house immediately. It offered the only shelter he could claim here for the next seventy-five years.

Nodding in satisfaction, he headed downstairs.

A squeal emanated from the music room. Peering through the door, he saw one of the Price girls trying to escape Dornbras's embrace.

He swore. Considering his new insights into the man's character, this situation could explode out of control all too easily. Had Dornbras learned that Max was on the verge of denouncing him? That was the most logical explanation for this insult. If he had nothing to lose, why ignore his own urges?

But perhaps Miss Ashburton was right. Dornbras might consider him too stupid to care. Maybe he believed that a little flattery would cover everything.

He would proceed as if nothing else were wrong, he decided grimly. Exposing his true feelings could hurt too many others.

"I thought I made it clear that my staff was not available for dalliance," he said lightly.

"She's only a maid." But he let her go—forcefully enough that she staggered into the wall.

"She is one of my tenants. You will leave her alone."

Dornbras shrugged, but his eyes promised vengeance. For the first time Max detected the spark of evil Miss Ashburton had mentioned. Goose bumps tripped down his spine. He kept his face impassive, though he would not have been surprised if a footpad with a knife had attacked him from behind.

Dornbras stalked off without another word.

Max sighed. Dornbras would take insult at the termination of the party, for there was no way to make it seem natural now, but that no longer mattered. He would have to protect the Prices as well as Missy and Hope. His groom would follow Dornbras until he could hire runners to look into the man's activities.

He turned to Daisy. "Are you all right?"

She nodded.

"Ignore the cleaning until everyone leaves on today's excursion," he ordered. "He needs time to recover his temper. You and your sister can help your mother in the kitchen for now."

"Thank you, my lord." She dropped a clumsy curtsy. "Has he pestered you before?"

"I only seen him once, my lord. His words was coarse, but another gentleman joined him before he could touch me."

"He will be gone soon. In the meantime, remain with your sister whenever you are working."

He went in search of Blake, who must make sure that Dornbras remained with the others today. He didn't want him preying on village maidens.

Max again awakened to pounding. This time Miss Ashburton's face was dead white. His heart sank.

"What is wrong now?"

"M-mother." Tears brightened her eyes. She was shaking. "Rose— She c-can't b-b-"

He'd seen her angry, terrified, laughing, and serious, but never before had she come close to hysteria. "Relax," he crooned, drawing her head against his shoulder. It nestled into the crook of his neck. "Cry it out. You're not making sense yet."

Her noisy tears made him uncomfortable, though these were neither false nor manipulative. He lightly rubbed her back, struggling to ignore her arms as they slid around his waist. There was nothing sensual about the move. In fact, he suspected that his willingness to hold and comfort her had smashed her self-control far more than whatever crisis had sent her here. She had been holding the household together for so long, that she might not remember leaning on another.

"Mo-mo-mo-" she sobbed, clinging harder.

Helpless, he carried her to the couch and settled her onto his lap—dangerous, for it teased his groin into readiness. When her sobs finally slowed, he poured a glass of brandy and shifted her to the seat beside him.

"Drink, Miss Ashburton," he ordered.

"Y-you m-must—"

"Pull yourself together, my dear," he urged, wrapping her hand around the glass. "I cannot understand you while your teeth chatter like rooks mobbing a cat."

She tried to smile.

"Good. Drink up. We will deal with the problem as soon as you relax."

He had to hold her hand in place so she could lift the glass to her lips. And very delectable lips they were, he admitted, thankful that she was no longer in his lap.

She choked on the first sip. He waited until she had managed two more before speaking.

"Can you explain now?"

Inhaling deeply, she nodded. "Rose woke me—she was sitting with Mother."

He kept his face placid, though the words tumbled ice into his gut. If Mrs. Ashburton died, the gossips would descend like crows, picking up enough tidbits to keep the shire talking for years.

"Mother is worse," she continued. "She is gasping for breath and burning with fever. I don't think she knows that anyone is with her, though I managed to feed her some tea just now."

"Easy," he murmured when she again began shaking. One hand rubbed her shoulder. "Let's take a look at her."

"C-can you send for the d-doctor?"

"I will go, but it would help if I could describe her condition."

She fisted her hands to keep them still. He helped her up, then padded after her, not waiting to find his slippers.

Mrs. Ashburton's room was stifling. Rose hovered near the bed, wispy gray hair dangling about her face and onto her worn robe.

"You can take a break, Rose," said Hope quietly, her tone offering no hint that she had been crying incoherently only moments before. His admiration soared. "Fix yourself some tea. I will call you if I need further assistance."

Max ignored Rose's departure as he stared at the woman in the bed. He could see where Hope had acquired her red hair and high cheekbones. The mother would have been just as delectable in her youth. But now she was gasping for air, her distress obvious.

"I will raise her," he said, recognizing the sudden tightness across his chest. "Pile pillows behind her shoulders. She will breathe better in a more upright position."

Hope complied.

"Dickie," mumbled Mrs. Ashburton as he laid her on the pillows. "Where are you?"

Max met Hope's startled eyes.

"Burning in hell," cried Mrs. Ashburton. "Don't hate me. Come back. Dickieeee . . ."

"Where will I find the doctor?" He backed away from the bed, hoping his touch had not triggered some unspeakable memory.

"The first house in the village."

He nodded. "Try to pour more tea down her throat. Do you need colder water?"

"No. This is quite fresh."

"I will be back as soon as possible. If you need anything, rap on my door. Blake will be there."

Her eyes widened in surprise.

He pulled her into a comforting embrace, pressing a light kiss to her brow. "You are not alone this time, Miss Ashburton. We will do whatever we can to pull her through, though I had no idea she was this bad. I can't promise success."

"I understand."

Mrs. Ashburton was again mumbling, drawing Hope back to the bedside. Max tossed on some clothes, then went to wake Blake. Fortunately his friend was alone.

He had not mentioned his real reason for establishing Blake in his room. Dornbras's fury had not abated since their morning clash. If anything, his tension had increased. The man was ready to explode, even if doing so meant alienating his host. He'd glared during dinner, making no attempt to be congenial. Nearly everyone had noticed, though manners prevented any mention of it.

So he could not risk leaving his room empty while he was out. Locking the door would do little good. Most of the room keys could open it. If Dornbras found an empty room, he would explore the wing beyond, with disastrous consequences.

So Blake must remain on guard.

A few words conveyed the situation. Blake did not even cavil at Max's use of the bedchamber.

Locking the door behind his friend, Max headed for the stables.

Hope sponged her mother's face and tried not to think about crying all over Merimont or sitting on his lap with her arms clinging to him.

She blushed.

Yet he had not taken advantage of her. He was far more complex than she'd dreamed. Instead of the shallow pleasure seeker she had expected, he was a very caring man. Yes, he could be infuriatingly arrogant, but he also tried to protect others from harm—a most unusual trait, in her experience. And tonight his sympathy and support had astounded her. Even his suggestion to prop pillows behind her mother's head and shoulders was working.

So how had a man so willing to help become so autocratic? She was still in shock that he was fetching the doctor himself rather than sending a servant.

Danger, warned her mind yet again.

But it was too late for warnings, she admitted. His touch had awakened something that she had never realized was sleeping, something bigger than that vague restlessness she'd felt in recent days, something specific, incited by his powerful shoulders and soothing caress. What would those shoulders feel like under her palms?

She tried to ignore the question, for speculation could only lead to disaster, but he had overwhelmed her senses and teased her imagination. It insisted on recalling the changes she'd felt under her hip when he'd pulled her into his lap.

She blushed.

Yet he had not ravished her. And that was not her only reason for questioning his rakish reputation. He'd been alone whenever she'd sought him out. He might merely be protecting her mother by indulging his appetites elsewhere, but she'd seen no evidence that he was pursuing the other girls. So why had he not taken advantage of her?

She wished she knew more about society. It was one subject her mother had been unable to teach, because she had never entered it herself. Were rakes less venal than she had been told? Merimont certainly fit none of the images her mother had painted. Nor did he resemble Millhouse or her uncle.

But this pointed out a new danger. By considering his differences from other men rather than noting his similarities, she risked forming a *tendre* for him.

A shiver touched her shoulders as she again recalled how he had held her—for comfort, she reminded herself sharply, though how she knew his motive was another question; no man had ever tried to comfort her. She should have recoiled from his touch as she'd done when Dornbras had grabbed her, but she had felt safe.

Safe? In the arms of an acknowledged rake?

This time the shiver was shock, for she had indeed felt safe. His chest was hard, his arms powerful—yet he had not turned that power against her, unless freeing a desire to feel those arms again counted.

She concentrated on cooling her mother. But every stroke elicited images of Merimont's hand caressing her. When the opening door drew her eyes to his return, she blushed.

"Where can we wait while Doctor Jenkins examines your mother?" he asked, drawing her from the bedside.

"Her sitting room." Passing through a pair of dressing rooms, she led him into the former master bedchamber.

"How is she?" He kindled a fire.

"Her breathing is easier, thanks to your suggestion." She suppressed her new awareness, though his genuine concern made that more difficult than ever.

"I am glad to hear it." He wandered restlessly about the room, fingering her mother's well-worn Bible, turning a collection of sermons over in his hand, touching the last living flower in a vase that had not been refilled in more than a week.

She cursed herself for neglecting her duties. She should have at least removed the withered stems.

"Is Dr. Jenkins prone to gossip?" he asked at last, pausing near the fire.

"No, which irritates several ladies no end." She managed a credible smile. "They are constantly after him to reveal details of everyone's infirmities, but he refuses."

"Excellent. That means he can check on Missy." He resumed his pacing—to the window, the tapestry frame, the fire, then back to the window and on around the room again. And again. She was ready to demand that he sit still when the doctor joined them.

"Her chill has turned into an inflammation of the

lungs," he announced bluntly. "I will be honest with you, Miss Ashburton. Such conditions often prove fatal, but we need not despair just yet. A friend recently sent a new remedy for just this situation."

"What is it?" asked Merimont.

"The root of the purple coneflower. He discovered it while visiting the Americas last year and claims startling results."

"I've never heard of it," said Hope.

"Not surprising. It is not grown here." He described its use.

Hope returned to the sickroom, her mind full of unanswered questions, but she was too tired to think. The news that a cure might be available had pushed fear aside, allowing exhaustion to rule.

Chapter Eleven

Max watched the fog enshrouding Redrock House pearl to lustrous silver. He had witnessed far too many dawns of late.

The night had been exhausting. First the scene with Hope, then his dash to the stables to saddle his horse—at least he could do that without waking a groom; his history of disobedience had taught him to saddle and harness his own cattle. Dr. Jenkins had been at home, thank heaven—he'd had visions of chasing over half the shire looking for him. But the man's reaction to finding Mrs. Ashburton at Redrock House had sent Max's heart plummeting to his toes.

He'd ignored the knowledge for days, though his friends had tried to warn him. Terrence had even gone so far as to leave, but neither had flat-out told him he was wrong. Perhaps they'd feared that he would refuse to listen—was his stubbornness really that ingrained? Or maybe they believed that his station put him above reproach, which might well be true. But looking at the situation through the doctor's eyes had forced him to admit that he had badly compromised Hope. He might be immune to censure, but she was not.

Abandoning the window, he held his hands over the fire in a futile attempt to warm them. He had moved into her home knowing that she had no acceptable chaperon, and he had often met with her alone. He had forced her to share a roof with five courtesans, to say nothing of Dornbras. If Blake had not rescued her, she would be ruined. Then he'd complicated matters by making it impossible for her to seek help without entering his bedchamber, where he had entertained her twice, clad only in a dressing gown.

He could still feel her in his lap.

At least she made an enticing armful. Honor demanded that he offer for her and press his suit when she turned him down—which she would, flaying him with that razor tongue in the process. He was not looking forward to that particular encounter.

His feet resumed pacing as he imagined it, halting abruptly when he spotted the incongruity in the image. It was not his offer that he found annoying. It was her refusal.

For the first time in his life, he faced proposing marriage. Why did she have to be the one lady in England who would not leap at his prospects? She did not merely distrust gentlemen. She feared them, he realized with another sinking sensation. Especially rakes.

Not that he was truly a rake. Devereaux and Millhouse were rakes. Mannering and Wroxleigh were rakes. Reggie was a rake. He had merely kept a sequence of mistresses, which was hardly unusual.

But that was beside the point. She feared him, along with all other men. He should have realized it sooner, though she'd tried hard to hide it. Mrs. Tweed had echoed her employer's beliefs when she'd described men as beasts and tools of Satan. He'd already known that Hope feared her uncle and considered all men alike. And her tirade against marriage had made her views clear.

Yet he must wed her, though proposing would be useless just now. He must first convince her to trust him. Perhaps he should flirt with her for a few days to soften her antagonism. She needed time to see him as a suitor, and he needed to show her that her fears were misplaced. He would never harm her.

At least the night had brought benefits as well as problems. For all his shock at the living arrangements, Jenkins had given Missy the same attention that he'd offered Mrs. Ashburton. And though he'd made no overt criticism, Max believed that they understood each other well enough.

"Those injuries were no accident," Jenkins had stated once he'd left Missy's room.

"I know. The culprit departed the moment I learned of the incident." He'd had to lie about that, for he wanted no one to go after Dornbras until Hope was safe from reprisals. He doubted that Jenkins knew the identities of any of the guests.

"I had not expected even that much consideration from you, my lord."

"He will pay in the end," he'd vowed. "Though the public reason will be different."

"One can hardly call him out over a courtesan," Jenkins had agreed dryly.

"How is she?" he'd asked, leading the way down the spiral stair, all the way to the first floor.

"Improving." Jenkins had then confirmed most of Hope's diagnosis, though the nose was, in fact, broken. "Not badly," he'd added. "But she should remain abed for another week."

"We will see to it."

Jenkins had nodded, then stared pointedly at the barricade across the hallway before entering the office.

"She will come to no harm," Max had promised, removing the chair he'd wedged against the other door— he'd not had time to arrange the bar. "But she is too anxious for her mother right now to consider her position."

Jenkins had left to check on other patients, leaving Max to brood over the complications in his life. But at least the doctor had provided an excuse to terminate this party. Two of those other patients were suffering from cowpox contracted to protect them against smallpox.

He nodded as boots clattered on the stairs. With luck, it would be Dornbras. If he handled this right, he could be rid of the man within the hour.

Dornbras's mother had died of smallpox shortly after his own mother had tumbled down the stairs—forming another bond between them at Eton and depriving Dornbras of his chief supporter. It had given the man a powerful aversion to illness. If he played his cards right, Dornbras would flee, insulting him enough to explain dropping the connection. If he was wrong, he would pitch them all into a scandal that would be discussed for years.

The first omen was good. Dornbras was alone in the dining room.

"Why the long face?" he demanded as Max entered. Perhaps he expected further comment on yesterday's contretemps, for his eyes seemed deadlier than ever—at least deadlier than Max had seen.

"The doctor's arrival did not awaken you?"

"Doctor?" He froze in horror.

Max shook his head. "Forgive me. It has been a troubling morning. I had forgotten that your room overlooked the rear gardens. One of the tenants has smallpox. Since his sister works here, the doctor is concerned about contagion."

Dornbras choked, spitting bits of egg across the table. "Sm— Con— What?"

"The doctor insists on examining each of us as soon as he fetches his wife to help with the ladies. It is a formality, of course. The girls show no symptoms, so it cannot have spread this far, but I promised we would cooperate."

"No." His face was turning green. "I cannot risk— He might quarantine the house. My plans— I must leave."

"I am sure you can go as soon as he verifies that you are free of disease. It shouldn't take more than an hour."

"I cannot wait. I should have left yesterday. Summon my carriage." He was practically running by the time he reached the door.

Max had no time to wonder why Dornbras had grabbed a vase on the way out. The sounds of gagging and retching echoed along the hallway. The man's fear was stronger than he'd thought.

He smiled, not the least sorry to have inflicted a little suffering on his erstwhile friend. Summoning Henry, he ordered Dornbras's carriage, then settled in to enjoy a good breakfast.

By the time he finished, Dornbras was gone. Rob would follow him. Not only would the groom see where

Dornbras went, but he could counter any rumors the man might start.

He was heading upstairs when Reggie appeared.

"It is time to terminate this gathering," Max said without preamble. "One of the tenants is ill—a brother to most of my staff. The doctor claims it is only cowpox, but I prefer to take no chances."

"Good thinking." Reggie nodded. "I don't trust country quacks. And this can only detract from our enjoyment. When do we leave?"

"Dornbras is already gone. I must remain until tomorrow. You can wait until then or go today. Your choice."

"What are the others doing?"

"I will speak with them now."

Max headed for Blake's room.

"What now?" Blake was still half asleep when he answered the door. "Is her mother worse?"

"Not so loud." He glanced along the hall before shutting the door. "As far as I know, she is fine. But I used the doctor's visit to terminate the party. Dornbras is gone."

"Already?"

"The maids' young brother has cowpox—at least we hope that is the worst of it," he said piously.

"You play rough. I take it he fled."

"Leaving behind everything he's eaten in at least three days. Reggie wishes to know everyone's plans before deciding whether to leave now or tomorrow."

"Encourage him to leave now, Max." Blake wrapped his dressing gown around him. "And ask him to escort the girls—he should enjoy that. I cannot leave you here alone. Someone is bound to call once the party ends. I am not the most acceptable chaperon, but it would be better than nothing."

"True, but Reggie thinks I am leaving tomorrow. How can you explain staying?"

"I have business in Exeter and will not return directly to London—which is true, by the way, though the business is hardly pressing."

"So he needs to leave today. I will encourage him to

do so, then. But it will be difficult to hide our presence if two of us remain. And Missy will also be here."

"How is she?"

"Improving, but Jenkins ordered her to remain in bed for at least another week."

"All the more reason for me to stay."

"Very well." He opened the door. "I will tell the girls to start packing."

But a new problem awaited him. Jeanette sported a black eye.

"Dornbras?" he asked grimly.

She nodded.

"What happened?"

"He tried to use force," she said.

"Tried?"

"She kicked him where it hurts the most," said Flo.

"Good for you." He nodded at Jeanette. "If I'd known, I'd have added to the injury before he left."

"He's gone?" asked Flo.

"Just now. He won't be back."

Jeanette's eyes widened. "He's a bad one," she said hesitantly.

"So I've learned. Any other injuries?"

"A couple of bruises."

"More than a couple," said Francine darkly. "She's lucky she escaped."

"And equally lucky he didn't come after her," said Max.

"We know. We kept the door locked, but he did nothing. He may have thought you would investigate if he made a fuss."

He noted that each of the girls had something at hand that could be used as a weapon—a vase, a penknife, a walking stick he'd left in the dressing room. "Forgive me. I did not know he was brutal when I invited him. Can you travel?" he asked, returning to Jeanette.

"If I must."

"She shouldn't for a few days," said Flo. "I think she's hurt more than she lets on."

"And returning to work with that eye will invite worse," added Francine.

"Then she must stay here until it heals." No wonder Dornbras had fled so adroitly. He must have realized that he could never hide this latest attack. And his own earlier claim that Missy had sought out the local doctor must also have raised fears. "Are you two willing to share a carriage with Sir Reginald?" he asked.

Francine smiled. "He's a nice one."

"Clean and playful," Flo agreed.

Two hours later, Max breathed a sigh of relief as Reggie's coach disappeared down the drive. His guilt had grown steadily since he'd left the girls' room. He should have recognized Dornbras's nature long ago. Instead, he'd basked in the glow of insincere flattery, exposing society to the man's cruelty.

His father had been right to condemn the friendship. And if he were honest, he had used the connection more to irritate his father than because he cared for Dornbras himself. Which did not reflect well on him.

This house party marked a crossroads in his life. It had stripped the scales from his eyes, forcing him to admit unpalatable truths. He had adopted his father's arrogance and stubbornness. He'd allowed an evil man to manipulate him. And his father was sometimes right. Montcalm might be overbearing, but his edicts tried to keep his heir out of trouble.

This party would also mark another change, for he must offer for Hope.

When had he started thinking of her so informally? he wondered, realizing that he was using her given name. But he knew the answer. When she had snuggled into his lap last night, something had shifted. Which was just as well, he decided when the memory raised renewed interest. Now he had to convince her to accept him.

Hope unlocked the office door and joined Merimont in the entrance hall. Relief had washed over her as she'd watched the departures. The first had been Dornbras, who'd looked positively green as he'd leaped into his carriage. The glimpse she'd caught of the man's eyes as the coachman sprang the horses had revealed stark terror. What had Merimont said?

The next coach had carried the redheaded gentleman and two girls. Their behavior had not changed since their arrival, with the girls giggling and the man indulging in bold caresses.

Not that she cared, she reminded herself, suppressing memories of Merimont holding her in his lap.

"How is your mother?" he asked, bolting the front door.

"Quieter, though her breathing remains labored. How did you know that raising her head would help?"

He smiled. "There is nothing magical about it. I suffered an inflammation of the lungs in childhood. Propping myself up was the only way I could breathe. It was one of the few times my father took my part against a doctor."

"I am grateful."

"Is she still delirious?"

She nodded as Merimont steered her back to the office, one hand resting lightly on her back. "Usually her feverish ramblings make sense," she said, half to herself. His touch did strange things to her spine. "But not this time. I believe she is trapped in some ancient argument and cannot escape."

"With Dickie?"

"I don't think so."

"Who is he?"

She turned to face him. "I've no idea. Last night was the first time she mentioned the name." Questions swirled through her head—the same ones she could see in his eyes. Not wanting to confide her mother's secrets, especially to a man, she changed the subject. "What did you do to Dornbras? He fled as if the hounds of hell were nipping at his heels."

"I wish they were." He ran his fingers through hair that already looked thoroughly disheveled. "I claimed Jenkins had warned us that one of the tenants had smallpox."

"They've all been inoculated. It is a fearful disease."

"His mother died of it, but I believe he jumped on the excuse to leave before his sins caught up with him."

Her heart stalled as he turned away. "What happened?"

"He struck Jeanette last night, though she managed some revenge of her own."

"Dear Lord!"

"It is my fault." His voice revealed genuine pain. "I never should have brought him here."

"Doing it a bit too brown, my lord," she said, trying to lighten his mood. "You may have mistaken his character, but you hardly conspired with him."

"I should have recognized his faults earlier."

"So you're not a saint." She smiled. "Be grateful. Hair shirts and scourging sound quite uncomfortable."

"You continue to amaze me," he said, shaking his head as he turned back to face her. "I expected a tongue-lashing when you learned of Jeanette's injuries."

"Am I such a harridan—no, don't answer that," she begged before he could open his mouth, for he would hardly have made such a comment if she were not. "I have accepted that there is little you can do against him at the moment. How badly was she hurt?"

"A few bruises, but she cannot return to London until they are healed. She is asleep just now. I will move Missy into the west wing as well. Blake and I will see after them."

"That is the most ridiculous idea I've ever heard. What do you know about nursing?"

"It isn't that difficult."

"But it would be highly improper for you to care for a female."

"Why?" His eyes gleamed. "Do you fear I'll ravish her?"

"Of course not!" she sputtered, blushing.

"Then perhaps you think she'll ravish me."

"I'm sure you would relish the experience," she said tartly, then blushed even harder when she realized what she'd said. "You are a very bad influence," she snapped.

He laughed. "Most ladies think me quite good."

"And conceited, as well." She drew in a sharp breath, trying to ignore the look in his blue eyes. It was far too dangerous to continue such banter. Straightening the papers on her desk gave her an excuse to put its bulk between them. "Do not offend propriety worse than you must. You can entertain them—with cards and the like," she added briskly. "But it would never do to see after their other needs."

"Ah." He pretended great enlightenment, though his eyes twinkled brighter than ever. "You do not think me capable of handling chamber pots and monthly courses."

"Oh!" She wished the floor would open to swallow her.

"I should not tease you," he said, running a finger down the side of her neck. When had he joined her behind the desk? "This will not be the first time I've cared for a female, though I beg you not to hold that against me."

"Your mistresses, I suppose."

"Others like Missy. I do not tolerate violence, no matter how lowly the victim." He tipped her head so she had to look him in the eye. "I am not the monster you think me, my dear Miss Ashburton. Caring for your mother will keep you busy. Blake and I can see after the others."

She stared into those blue eyes, seeing only sincerity. "Very well, but I will also keep an eye on them."

"If you insist. We will remove the barricades, then bring Missy to the west wing. It will be easier for all of us once the house is united."

What was he saying? she wondered, panicking when sparks flew down her arms from his caress. Why was she standing here while he seduced her?

"I must check on Mother," she said, bolting without another word. She thought a shout of laughter erupted behind her, but her ears were buzzing too loudly to be sure.

Silly fool, she berated herself. Not only had she fled like the veriest ninny, but she'd revealed her nervousness. He must think her the pattern card for frustrated spinsters everywhere.

And she was. She must avoid him to guard against further silliness. This was a momentary aberration, brought on by finding herself in a man's embrace for the first time in her life. If she'd had a father, last night would have meant nothing, for Merimont had offered only comfort.

But the uncomfortable sensations returned when she discovered that he was removing the barriers. They had kept her safe. Now she would never know when she might run into him.

Chapter Twelve

Hope stood at the kitchen table briskly kneading bread and glaring at a back door that had admitted no one this morning. What else could go wrong?

Even before Merimont had finished removing barricades yesterday, Daisy Price had raced into the library to report that her father had fallen from the barn roof. All the Prices had rushed home, leaving no staff beyond Mrs. Tweed, Rose, and Henry.

At least Mr. Price was alive, she reminded herself, lest this latest disaster drive her into a melancholy as bad as her mother's. But he'd snapped his leg and would be unable to rise for weeks. Mrs. Price had to look after him and their sons—which must also require Daisy and Annie's help. The girls had not reported for work today.

Frustrated beyond bearing, she pounded the dough. Imagination turned it into Dornbras, into the evil humor infesting her mother's lungs, into Merimont—she distrusted his sudden affability and his penchant for sneaking close enough to touch her—into her uncle for catapulting her into this imbroglio, and finally into Mr. Price's broken leg, which deprived her of any usable staff.

Her stamina had already been stretched to the limit by nursing, cleaning, and cooking for four. Having to cook for ten more was the last straw. Her own efforts in recent days had dwindled to bread, porridge, and whichever boiled meat she used to make her mother's broth. She'd even been too exhausted to add turnips, carrots, and onions to the joint to make a stew. Now she had to produce regular meals for two lords, herself, her mother, two courtesans, and eight servants, none of whom could help her.

Giving the dough one last whack, she shaped it into loaves and was covering them with a cloth when Merimont walked in.

"What are you doing down here?" she demanded sharply.

"Helping you cook breakfast."

She stared.

"It has not escaped my notice that you do most of the work, Miss Ashburton," he said matter-of-factly. "As you pointed out last week, Rose and Mrs. Tweed are too old to be effective. I've sent to London for a staff. In the meantime, we must all lend a hand."

"But—"

"But what?" he asked when she stopped.

"But you're a man."

"You have excellent eyesight, Miss Ashburton." His eyes danced with laughter.

"That is not what I meant." Feeling the heat rise in her face made her blush even harder. "What do you expect to do? I doubt you've been in a kitchen longer than it takes to steal sweets."

"True, but you can guide me. Learning will be fun."

"You have a very odd notion of pleasure," she snapped, flustered as he moved around the table to stand so close that she could feel his body heat despite the roaring fire only ten feet away.

"I have an excellent understanding of pleasure," he murmured.

Ignoring the suggestive tone, she snatched up the pot of oats and barley that had been steeping overnight and hung it above the fire, adding a pinch of salt from the box fastened inside the fireplace. "You already offered to nurse Missy and Jeanette. Why have you abandoned them?"

"I haven't. Unlike your mother, neither needs constant attending. Now that the Prices are gone, I will be more useful elsewhere."

"You can distribute coal and carry out ashes."

He grinned. "Henry is doing that."

"Then you can empty chamber pots," she said maliciously, trying to force him out of the kitchen so she could think. Somehow, he'd closed the distance between them.

"Wilkins has volunteered for that chore."

"Your valet?" What had he done to the poor man to gain such cooperation? "He is even more arrogant than you are."

She regretted the words as soon as they escaped her tongue, though valets were notoriously haughty. All humor faded from Merimont's eyes, leaving them almost bleak.

Abandoning his attempt to crowd her, he paced to the door and back.

"This situation is not one any of us would choose, Miss Ashburton. But you cannot do everything yourself. I admit that I've never had to perform such chores, but I will do what I can, as will the others. Jeanette is ensconced on a couch in Missy's room. She is not that badly injured and can help Missy. When I checked your mother, Rose was asleep, so I sent her to bed. Blake will sponge down the fever until Mrs. Tweed awakens."

"No!" The protest was out before she could stop it.

"He will not harm her," he said quietly, though steel threaded his voice. "Do you want your servants to collapse from exhaustion?"

"Of course not, but you don't understand. If Mother finds a man in her bedchamber, she'll die of shock. She is not fond of men in the best of times and barely tolerates Dr. Jenkins. Seeing a strange lord would send her into hysterics."

"So that's where you learned it," he said, tossing his jacket onto a chair and rolling up his sleeves.

"What?"

"Your fear of men. Don't deny it," he continued as she opened her mouth. "I can see it in your eyes. But while a few are dangerous—Dornbras, for example— most are not."

"So you say, but I am a better judge of what might harm me, my lord. In my experience, the higher a man's station, the more likely he is to hurt others, especially females." She glared from his abandoned coat to his bared forearms.

"I will never hurt you," he said, noting her gaze. "But neither do I wish to destroy my coat while cooking breakfast. You obviously have little experience with gentlemen. Do you know any aside from your uncle and Millhouse?"

"A few, but they are enough to put one off the entire gender. And you know nothing about Mother. Please stay away from her. Even knowing you are in the house would horrify her. Do you wish to prevent her recovery?"

He frowned. "Why would she react so strongly?" he finally asked.

"She has suffered greatly at the hands of men. It is not your place to judge her reactions."

"Perhaps not, but don't make the mistake of judging every man by your mother's experiences."

She glared, furious at his self-serving use of facts he did not understand. "Stay away from Mother!" she snapped.

"Very well. Blake will remain only until Mrs. Tweed awakens, but if you wish to keep us out of her bedchamber, then you must allow me to help here. You cannot expect Mrs. Tweed and Rose to handle all the nursing."

He was right, she conceded. Feeding fourteen people would consume most of the day, and she knew better than to ask her own servants to help with more than cleaning. They lacked the strength to lift heavy pots, the coordination to work close to a fire without burning themselves, and the steadiness to handle a knife. "If you insist. But you will regret it. There's an apron in the pantry."

"I don't need one." His smile warmed her clear to her toes. "So what is for breakfast?"

"Ham, which is already sliced."

"Do we have eggs to go with it?"

"Not unless you wish to gather them. I've not had time to check the poultry yard." She enjoyed the horror in his eyes. He must have encountered irate chickens before.

"What else?"

"Toast. Can you slice bread?"

"I can try." He picked up a knife.

Within minutes, she was convulsed in laughter.

"How dare you insult me?" he demanded.

"Look at the mess you've made." She pointed to the table. Half a loaf of bread had been reduced to crumbs. "How can anyone mangle bread so badly?"

"It *tastes* the same." He popped a chunk in his mouth, then chuckled. "But this knife must be the dullest in Christendom. It's as well I didn't use it on Dornbras. It would have bounced off his thick hide."

"Don't blame the knife, my lord. I sharpened it this morning. It is your technique that is wanting."

"So show me what I'm doing wrong."

"Very well. But you must stir the porridge," she said, shaking her head. "It cannot be left unattended. Can you manage that?"

"Definitely."

"Good. Keep it moving," she ordered, handing him the spoon. "Else you will make lumps."

He replaced her at the fireplace, allowing her to examine the remains of the loaf.

"What a mess," she grumbled, sweeping the crumbs into a pile. She could put them in a pudding for dinner, but they would be short of toast for breakfast. "You must remain in control if you wish to slice food evenly," she told Merimont. "Hold the knife straight, with a firm grip on the handle. You allowed it to wander in all directions." In moments she had cut the remainder of the loaf and was arranging the pieces on the toasting rack.

"Stirring food is hot work," Merimont complained.

"If you had deigned to wear an apron, you could wrap it around your hand to protect against burns. Keep the porridge moving," she added when he paused.

"My back hurts. I have to bend forward to reach it."

"It is part of the fun of learning a new skill," she reminded him, positioning the rack near the fire. "No one asked you to help."

"Surely there is a more convenient place to hang this pot."

"Larger kitchens offer more options, but Redrock has always been small. I could hang the pot higher, but that would leave it too far from the fire to be effective. Of course, you could always install one of those new patent stoves. The chandler bought one a few months ago. His cook has praised it ever since. Pots rest on a flat surface at a convenient height, and the oven can be heated in an hour instead of requiring two days. It needs daily blacking to prevent rust, but he considers that a minor problem." She adjusted the spit holding the joint for dinner and straightened the drip pan that Merimont had kicked askew.

"You have flour on your nose," he said, abandoning his complaints as he reached over to rub it away.

She jumped. "Pay attention to the porridge," she grumbled, flipping the toast rack to brown the other side.

"I am." His finger traced her ear.

She reached for a towel as an excuse to evade that pesky finger, made an unnecessary adjustment to the spit, tossed a few more coals on the fire, then carried the toast to the table.

"I had intended to move into the dower house," he said, surprising her with the change of subject. "But it seems beyond repair. Watts agrees. The rot is so pervasive, we would have to gut it, yet even the stone walls have problems. The rear is so bowed it should have collapsed by now. How can you claim even two rooms to be usable?"

"Only for a few days. Does that mean you will move to the White Heron?"

"No. I will remain here for now." He gestured with the spoon. "The dower house must come down. It is dangerous. And unless you marry, I will need to replace it."

"We've already discussed this, my lord. I have no intention of wedding," she said sharply, though her heart sank. She had thought his sudden warmth was an attempt to seduce her, but he must be trying to drive her into another man's arms—had someone mentioned Squire Foley's halfhearted courtship? "Mother will recover soon. Once Missy can travel, I expect you all to leave. If you wish to remain in the area, you must move to the White Heron until the dower house is rebuilt. You have already stayed here longer than is proper."

"Rebuilding will take at least a year, so you'd best become accustomed to me." He held up both hands to halt her protest. "I will not harm your mother, as she will admit once she's met me. She cannot be as fragile as you claim."

She cursed under her breath, barely restraining herself from heaving a lump of bread dough at his head. "Pig-headed fool. He is worse than I thought," she muttered, seething. "He will push Mother into an early grave, then force me out so he can take my home for himself."

He blanched. "You can't believe that."

"Why should I think well of you, my lord? You ignore inconvenient facts and make decisions based solely on your desires. When will you admit the world does not conform to your expectations? The facts are irrefutable, sir. You will not break the lease by forcing me to wed. I don't care who you bribe to offer for me. I will never marry, and neither rape nor seduction will change my mind. Nothing will induce me to endure what Mother went through."

A loud sizzle interrupted his response. "What the—?" He stared in amazement as porridge boiled in a seem-ingly endless stream down the sides of the kettle and onto— "My boots!"

Hope swore. Grabbing the spoon from his hand, she jerked the pot away from the fire. Fanning and stirring soon soothed the remaining porridge into submission, but not before half of it was lost.

"What happened?" he demanded, scrubbing at his boots with her best towel.

"You stopped stirring. I told you to keep it moving," she snapped, mentally cursing. Breakfast would be skimpy indeed. Little toast. Less porridge. "You'd better gather some eggs," she muttered, then jumped when she realized what she'd said. "No, don't. You'd break most of them and probably scare the hens into refusing to lay."

"There goes that razor tongue."

"You deserve a scold." She glared at him as flames licked at the spilled porridge, pouring smoke and the stench of charred oats into the kitchen. "If you help any more, we will all starve."

His eyes moved from the pile of crumbs to the blackened mess in the fireplace. An unexpected chuckle burst from his throat. "I can't believe one person could do so much damage in so short a time."

"You are a man," she said darkly, though she could feel a smile tugging at the corners of her mouth. "You can't keep more than one thought in your head at a time."

His laughter increased. She thought she heard *lead me a merry dance,* but the words were too distorted to be sure. And his laughter was contagious. Before she knew it, she was chuckling with him.

"Egad, what a mess," he said when he finally caught his breath. "Dare I offer to clean it up?"

"I think not. You would doubtless fall into the fire, and then I'd have another patient to nurse."

But he wasn't listening. Already, he was scraping away at the hearth.

Shrugging, she dumped the bread crumbs into the porridge and added several chopped apples. Slicing cold mutton to go with the ham, she retrieved a tart she'd planned to use for dinner and decided there was enough to feed this odd collection of guests.

Leaving Merimont to do as he wished, she carried the meal into the servants' hall, then filled her mother's bowl with broth that had remained safe in the warming box and made her way upstairs.

Max frowned as he drove toward town. So far his efforts to earn Hope's regard had been a disaster. She didn't believe anything he said, was clearly suspicious of his motives, and wanted nothing to do with him. So how was he to win her hand? He'd never before met any female who went out of her way to avoid him and made him feel like a bungling fool in the process.

Her interpretation of his flirtation had seemed outrageous until he reread the lease. Then he cursed himself. He'd only noted Mrs. Ashburton's rights the first time, but Hope must know that her mother's chances of surviving an inflammation of the lungs were slim. Her own claims to Redrock disappeared upon marriage. Obviously she expected him to force her onto the first man he could find.

"Absurd," he mumbled. Even if he had no obligation to wed her himself, he would never have considered doing so. While it was true that he'd intended to introduce her to society, he had not expected that to affect her rights to Redrock House.

But her fear of marriage went beyond the question of Redrock and her income. He could still hear her voice— *endure what Mother went through.* She hadn't explained, nor had she spoken about her family's past. It was something he must investigate, for he suspected that it held the key to understanding her. Her mother feared men and had taught her to do the same. Until he knew why, he could not prove she was wrong.

In the meantime, he must win her friendship, kindle at least a little interest in more, and help with the work until the London servants arrived, though he had to admit that his efforts to date had been less than useful.

A grin tugged the corners of his mouth over the breakfast debacle. If anyone had suggested that he could be amused by his own ineptitude, he would have called them out. But this was too ridiculous for words. How had he bungled something that looked so easy?

The mess had been surprisingly difficult to put right— leaving him reluctant to ever consume porridge again. What must such horrible stuff do to his innards? By the time he started scraping it up, it had become a gluey mass that stuck to the hearth stones tighter than mortar. In fact, if the dower house had been constructed of burnt porridge, its walls would never tumble down.

His boots were ruined. Leather did not tolerate being doused in boiling porridge, then scraped bare. No amount of polish would restore the finish. He cursed, though he had learned an important lesson from the incident. If he ever ventured into a kitchen again, he would not go near a porridge pot.

Pulling up in front of the apothecary shop, he consigned his team to Hope's groom, Ned.

He had volunteered to replenish Hope's supply of

herbs, but his real reason for visiting the village was to learn more about Mrs. Ashburton. The garrulous apothecary seemed a good place to start.

"Good morning, sir," said Mr. Winters, his curiosity obvious as Max strode through the door.

"I am Lord Merimont, new owner of Redrock House." He extended his card.

"My lord." His eyes brightened.

"I stopped at the manor this morning," he said carefully. "Mrs. Ashburton's condition has improved somewhat, though she remains feverish."

"I heard Dr. Jenkins called on her two days ago."

"So I understand." He lowered his voice as if sharing secrets. "He advised that she be told of the change in ownership, since she has never liked Ashburton."

"Few people do," said Winters. "I've never heard him say a word in favor of either mother or daughter. You've no idea what they've had to endure, for all he's a lord. You must have seen what he did to Redrock."

"Why would anyone behave so recklessly?"

"He's a bad one," muttered Winters. "Like his brother, by all accounts."

"Did you know the brother?"

"I was but a lad when he arrived, apprenticed to my uncle in Portsmouth. Da hated the man. Never explained why, though, other than to mutter about arrogant lords." His eyes sharpened with curiosity.

"Ah, well, such ancient history hardly matters," said Max, abandoning the topic before Winters decided his interest was too intense. "Mrs. Ashburton needs headache powders, willow bark, and lavender."

"You spoke with her?" Though he was reaching down the herbs from a shelf, his attention remained focused on his customer.

"With the housekeeper. It would be highly improper to visit the sickroom," said Max repressively.

"Then why call at the manor?"

"To let them know that I will be gone for a few days." He'd decided that removing himself from the manor—at least in the public eye—would be necessary. Convincing Hope to accept him would take longer than he'd expected. Neither of them needed callers just now. "Since I had to come into the village myself, I offered to stop here and save them a trip."

"Of course."

Max could see new questions hovering on the man's lips, but he gave him no chance to ask them. Collecting his purchases, he bade him good day and left.

So Hope's father had been a bad one, hated by the local merchants—not that the information would do him much good. Hatred could merely mean that the man neglected to pay his accounts on time—a likelihood if the quip about arrogant lords meant anything. Comparing him to the current Ashburton added nothing to his knowledge, for he did not know much about that man, either.

Similar visits to the butcher, the chandler, and the coal merchant elicited nothing useful, though the collier recalled Hope's father as a well-spoken man who enjoyed hunting. But since he also described the current Ashburton as likable, Max had to question his judgment.

He was leaving the lending library when a young lady nearly ran him down. An enormous bonnet framed dull brown curls, distracting the eye from a walking dress embellished by enough ruffles and ribbons for three gowns. He doubted she was a day over seventeen.

"Lord Merimont," she squeaked, clutching her hands to her throat. The gesture clearly rose from surprise rather than fright, for she batted her lashes and smiled. "Welcome to Devonshire, my lord, though it was quite naughty of you to keep your arrival so quiet. I only heard about it this morning. Mama will insist that you dine with us. She was so disappointed that prior commitments kept you from our table in London. How long will you be staying?"

Warning bells pealed in his head. She was like a hundred other chits who aspired to become Marchioness of Montcalm. "My business is already complete," he said coolly, backing a step as if to better examine her. For once, he wished he carried a quizzing glass. It was a marvelous tool for depressing pretensions. "I fear I do not recall your name."

"Miss Agnes Porter, as I told you at Lady Marchbanks's rout," she said, dimpling. "Your compliments were quite delightful, though Mama considered them a trifle warm for propriety—Papa would have discussed that with you if we had not been called home unexpectedly." She had again moved close enough that he could count every thread on her gown. It was time to put a stop to her fantasies.

"If your parents construed words uttered at a rout as warm, then I must assume they are mushrooms, Miss Porter," he said pointedly. "The flirtations bandied about society drawing rooms are meaningless, as everyone who belongs there knows. Not that I can imagine flirting with you. I have no use for schoolgirls."

Ignoring her gasp, he leaped into his curricle and sprang the horses, wanting only to move as far away from Miss Agnes Porter as possible. He would wager Redrock House that she was the sort who could twist a casual greeting into a compromising affair if it suited her purposes—like Miss Timmons, who had pursued Wrexham so assiduously last Season that he'd been forced to flee London. Rumor claimed that her coach had suffered a breakdown outside his estate barely a week later.

The moment he returned to Redrock, he ran Hope to ground in the library. "Who the devil is Agnes Porter?" he demanded.

"Don't you know?" She grinned almost evilly, cocking her head to one side. "She has spoken of you so often that I thought you bosom bows—though I must admit that her tales sound somewhat contrived. I cannot believe that an earl would look twice at her."

He relaxed. "She claimed we'd met, but I've no recollection of it. Who is she?"

"Her father is a local squire. She and her mother accompanied him to London last spring, staying with her widowed aunt for a fortnight."

"Does this aunt have a name?"

"Lady Fitzcummings. I doubt she is as well connected as Agnes claims, but she did take Agnes to several small parties and at least one ball."

"Ah. Fitzcummings. That would explain it. I've only seen the woman twice, but her husband was a remote connection of Lord Marchbanks, which would account for her invitation to his wife's rout."

"Yes. Routs can satisfy all manner of obligations to people one would rather avoid."

He laughed, but the memory of Miss Porter's fluttering lashes quickly sobered him. "How serious are her delusions?"

"You should be safe. Her head was in the clouds even before going to London. And while her claims sound warm enough, I doubt she cares for you personally—or even for your title. Her dreams do not move beyond escaping Devonshire. I suspect she is enamored of your reputation as a dashing rogue."

He swore.

"Be kind. The girl is entitled to a few dreams. Her best prospects for marriage are Squire Foley, who seeks a mother for his children so he can concentrate on his dogs and horses, and Mr. Hemple, heir to an inhospitable farm hacked from the wilds of Dartmoor."

"Which makes her dangerous now that I am here in the flesh and not merely a name glimpsed in the distance. I've met many deluded girls. Fortunately, I had already told Mr. Winters that I am leaving. When she calls, tell her I am visiting friends."

"She would never call while Mother is so ill."

"She will call. She will do more than call if she suspects I'm here."

"Like what?"

"Crawl into my bed and scream rape," he muttered.

Hope shook her head as Merimont left the library. Did he really believe that every female in the country was after him?

Yet he was proved right less than an hour later. She was spooning broth into her mother's mouth when Mrs. Tweed rapped on the door.

"Mrs. Porter and Miss Agnes to see you," she said, extending their cards.

Hope sighed, handing her the bowl. "You stay with Mother."

She refused to straighten her hair or prepare a refreshment tray. They must know this was not a propitious time to call. But she greeted them politely enough.

"I hear Mrs. Ashburton is improving," said Mrs. Porter, settling into a chair.

"The crisis has passed, though she remains very ill."

"Mr. Winters claims she is well," said Agnes, her tone clearly calling Hope a liar.

"You must have misunderstood. Improvement is hardly the same as recovery," said Hope shortly. "She is now aware that I am in the room with her, which is more than she knew two days ago. Yet I doubt she recognizes who I am."

Mrs. Porter colored and began a comment on the weather, but Agnes again interrupted. "I heard that Lord Merimont owns Redrock."

Hope cursed herself for dismissing his fears. Agnes's eyes were no longer dreamy. They'd turned calculating and fanatical. "He does. Watts thinks the tenants will benefit, so we are pleased with the change."

Agnes peered about the room as if Merimont might be hiding behind a drapery, but she said nothing more while Hope steered the conversation to the vicar's Sunday sermon, neighborhood gossip, and Agnes's upcoming trip to Bath. Only after Hope stared pointedly at the clock for the third time did Mrs. Porter raise the purpose of her visit.

"We are planning a dinner party on Friday, Miss Ashburton. Will you be able to join us?"

"I cannot leave Mother alone," she said in a vast understatement.

"But Lord Merimont will wish to attend," said Agnes warmly. "He must already find the country boring. I know how much he loves town."

"If you say so. I barely know the man, but I understand he left this morning and does not expect to return for at least a fortnight."

Agnes opened her mouth as if to protest, but a jab from her mother's elbow kept her quiet. The pair finally took their leave, though Hope feared she had not seen the last of them.

Chapter Thirteen

A week later Max turned away from the window to resume his seat in the doorway of Mrs. Ashburton's dressing room. Even Hope had finally admitted that she and her servants could not handle all the nursing, so he and Blake were keeping watch at night. The woman was sleeping better, though she was still troubled by chills or fever. He was under strict orders to stay in the shadows and awaken Hope if her mother underwent any change.

His own situation was increasingly frustrating. Having put it about that he was leaving, he and Blake could not venture out. And his efforts to soften Hope's antagonism were going nowhere. While she was more relaxed than before, he had only to mention the house, her plans, marriage, or pleasure for her to withdraw into a prickly shell that he could not penetrate.

Normal flirtation did not work. She recoiled from every touch, retreated from any hint of warmth, and refused to indulge in any of the conversational gambits London society took for granted. It had been a mistake to crowd her, he admitted now. He had not understood the depth of her fear. No matter how pleasurable she found his touch, terror was stronger, so flirtation merely drove her away.

Yet they had grown closer, though he wasn't sure why. She delighted in pricking his pretensions. The breakfast fiasco had not been his only disgrace. There was the day he'd polished the drawing room tables with lemon wax, then used the same rag to wipe a smudge from the mirror. While removing the mess he'd left, she'd kept up a scolding monologue on the subject of inept lords. So why had he been laughing by the time she finished?

The same thing had happened when he'd spilled coal all over the entrance hall, landed on his backside in a pool of soapy water from a bucket he'd knocked over, and demonstrated a singular ineptitude for opening wine bottles. He should have been mortified by his lack of skill—or at least furious at having to perform such menial tasks. Instead, he found amusement in the absurdity of it all, sharing her delight in laughing with him.

She was a different person when she laughed. For those brief moments, she forgot her mother's illness, forgot her uncle's persecution, even forgot her fear of rakish gentlemen. He longed to bring more laughter to her life, freeing her from the cares that weighed on her shoulders.

But he could do nothing until she accepted him—if she ever accepted him. His lack of progress pressed heavily on his spirits. He could not postpone his offer much longer. Already Mrs. Ashburton had regained awareness of her surroundings. The neighbors would soon discover that he was here. And he had yet to decide what Ashburton might be up to—or Dornbras, he admitted, wondering where that gentleman was; he'd heard nothing from Rob in three days.

The Porters had returned twice since their initial visit. He had concealed himself in the music room during yesterday's call, listening through the door Hope had left open. The result was enlightening, though it did nothing to make his situation any easier. Squire Porter was ambivalent about pursuing a match. While he would clearly welcome the connection, he was worldly enough to know it would never come about without trickery. His wife was more inclined to believe Agnes's claims, which now included clandestine meetings in London. The girl herself was dangerous. Whether she was merely greedy or actually believed her fantasies did not matter. She was a determined miss whose parents probably found it easier to oblige than to oppose her.

Two hours later, he'd glanced through a window to see her sneaking around the house, testing the doors and windows. Thank heavens they were keeping them firmly locked, even in daylight. Since Henry was now sleeping in the attics, the only people needing admittance were the grooms and coachmen, who ate in the kitchen twice a day.

But knowing that Agnes was determined to trap him increased his irritation. He could not leave the house for fear she would accost him. He dared not even take a turn about the terrace. Beleaguered, besieged, and disgruntled, he stared at the sickbed.

He needed to settle with Hope before his life grew even more complicated. If only he could think of a way to convince her.

Blake watched Max descend the stairs. His friend's face grew glummer every day.

"Has Mrs. Ashburton suffered another setback?" he asked.

"No. She is doing better this morning."

"Then what put that frown on your face?"

"She will be up and about in another week. Hope won't tolerate us here after that."

Blake noted the use of her given name, but said nothing. Max was so stubborn that he probably hadn't figured out he was in love with her. "Then we must leave," he said calmly, trying to force Max to think instead of react. "Jeanette returns to London tomorrow. Even Missy will be fit enough to travel in a few days."

"So we let Mrs. Ashburton's irrational fears drive us away?"

"They may be a little exaggerated, but I'd hardly call them irrational. You know how difficult her life has been."

"No more than many others. Yes, she lost her husband at an early age. But despite Ashburton's crimes against the estate, she has hardly been living in a hovel. So why does she fear men?"

Blake stared. "Ashburton despises her. He would gladly destroy her."

"How do you know?" Anger threaded the voice.

Well, well. Max was more firmly caught than he had realized. "Why not ask Miss Ashburton?"

Max cursed, clenching his fists as if he wished to strike

something. Blake sighed and led him into the music room. "Start at the beginning. What is wrong with you today?"

"I have to offer for her."

"Agreed. No matter how fine a face you put on the last fortnight, you've ruined her in the eyes of the world. But is offering so bad?"

"Not really, but she'll turn me down. Her mother's history might provide a clue to how to convince her, but she won't discuss it." He glared.

Blake shook his head at his friend. "She must know what you will do with the information."

"Then why tell you?"

"Don't wish me to Hades, Max. She cares nothing for me beyond friendship, and I prefer it that way. We discussed her family briefly during that walk to the village the morning after we met. At the time, she did not realize where this must end, but she hardly told me anything." He hid a smile, for the only reason she'd answered at all had been to balance the information she had extracted about Max.

"So what did she say?" His voice had become a feral growl.

"Don't hold her openness against her. She accepts my friendship because she needs someone safe to talk to."

"Safe? Why would she need safety now? Dornbras is gone."

Blake paused long enough to make Max nervous. Pushing two stubborn mules together was tricky, but necessary. "She is so afraid of repeating her mother's mistakes that she cannot overlook your reputation. What do you know of Ashburton?"

"Her uncle?"

He nodded.

"He enjoys gaming, is clutch-fisted with his family, and has done his best to ruin this estate."

"He also enjoys wenching and is much like Dornbras, though less public about his worst habits. He is miserly with his family because he despises them. As near as I can tell, he blames everything wrong with his life on Hope's mother—and on Hope, by extension."

"How the devil does he justify that?"

"She doesn't know—or won't say. The only facts she revealed are that Edward revered his brother. Arnold wed her mother while Edward was on his Grand Tour—her tone hinted that the marriage was unhappy. After Arnold died, Edward was recalled and forced to wed a woman he despises."

Max began pacing. "He can hardly blame Hope for that. Even Ashburton is not insane enough to persecute two innocent females just because he hates his wife."

Blake shrugged. "That's all she told me, though Mrs. Tweed sometimes mutters about that evil man, apparently referring to Hope's father."

"Hope did mention that her mother's marriage was forced, but there has to be more to the story. And it must be something big. Ashburton has done his best to destroy them since he acquired the title. So why give the estate to me?"

"I thought you won it in a card game."

"So did I at first, but I have no memory of playing out the hand. He announced that I'd won, handed me a small fortune, then sauntered out, looking like a cat with a mouth full of feathers. Brummell and Alvanley were surprised at his reaction."

"Interesting. I can't imagine what purpose that would serve, but if there is any chance he cheated, you need to investigate. He is not a man to act without purpose, especially when it means abandoning something of value."

"Not entirely of value. I thought he might have surrendered it before it started costing him money, but he could have prevented that easily enough."

"Does he hold some grievance against you? Perhaps he is hoping to compromise you into wedding someone your father might not approve."

"I've rarely met the man and can't imagine why he would plot against me." He frowned suddenly. "You described him as being like Dornbras. Are they friends?"

"I don't know. I've avoided Dornbras for years, except when you forced us together. Why?"

"It was Dornbras who suggested this house party."

Blake thought back to that scene at White's. "So it was. But why would that matter?"

"It might not, but it is another fact to consider."

"If you are going to offer for her, you'd best do it soon."

"Today. If only I could think of a way to convince her. She never reacts the way I expect her to."

Blake grinned as he followed Max downstairs. Maybe he could reassure Hope that Max would never harm her. He'd already revealed some of Max's soft spots. And she had to feel an attraction. He'd watched her avoid Max even as her eyes followed his every move.

Max ignored the chatter during breakfast. His talk with Blake had raised some interesting points. Though he doubted Ashburton had a grievance against him, the man might be using him to hurt Hope. As evidence, there was that odd remark Ashburton had made about Redrock's amenities . . .

Whether Dornbras was involved was irrelevant—this scheme could have nothing to do with Dornbras's original one. And Ashburton could hardly have anticipated the events that had led him into gaming at Brook's that night. He had merely met Ashburton's needs. But what did the man hope to accomplish? And how could he convince Hope that he'd known nothing about it?

Someone pounded on the kitchen door, pulling his thoughts back to the room. Was something wrong in the stable, or had Agnes devised a new way to run him to ground? Perhaps he should slip out of sight.

Henry went to open it. "What are you doing here, Jack?" he demanded as a boy burst in.

"Henry's brother," explained Hope in an aside. She motioned Henry to silence. "Is there a problem?"

Jack nodded. "Pa sent me. He saw Lor' Ashburton crossin' the river."

She blanched.

"Lord protect us," squeaked Mrs. Tweed.

"Is he coming here?" asked Max.

"Why else would he be in the area?" Hope's eyes looked huge.

"He no longer owns the estate," said Blake firmly. "So he cannot expect a warm reception."

"And he is not your guardian," Max reminded her. "You needn't see him at all, if you don't wish to."

"It is not that simple." She turned back to Jack, thanking him for his information and sending him off with a slab of bacon for his family. When she returned, her face was white.

Max caught Blake's eye, suddenly understanding Ashburton's scheme. He had sought to place his niece in a compromising position that would shackle her for life to exactly the sort of man she hated—rumor declared him a womanizing drunkard, though it was all exaggeration. At the same time, Ashburton could strike another blow at his sister-in-law. Seeing her daughter forced into marriage as she had been would surely send her into a decline.

But he would not tolerate such manipulation. Nor would he allow Hope's reputation to be smeared across the realm, as Ashburton would surely do.

He would wed her, of course, but not under so public a shadow. Even marriage would not restore her reputation once Ashburton finished with her.

"How long will it take him to reach here?"

"Another hour, for the road swings west to avoid Dudley's Bog, and I doubt he'd risk putting his carriage to the farm track."

"We have time, then. We are not here." He turned to the servants. "Wilkins, you and Harris pack our belongings. Henry, take Missy to her old room on the nursery floor, then help carry the luggage to the attics. Mrs. Tweed, can you and Rose make the bedchambers appear unused in case Ashburton decides to explore?"

She nodded, momentarily energized by the danger that faced her employer. "Opening windows will dissipate your scents. If he asks, we are taking advantage of warm weather to dry out a leak."

"Excellent."

"I will put the food away, then help upstairs," said Jeanette.

"Perhaps I can claim Jeanette is a nurse brought in to help with Mother," said Hope.

"Not a chance," said Blake. "Ashburton knows every courtesan in the country."

Max nodded. "He probably knows everyone I invited. I don't think this visit is an accident."

Hope's eyes widened. He could almost read the thoughts parading through her mind—concern that disturbing her mother might bring on a fatal relapse, suspicions about what Ashburton might hope to achieve, uncertainty over the effect this might have on the rest of them.

But overriding everything was a stark terror that drove icy knives deep into his soul.

Hope pulled her eyes from Merimont's mesmerizing gaze as the servants hurried out to begin covering their traces. She knew her face was white. She could only pray that it recovered some color before Uncle Edward arrived.

Since he had no legitimate reason to call, he must be planning to cause trouble. This must be why he had wagered away the estate. If he was stupid enough to believe that a new owner could break the lease, he would try to goad Merimont into throwing them out so he could gloat over their plight. But she could deal with that.

What she feared was Merimont's house party. Watts had long ago admitted that he was expected to report any visitors to the manor. He had never had cause to do so—and he was thrilled to have Merimont in charge now—but Uncle Edward might have set up more than one spy in the neighborhood. If he knew, he would cause as much trouble as he could.

"We haven't time to warn Watts," she said, turning to Merimont. "Will he reveal your presence?"

"Since he now works for me, I doubt he would tell Ashburton anything," he replied firmly. "He is less than complimentary about the man. In any event, he is surveying timber today and should not return until late."

"I can only hope."

"Why not refuse Ashburton entrance?" asked Rockhurst. "He has no reason to expect hospitality after the way he has treated you."

"Turning him away would merely pique his curiosity. And Mrs. Tweed can hardly claim I am out. He would insist on awaiting my return. He knows I never spend the night elsewhere. Asking the staff to deal with him will guarantee that he moves in."

"And we cannot have that," said Merimont. "But you should not see him alone. He hates your mother, and thus you. That makes him dangerous."

"This will hardly be the first time I have faced him," she said, shrugging, though she recalled all too clearly her narrow escape on his last visit. But that was not a memory she wished to share. "Mother has been blue-deviled since Grandfather's death, so I have been the one to meet with him. She rarely did more than share meals with us."

"What if he wants to harm her?" Merimont demanded, surprising her with his insistence. "You need a way to enforce your wishes."

"I don't see—"

"At least listen to him," put in Rockhurst quietly.

Hope glared at Merimont. "Your fears are exaggerated," she insisted.

"Perhaps, but it is better to plan for all contingencies. I do not know Ashburton well, but I have seen his sort before. The only argument they understand is force. You are not strong enough."

"I do not understand what concerns you." Though she feared that she did. Uncle Edward had made it clear that he would restore Redrock if she consented to be his mistress. Might he use force to achieve that end? It was the only form of ruin left to him.

"Do you want him to move in?" He nodded at her gasp. "You cannot allow him under this roof. Aside from the effect on your mother, if he discovers us, he would destroy both of your reputations."

"To say nothing of yours." She glanced from one man to the other. "I care little on my own account, but I will not tolerate having him injure you. Yet you can hardly protect me. He would recognize you in a trice. I will have to rely on Henry."

"Inadequate. For all his enthusiasm, he is too young. But Wilkins can pose as your butler. Ashburton has never met him."

"He knows I have no real staff. Henry I can pass off, as he is a tenant."

"But your situation has changed, Miss Ashburton. Under the lease, staffing the estate is my responsibility. I prefer a full complement of servants so the property remains in good repair."

She nearly choked.

"Just in case Ashburton has checked the names of my servants, you may call him Reeves," he added. "That name is connected to none of us. And he is powerful enough to eject Ashburton if necessary. Your uncle is soft from too much wine and too many hours of idleness."

"Very well." She didn't like it, but she had to admit that having Wilkins nearby would help her relax.

Max watched her leave, then turned to Blake. "Suppose she cannot turn him away."

"We can probably manage one night in the attic. Locking all the doors will protect us." He frowned. "Of course, Ashburton's groom will spot our carriages in an instant."

Max groaned. "You had best visit the stables. Lock the carriages away and find a way to explain the horses. The fences are too shoddy to risk turning them out to pasture." He ran his fingers through his hair. "I wish I knew his purpose."

"As do I."

Max went upstairs to help clear bedchambers. At least he didn't have to fret over Mrs. Tweed or Rose. They hated Ashburton at least as much as Hope did.

He disliked sending her up against her uncle with only Wilkins for protection. He ought to be doing it himself. Skulking about the attics while Hope was in danger made him feel like a coward. But he could not take chances until he understood the man's purpose.

Fear and regret bedeviled him as he scrambled through the next hour. If only he had settled with Hope so he had a legal right to protect her. Yet revealing his intentions might play into Ashburton's hands. What was the man's goal? Even if Hope successfully turned her uncle off, could they prevent him from settling in the village?

One crisis at a time, he admonished himself, tossing dustcovers over furniture. First he had to erase evidence of his presence. And the White Heron was small, he recalled. It wasn't the sort of inn Ashburton would approve. He was a man who puffed up his consequence by ostentatious display and loud complaints about perceived slights.

"Thank you, Reeves," said Hope as Wilkins set the tea tray on a convenient table. She poured, making sure it was very weak—her uncle disliked weak tea above all other beverages.

"I would have preferred wine," he said, setting the cup aside.

"We have no reason to stock wine," she said smoothly. "We rarely entertain."

He frowned. "My man can procure some from the village."

"That isn't necessary. You won't be staying."

"Of course I will. I am your uncle."

"A connection neither of us wants." She swallowed tea to give her time to remove the irritation from her voice.

"Your mother would insist that you offer hospitality to family," he swore.

"An odd notion that proves you know nothing about her, sir."

"*Lord* Ashburton. You will address me by my title, girl."

She ignored him. "Mother is ill, which is another reason you cannot stay. You might expose her to the cowpox sweeping the area—if it is merely cowpox," she added lightly, grateful to Merimont for suggesting this excuse. "She is too weak to throw off another malady."

He paled. "Watts should have notified me immediately."

"Why? The estate is no longer yours."

"Aha!" A triumphant smile twisted his mouth. "I was right. Merimont is here. No one will believe that you refused the advances of so unprincipled a libertine."

She forced a shrug. "Why should I care for the opinion of people stupid enough to believe a word you say? Most will not, for he stayed only long enough for tea. Lord Rockhurst accompanied him."

"I am aware of that. So did Sanders, Dornbras, and Sir Reginald, to say nothing of their female companions." His eyes gleamed.

"You are misinformed." It was difficult to remain casual under such provocation.

"Hardly. Dornbras mentioned the orgy before leaving town."

"Then he must have mistaken its location."

"The man never misses a thing," he growled.

She shrugged. "I wouldn't know about that. Lords Merimont and Rockhurst informed us of the change in ownership, then spoke with Watts. Merimont was unhappy about the estate's condition, as you must have expected. He issued a spate of orders before leaving, one of which augmented my staff. A butler showed up last week, and I received word yesterday that a cook and several maids will soon follow."

"You lie! The stable is full of horses. Where is he?"

"You are offensive, sir," she snapped, thinking furiously. "I often supplement our income by boarding horses for neighborhood house parties."

"Watts never mentioned it."

"Why should he? You forbade him to bother with the house and grounds. Since the stables fall under my control, what I do with them is my own business."

"You won't best me, girl. No one will believe Merimont remained here long enough to check the books, yet did not stay either here or in the village."

She shook her head pityingly. "This discussion is pointless, sir. I doubt he examined the books, for he and Lord Rockhurst were merely paying a courtesy call. His orders correct obvious problems—broken fences, a roof leak, repairing the dower house, removing deadwood from the park. With harvesting done for the year, he has plenty of time to consider next year's planting. Or he may let Watts deal with it. His rumored interests hardly include agriculture. But I suppose we will learn more when he returns."

"When?"

She shrugged. "I did not ask, though I cannot imagine we will see him until the dower house repairs are complete. If you truly care, write to him—not that I can see that this is your concern."

"It will be. You are naïve indeed if you think he will settle for that ruin down the road. He will throw you out like the refuse you are," he said with a satisfied sneer. "You will come crawling to me, begging for support."

She shook her head. "Our lease is unbreakable, as you should know. But you needn't fear any requests for help. Mother needs peace of mind, something you would never allow her."

"Such a dutiful daughter." He rose to loom over her chair. "Don't pretend with me, girl. I know you too well."

"Another delusion." She ignored his attempt at intimidation, grateful that Wilkins hovered nearby. "You will wish to leave if you hope to reach a comfortable inn before dark."

Merimont had been right, she admitted, watching her uncle's face turn purple. The man had expected to ruin her. Why did he hate her? She posed no threat to his pocket, his family, or even his reputation—which he was tarnishing with no help from others. She lived hidden away in the country, unknown, without power, and had met him only a dozen times in her life.

Wilkins appeared in the doorway. Ashburton stepped back a pace, glaring.

"What is it, Reeves?"

"The coachman is unloading luggage, Miss Ashburton. Should Mrs. Tweed prepare a bedchamber?"

"Not today, Reeves. My uncle was just leaving."

"But—" Ashburton glared.

"The subject is closed," she said firmly. "I cannot accommodate guests at this time. You forfeited your right to shelter when you wagered away the estate. Now that you know we will make no demands on you, there will be no need for further contact."

"This way, my lord," said Wilkins, sounding like the haughtiest of butlers.

Ashburton spluttered. For a moment, she feared he would refuse. But he finally left.

She collapsed.

"Sherry?" asked Wilkins, returning with a tray after locking the front door. He proffered the decanter that usually sat in the office.

"Thank you, Wilkins. I have never seen him more furious."

"I took the liberty of asking Ned to follow him," he said, naming her groom. "If he remains in the area, you will wish to know where."

His words echoed long after he left. She had grown complacent in the last fortnight, but Uncle Edward had not washed his hands of them. Why hadn't she realized that ten years of petty revenges would never balance a quarter century of hate?

Chapter Fourteen

Two days later Max found Hope in the library thumbing through an herbal. She'd hardly spoken to him since Ashburton's visit.

He suspected that her uncle was behind her sudden coolness. She must now recognize what he'd acknowledged a week ago. She'd been compromised. Despite her denials to Ashburton's face, everyone in the area knew about the house party. The locals might believe that she had moved out for a week, but the discrepancy was bound to come out.

Ashburton would twist the tale into a serious scandal. Despite her innocence, she would bear the stain of loose conduct for the rest of her life. Wedding him was her only choice.

Knowing that she needed time to absorb that truth, he had allowed her to avoid him, spending his days with Watts. The changes they'd made since Ashburton's visit had made avoidance easy. He had dispatched Jeanette back to London, then moved into his original bedchamber to keep from disturbing Mrs. Ashburton. Missy and Blake shared the west wing with him, leaving Hope and her mother as the sole residents of the east wing. The house was as divided now as before he'd torn down the barricades.

Mrs. Ashburton had improved enough to take solid food and converse rationally. Sharing meals with her mother kept Hope out of sight. But it was time to press his suit.

He told himself that she would be expecting it, yet he was uneasy, for she rarely reacted as other ladies did. And now that he'd come to the point, he was even more uncertain. How harshly had Mrs. Ashburton depicted marriage? The facts Blake had divulged raised more questions than they answered.

She ignored him as he crossed the library, her expression announcing that she did not wish to see him.

"Is something wrong?" he asked.

She shrugged.

"Has your mother relapsed again?"

"Not really."

"Does she need the doctor?" He felt foolish quizzing her, but she gave him no choice.

This time she met his eyes. "Her fever is gone, and she is breathing easily, though she is still too weak to stand. But blue-devils plague her."

"They often accompany serious illness." He kept his voice calm and refrained from crowding her. She would flee from any sign of coercion just as she'd fled from his touch and his compliments.

"It is not just this illness," she said, responding to his silent encouragement. "Her melancholy has deepened every year since Grandfather died. This latest malady was the final straw. She is making little effort to recover, even claiming that unconsciousness is preferable to thought." Her eyes brightened suspiciously.

He recognized her problem. It was not just the idea of losing a beloved mother. Loneliness must loom as an equal terror. Her lack of supportive family was a point he could use in his favor, but first he must address Mrs. Ashburton's blue-devils. "You can hardly blame her for growing weary of the struggle," he said gently. "Mrs. Tweed told me how often she has been ill. Having only Ashburton to call on cannot be easy."

"We don't." She frowned. "Even you should realize that he would never lift a finger to help unless he could turn the situation against us."

"I phrased that badly. I meant to say that most people can rely on family in times of trouble, but you lack that option. Knowing that he can disrupt your lives must be disheartening, at the very least."

She nodded. "Grandfather protected us during his lifetime and did what he could to defend us after he

died. Or thought he did." She stared out the window so
he could no longer see her face.

"How did he fail you?" he asked, curious because
the lease had provided more safeguards than he would
have expected.

For a moment he thought she would change the subject, but she finally answered. "He did not expect to die.
He was healthy, active, and came from a long line of
graybeards. The lease protects our home, but he made
no arrangements to ensure his other plans." She laughed
without mirth.

"Other plans?"

"I was to spend a year at a school for young ladies,
learning how to go on in society—Mother was little help,
as she had not come out before her marriage. Then we
were to attend the Season in London. Mother was ambivalent about it, but Grandfather convinced her that it
was for the best. Yet in the end it didn't matter."

"What happened?" He moved a step closer.

"Grandfather died a month before I was to leave. He
suffered a fit while heading home after a visit. Since his
will made no mention of school or Seasons, Uncle Edward canceled them."

"So you lost your chance to marry."

"In retrospect, that was for the best. Grandfather
never realized that Uncle Edward would turn on me as
he'd already turned on Mother. Had I gone to London,
Uncle would have turned society against me. Even with
Grandfather's support, the situation would have been intolerable." She returned the herbal to its shelf. "Mother was
shocked to discover his animosity after Grandfather's
death. That was what started this melancholy."

"What did he do?" His heart chilled as he considered possibilities.

"Refused to pay tuition, refused to provide either the
Season or the dowry his father had promised, then made
sure that the estate yielded so little that we could not
afford even a short trip to Bath. He swore that he would
destroy me if I dared go to town." She shrugged.

"So you stayed here and blamed your grandfather?"

"Not exactly. By then, I had learned that he was no

better than other men. He wanted me off his hands, so he ignored his son's hatred and the pain I would have suffered from being held up to public ridicule. He was probably plotting to find Mother another husband, so he must have regretted giving us Redrock."

"Not all men are schemers, Miss Ashburton. Perhaps he thought she would enjoy meeting her peers. London is quite entertaining, and she had never been able to enjoy it. How old was she when she married your father?"

"Sixteen."

"No wonder she was not out."

"She would never have had a Season. Her father considered London a den of iniquity unsuitable for gentlemen, let alone ladies."

"Is he a Puritan?"

She absently straightened a pile of newspapers on a table, preventing him from seeing her face. "He was a vicar before inheriting an estate."

"But even a rigid-thinking vicar would support her against Ashburton's spite—or has he passed on?"

"I've no idea, but I doubt he would lift a finger for her. He thinks her dead."

"Then he should be pleased to learn that she is well."

"You misunderstand." Her tone hardened. "The family disowned her twenty-seven years ago. To them, she is dead."

He stared. Twenty-seven years would have been about the time of her marriage. Had she eloped? But Hope's words answered one of his questions. Only someone harshly religious would have arranged a private sitting room as Mrs. Ashburton had. He'd been surprised at the stark gray walls and sparse, uncomfortable furnishings. The tapestry frame had contained a nearly finished rendering of a brutal Judgment Day in which few souls were awarded redemption. The only other personal items had been a well-worn Bible and a book of sermons.

But he knew better than most that parental regard always overcame anger in the end, no matter how severe the transgression. "I am sure he uttered harsh words at the time, but cooler heads would eventually have prevailed," he said soothingly, moving around until he could see her face. "Even my own father, who is far from pleased with me, would never bar the door."

"He can't. You are his heir. Whatever his own feelings, he has no choice but to accept you." The bleakness in her voice pulled him up short.

"You are serious."

She nodded. "Mother rarely talks about her family, but I have learned a little over the years. They are very rigid thinkers who will never forgive the stain she put on the family name."

"Stain?"

"Father seduced and abandoned her, leaving her with child," she said bluntly.

"What a cad!"

She shrugged. "Her father did not tolerate sinners, so he threw her out with nothing but the clothes on her back. Only the eight shillings she'd concealed in her hem kept her from starving on the long walk to Sussex."

He could feel the blood drain from his face. Such cruelty was so far beyond his own battles with a man he had long considered an ogre that he could barely comprehend it. For the first time in his life, he admitted that his father truly cared about him. Despite their differences, Montcalm would not dream of treating him so badly. If he'd truly despised his son, he could have canceled his allowance years ago, or even incarcerated him.

Hope continued. "She wrote home twice—once to announce her marriage, and again, after Father died, to reveal my birth. They did not respond. I was a sickly infant, so she put them behind her and concentrated on me."

"How long had she been wed before you were born?"

"Three months." Again she turned her back on him. "When she arrived at Ashburton Park, Grandfather was furious—or so he claimed. Mother never talks of those days, but he told me the tale before he died. He forced Father to wed her, then settled them here, canceling Father's allowance so he would have to remain and meet his obligations."

"A huge demand."

"An impossible demand," she countered, whirling to glare at him. "Father was an arrogant, selfish drunkard who exerted no control over his behavior and rarely looked beyond the desire of the moment. When he met Mother, he wanted her. So he took her. He was furious to be thrust into marriage five months later with a girl he'd all but forgotten. My birth was several weeks early because one of his beatings initiated labor."

He cursed, but she ignored him.

"Mother named me Hope because she hoped I would survive long enough to be baptized. Father refused to summon either a doctor or a vicar, lest his own crimes come to light, so she lay near death for nearly a month, with only Mrs. Tweed to attend her. When Grandfather discovered the truth, he summoned Father home."

"For a tongue-lashing, I suppose."

"Father was already furious that his great sacrifice had not produced an heir. Their confrontation exploded into a fierce argument, though Grandfather declined to give me any details. In the end, Father bolted for the local inn, where he added several bottles of wine to what he'd already consumed. On his way back to the Park, he tumbled into the river and drowned."

"Your mother was better off without him," he said frankly. "As were you."

"I know. Dealing with Uncle Edward is difficult enough. At least he does not resort to violence when in his cups." She picked up a feather duster and attacked the mantel.

That explained Hope's fear, he realized. None of the men in her mother's life had been pleasant, but those who were closest had invariably caused pain—the father who threw her out; the husband who first ruined her, then nearly killed her; the brother-in-law who made her life as miserable as possible. Even Hope's grandfather had failed her. No wonder she feared placing another man in a position of power.

He touched her arm, turning her to face him. "You have been poorly used by men all your life, haven't you?"

"No more than others."

"Much more. Most people are not like that, Miss Ashburton. I will never treat you thus," he vowed, then continued before she could respond. "But I do not understand why Ashburton hates you—or your mother, for that matter. Surely his father explained what had happened."

She smiled wanly, then took a seat, motioning him into a chair well out of reach. "Uncle Edward adored his brother, emulating him in all things. In his mind, Arnold could do no wrong."

"Was he blind and deaf? Surely others derided Arnold's excesses."

"Just as others deride Dornbras?" she asked, a twinkle briefly lighting her eyes. "I understand that Lord Rockhurst has long railed against him."

"Touché, my dear. Some of us are indeed blind, though at least I have seen the light."

Her humor faded. "Uncle never has. He twists his memories to make Father a saint, explaining criticism as jealousy or a way to deflect attention from the speaker's own misdeeds. He blames us for Father's death and for ending his Grand Tour—he hated abandoning those signorinas. Since Grandfather made him settle the succession the moment he returned, he also blames us for saddling him with a managing wife."

"He blames you for his wife?"

"Of course." Surprise threaded the words. "Like most men, he cannot attribute his problems to fate, let alone admit fault. We have become his scapegoat for everything wrong in his life. Grandfather's death shortly after leaving here added another grievance—we had parted in anger, contributing to his fit."

He heard the guilt. "You cannot believe that you killed him."

"Uncle Edward does." She shrugged.

"So he prevented you from entering society and did his best to ruin you."

She nodded.

"But he can no longer hurt you," he reminded her softly. "You are free to pursue the life he held hostage.

It is not too late to seek marriage and a family of your own."

"I have no interest in such affairs," she vowed, though he thought a hint of longing briefly flashed in her eyes. "And you haven't been listening. As long as my uncle breathes, he will destroy me if I dare enter society. Besides, Mother needs me. Who would nurse her through her next illness if I abandoned her?"

It was not the response he wanted, though he would welcome Mrs. Ashburton into his home. And while she had been unexpectedly candid, he still had questions. Even considering his own experience with blind stupidity, her explanation for Ashburton's was inadequate. The man was not actually insane, so why was he still threatening her?

But Hope was clearly through confiding in him, so he turned the topic. "What were you looking for in the herbal?"

"A tonic that might restore Mother's strength."

He doubted such a thing existed, but this was not the time to quibble. "Revealing that Redrock will recover its former prosperity might help."

"I can hardly explain that without telling her that you now own it. She can barely manage to eat. How can I burden her with new troubles?"

"You consider my ownership trouble?"

"Let's see—" Laughter filled her eyes as she ticked off points on her fingers. "Your first reaction was to break the lease. Then you moved in, exposed me to censure from my neighbors, provided me with two additional patients, brought my uncle's wrath onto my head—"

"Enough," he begged, chuckling as he covered his head to protect it from her barbs. "I am a depraved devil unfit for human society, a traitor to every decent thought, a Jonah, a—"

"Doing it far too brown, my lord," she said, joining his mirth.

"A bit, but so are you. I admit to inadvertently wronging you—and will do all that is possible to rectify my errors—but I've done nothing to harm your mother. Nor will I. Tell her of the change. Knowing that Ashburton can no longer meddle in her affairs could provide peace of mind. Tell her I am restoring the estate. Since she receives half the income, her finances should improve. I cannot let Redrock languish, as it will supply all of my own income."

"So I've heard. Why does your father want you at home?"

"To turn me into a boring, disapproving recluse like himself."

"Impossible. You are far too alive to bury yourself in the country."

"That is not strictly true. I would not bury myself as he does, but neither am I happy living in town. London society is more interesting in small doses than as a steady diet. And I am fascinated by innovation, particularly in agriculture."

"Then I would think your father would be pleased."

"He doesn't trust my judgment," he admitted, pacing to the window and back.

"Why?"

He nearly tossed out his usual reply—stubbornness— but she needed to know the truth. "He cites youthful indiscretions to prove me incompetent—like the Horseley ball and the Ashleigh affair."

"Wasn't that a ridiculous wager over walking backward from London to Brighton, or some such thing?"

"Not quite that stupid, but how did you know of it? It happened at least ten years ago."

"Agnes. She has repeated every scrap of gossip about you for months."

He groaned. "No wonder you think me depraved. But the truth is rather tame. It was not I who proposed the wager—Ashleigh's walk was from Hyde Park Corner to Chalk Down, by the way; silly, but hardly impossible. I backed him for the grand sum of ten guineas, for I knew how stubborn he was. He would die rather than admit defeat."

"So you are again claiming sainthood?" She smiled.

"No. There are any number of things I would do differently if I could go back, but we can only live in one direction. Where Father and I differ is that he prefers not to live at all. We even disagree on planting and harvesting. He refuses to accept that new ideas might actually be better." He sighed.

"So you came to blows, so to speak, and now you have no allowance."

"We will make up this quarrel eventually," he admitted. "Part of it was my fault for not explaining my intentions." Where had that admission come from? Portraying himself as a hotheaded fool would hardly make her more amenable to wedding him. "Sooner or later, he is bound to realize that the incidents he most despises happened long ago."

"And that you are now dedicating your life to productive occupation and a sober existence?" She burst into laughter on the final word.

He joined in. "Not quite that staid, God help me."

"I didn't think so. But you are right about Mother. Despite your questionable reputation, knowing that Redrock has changed hands must be good news."

Smiling, she headed upstairs.

Good news. He had taken a huge step toward winning her hand today. Warmth spread through his chest.

Max stood in the library doorway as Hope and Blake returned from a walk in the garden. She laughed, looking more carefree than he had ever seen her. His teeth clenched as Blake patted her hand. Despite the man's protestations of disinterest, he was being far too friendly.

Blake headed for the stables, leaving Hope to enter the library alone. How many other assignations had they conducted under his nose?

Fury built a red mist before his eyes—fury at Blake for courting her when he knew she was spoken for, fury at Hope for turning brighter smiles on Blake than on the man she must wed, and fury at himself for not settling this sooner.

"Am I to wish you happy?" he demanded when she reached the door.

"What are you talking about?" The light drained from her eyes, revealing deep weariness.

He had no right to be irritated with her, but he couldn't stop his words. Every time he thought he understood her, she proved him wrong. This morning, she had seemed to favor him, but that had been wishful thinking, he saw now. She was far warmer with Blake.

So let Blake have her, urged the voice.

But he couldn't. She was his responsibility. And Blake insisted that he didn't want her. "You and Blake have certainly become close," he snapped, ignoring her sudden pallor. "How can you wander about in his company without a chaperon?"

"You've never complained about meeting me without a chaperon."

"And look where that's gotten us! I've compromised you so badly that we will have to wed if I'm to have any hope of redeeming your reputation. But even that won't help if you insist on throwing yourself at every man you meet."

"You are mad." She backed a step.

He grabbed her shoulders so she couldn't run away. "You are staying here, Hope. We need to settle this."

"There is nothing to settle."

"You cannot ignore facts," he insisted. "I've compromised you."

"Fustian. I've done nothing wrong."

"What about coming to my bedchamber in the middle of the night?" he pointed out, furious to see denial stamped on her face.

"No one will ever know about that."

"Don't count on it. Truth always comes out in the end."

"No."

He snorted. "Pay attention, Hope. Nothing escapes the gossips. They will twist every word, every glance, every denial into new scandal. Can't you hear Mr. Winters chortling over your downfall, or Miss Porter telling the world that you are my latest conquest. And what do you think your uncle will do?"

"I don't care." Tears brightened her eyes.

"But I do." He held her gaze for a long moment. "I

won't have either of our names dragged through the mud."

Pulling away from his grip, she retreated to the far side of the room. "You will have to live with suspicion, my lord." Her voice was firm. "I would rather be the subject of endless gossip than wed you, so you can give up this silly notion and leave. You won't circumvent the lease so easily."

"Damn the lease!" he snapped, temper shattering as he strode after her. "You can't avoid the truth by confusing the issue. Or is it Blake? Have you decided that he will make a more conformable husband?"

"What?" She blanched.

"Forget Blake," he growled, backing her into a corner, even as a voice in his head warned him to calm down. "He has no interest in acquiring a wife, so throwing yourself at him merely marks you as a forward hoyden."

"How dare you twist the facts and assume others behave as you would? If any tales are bandied about, I'll know who to blame. You are despicable."

"No. I am realistic. You are the one who is hiding, Hope. You claim not to care, yet merely mentioning impropriety has you in tears." He reached out to wipe the evidence from one cheek. "You know we must wed. Instead of arguing about it, we would be better served to work out the details."

"Arrogant, conceited fool." She slapped his hand away. "Pay attention. I have no intention of wedding anyone, least of all you. I'd become Uncle Edward's mistress first."

"The hell you would!" He jerked her close enough to glare into her eyes. "You are mine, Hope. It's time you admitted it."

Something kindled deep in the gray that was neither fury nor fear. Giving himself no time to think, he took what he'd wanted since arriving at Redrock. His lips crushed hers as he plundered her mouth.

For a long moment, Hope was too surprised to move, but as his tongue boldly twined with hers, she sagged against him, relishing his kiss as if it were food and she was starving.

Her senses reeled from an emotional onslaught she'd hardly followed and didn't understand. When she'd spotted him in the library doorway, her first reaction had been joy, quickly stifled because she dared not reveal her growing obsession. After avoiding him for two days, she'd been horrified to discover that she missed his flirtatious banter and myriad touches. Hardly an hour had passed when he wasn't in her thoughts. She still couldn't believe she had told him so much about her family that morning, but once she'd started talking, she hadn't been able to stop.

But the joy had been short-lived, overwhelmed by fury at his words. How dare he dictate her choice of friends or imply that her behavior was improper, especially considering his own disreputable conduct. Then he'd had the gall to demand that she wed him, making it clear that offering was an unwanted obligation. And he'd exaggerated this supposed compromise, for they'd done nothing but talk. She knew his real purpose was to gain unfettered access to Redrock. When she'd refused, he'd turned to seduction to force compliance.

She tried to pull away, but her body would not cooperate. It was reveling in sensations she'd experienced only in dreams.

Light flared deep in his blue eyes as he trailed kisses across her cheeks, brightening the color and blurring the pupils. But it wasn't the cold light of evil. Her breasts tightened, spilling heat into her womb that weakened her knees. Her hands had somehow become entangled in his hair, combing the unexpectedly soft waves with sensual delight.

"Damn you," he growled as his lips returned to hers.

When his hand slid down to cup her backside, she pressed closer, moaning. He deepened the kiss until she remained on her feet only because he held her upright.

As suddenly as it had started, it stopped. He froze, thrusting her away, a look of horror on his face.

Reeling from his sensual assault, she said the first

thing that popped into her mind. "What an odd way to protect my reputation."

"That's not—"

"But what else can one expect of a rake?" The heat in his eyes made her furious. He might want to be different, but under his charm he was just like her father, seducing anyone he met. And she'd nearly let him. Horror burst along nerves still aflame from his caresses.

"Forgive me. That was unconscionable."

Her temper exploded. "Do you think that can make up for assaulting me?" she demanded. "How arrogant! You are no better than any other gentleman. You do whatever you please, then dismiss the mistakes with a laugh and an apology."

"That's not what I meant," he snapped.

"Do you think me stupid? You care nothing about me or anyone else. Your only goal is to acquire Redrock and protect your own precious reputation from Uncle's spite."

"You can't believe—"

"I believe my eyes, sir," she said, determined that he would not cajole her. "You are just like my father, attacking women to prove your own prowess—"

"Then why would I stop?" he demanded furiously.

But she dared not listen. His seduction might have been protracted, but it was just as deliberate as other men's—the flirting, the touches, the laughter and warm glances. "Leave, Lord Merimont. Move in with Watts, or stay at the White Heron, or go home and make peace with your father. Just take yourself away, and don't return. If you have a shred of decency, you won't come here again."

Tears threatened to spill down her cheeks, so she fled, slamming the door behind her.

Damn him for being just another conscienceless rake-hell, claiming concern one minute, stealing kisses the next. And damn her for wishing he had not stopped. God help her, she was no more immune to a charming rogue than her mother had been.

Max watched her go, still reeling from desire. Why the devil had he kissed her? That was not how he had intended to broach the subject of marriage. He had not played a hand so badly since . . . since his last confrontation with his father. Again he had started in the middle, rushing his fences and becoming so embroiled with side issues that he had lost sight of the facts that should have supported his argument.

Damn! Never had a kiss affected him so deeply—and never had he lost control so thoroughly, pressing her far beyond propriety.

But despite her obvious innocence, she had responded like no one he'd ever encountered, with more passion than he'd ever suspected she had. That was what had brought him to his senses. The last thing she needed was to be seduced like her mother.

Her response had terrified her, but she'd already taken her revenge. Her scorn had flayed the flesh from his bones, leaving him a quivering wreck. And she was right. He had bungled this in every way possible, digging himself into a pit so deep he could barely see daylight.

His only ray of hope was her response. Part of her would want to repeat the experience—not that she would listen anytime soon. She would cling to the fiction that he was like every other man. Somehow he must convince her that he was different.

Leave . . . don't return. What a pickle. Ignoring her demands would give her a new grievance. Yet obeying would eliminate any chance of changing her mind.

Become Uncle Edward's mistress . . .

His hand shook. Had he driven her to desperation? Surely she hadn't meant it. But the uncertainty was already eating at him. He couldn't live with her rejection.

Because he loved her.

Staggering to a chair, he sat with his head in his hands, hurling every curse he'd ever heard at himself.

He'd made a worse hash of this than he'd thought. If only he'd considered his feelings earlier. But he hadn't, constructing arguments as if this were a duty he must perform. Instead of offering the one thing that might have made a difference, he'd tried to force her into submission, using words that made his offer sound like the same punishment her father had faced.

He deserved worse than a tongue-lashing—like a long, lonely life without the woman he loved. And unless he could find a way to convince her he cared, he might face just that.

Chapter Fifteen

Max hardly noticed when Blake entered. His thoughts were chasing his feet as he paced circles around the library. He loved Hope but had no idea how to approach her. Her response to his kiss had seemed genuine, yet he had no experience with innocents. Was she truly interested or merely curious? And how was he to explain her warmth with Blake, when she alternated between spitting fury and cool disdain with him?

The irony was clear, taunting him whenever her words echoed in his mind. After years of dodging greedy misses eager to force him to the altar, he'd finally met one with a legitimate claim, and she didn't want him.

"Why the long face?" asked Blake.

"I've buried myself in a hole I may not be able to crawl out of," he admitted, stopping at the window.

"Which particular hole are we discussing?"

"I love Hope."

"Congratulations. You finally recognize what's been staring the rest of us in the face for a week."

He snorted. "Condolences would be more appropriate. She hates me."

"That is not my impression."

"Then how would you describe it? She considers me an arrogant degenerate. When I offered for her, she swore she'd rather become Ashburton's mistress than wed me."

His fury returned as he realized the significance of her words. It was another grievance that would need redressing if Ashburton returned.

"—you say?" asked Blake.

"What?"

"I asked what you said to elicit such a ridiculous vow." Blake was grinning.

"Enjoy yourself," he grumbled. "But I'll remember this."

"How badly did you blunder?"

"She stormed out of here, slamming the door hard enough to wake the dead."

Blake shook his head. "What did you do, Max?"

"You mean after informing her in the midst of a tirade worthy of my father that she had no choice but to wed me?"

"You didn't!"

"I did," he admitted morosely.

"And then?"

"I kissed her."

Blake laughed.

"It's not funny."

"Your face is hilarious. I never thought you capable of blushing." He laughed again.

He wanted to punch something, but a moment of thought stopped him. Blake was right. He was blushing. Chuckling, he took a chair and relaxed. "That's not the worst of it. I compounded the insult by apologizing."

Blake was laughing too hard to remain on his feet. "Of all the cow-handed, idiotic things to do."

"I'll give you no argument on that."

"So how will you dig your way back into her good graces?" asked Blake, stretching his legs toward the fire.

"Maybe you can put in a word for me. At least she likes you."

"Are you still ranting over that? I told you we were merely friends."

"Which means we are not. You saw her this afternoon—laughing and relaxed with you, then turning to stone the moment she saw me."

"Why should that surprise you? Your face could have slain armies. But now that you've admitted you care, maybe you will finally move past this irrational jealousy."

Max started to protest, but reined in his temper before he made a bigger fool of himself. Jealousy had started today's argument. "So what do you talk about?" he demanded shortly.

"You, mostly." Blake grinned at his surprise. "Today she asked about your reputation for debauchery. Missy mentioned your crusade to help unwilling girls escape brothels—she wants to go to America and start a dressmaking business, by the way, but her savings are hidden in her room in London."

"I'll take care of it. Was Hope surprised?"

"No. She had already concluded that much of your reputed wildness derives from frequenting disreputable neighborhoods for reasons beyond the obvious."

"Yet she threw that very reputation in my face only minutes later."

"Have you never lashed out to wound when in the throes of temper?"

"Maybe."

"Relax. She is fighting against it, but I would stake my fortune that she harbors a serious *tendre* for you."

"So she treats me like vermin and laughs with you," he grumbled. "Yet you embody everything she hates about me."

"You are hopeless, Max. You often speak with Lord Westbrook at White's, don't you?"

"What has that to do with anything?" he demanded. But Blake's expression finally forced a reply. "You know I do."

"He is very like your father, yet not once have I seen you lose your temper with Westbrook. Or contradict even his most inflammatory statements. Or rant in private over his stupidity."

"Why bother? The old bore will never change."

"Yet when Montcalm makes exactly the same claims, you explode in fury."

"His remarks are always personal. Westbrook's aren't."

"But they are," said Blake softly. "You ignore Westbrook because he can't hurt you. It is easy to brush aside his suggestions. That is not true of your father."

Max pursed his lips, his heart lightening as he realized Blake's point. "So Hope can relax with you because you pose no threat. But that means she sees me as threatening."

"Aren't you? Setting aside your more obvious crimes, she fears depending on others, especially men. Caring for you gives you the power to hurt her. Besides, she has no idea how to deal with attraction. She has little experience with people in general, and virtually none with men. Ashburton's influence kept her out of society."

"And her father was far worse than we thought," Max admitted. "He seduced and abandoned her mother, was forced into marriage when his father discovered that she was increasing, then released his frustrations by beating her."

"Good God!"

"I should have realized that only something that bad could produce such deep aversion. To Hope, marriage is a threat—which makes my introduction of the subject even more cow-handed. I've been trying to find a way to prove I care. At this point, she would distrust anything I say. I've never seen anyone so angry—not even me at my worst."

"Don't look to me for suggestions. I haven't any. She is not the sort who welcomes gifts, she distrusts charm, and she is so concerned about her mother that her mind is usually elsewhere. How did she respond to your kiss?"

"I think she scared herself."

"That's hopeful."

"Her mother . . ." Max nodded as an idea unfurled in his mind. "Her mother is isolated, alone, and terrified of the future. Her family disowned her. I think the estrangement weighs heavily on her mind. It might even explain her deliriums."

"What are you thinking?"

"Mrs. Ashburton's father sounds like mine, only colder. There must be other family members, though Hope knows nothing about them. I cannot believe they are all vindictive. I want to heal this estrangement, and not just for her peace of mind. If Ashburton is as venal as I suspect, she needs more than me to protect her. Even the worst interpretation of the facts Hope knows

cannot justify her uncle's hatred, so more must lie behind his spite than they suspect. And that makes him
dangerous."

"Agreed, so what do you have in mind?"

"I want to visit Mrs. Ashburton's family. If they will
stand behind her, even Ashburton must think twice
about attacking."

Blake nodded. "It is worth a try. When do we leave?"

"*We* don't. According to Ned, Ashburton is in Exeter,
so he will likely return. You must protect Hope and her
mother until I return. Wilkins will stay for the same
reason. I will see if Mrs. Tweed knows who the family
is. But I don't want to mention my quest lest it raise
hopes that will come to naught."

"Very well, but leaving without an explanation could
dig that hole deeper."

He grinned. "I doubt it. She told me to go away.
Obeying might actually work in my favor."

Max inhaled deeply before wielding the knocker. It
was well before calling hours, and doubts were already
assailing him. Perhaps he should have waited for a more
conventional time. Or maybe he should forget the whole
thing. In the week since he'd left Redrock, Hope could
have hardened her heart beyond recall, or her mother
could have sickened and died.

But he could only continue as planned and hope for
the best.

Mrs. Tweed had never known Mrs. Ashburton's family
name, so it had taken him several days to discover her
parentage. He'd gone to London, where luck had led
him to the previous Ashburton's solicitor.

Mrs. Ashburton had been born Catherine Anne Godfrey, daughter to Sir Quentin Godfrey, whose estate was
fifty miles from Redrock.

Unsure of his welcome, he had taken a room at an
inn when he arrived after dark. But that had yielded an
unexpected benefit. The innkeeper recalled Sir Quentin's daughter.

"Quiet little thing," he'd said as he served dinner in

the private parlor. "Seldom saw her except at church. Her pa don't hold none with mixin' classes."

"I've heard him described as puritanical." He relaxed with the first bites. The stew was flavorful, and the bread fresh.

"That's the effect, but not the cause, if you take my meanin'."

Max raised a questioning brow.

"The man's worse than Lord Castleton for lovin' power," he said, naming a neighboring marquess Max knew to be a strict martinet. "He kept his children in seclusion and railed so often against the corruptin' influence of libertines and the merchant classes that we were amazed he allowed the boy to attend school. The girl didn't even have a decent governess. He never woulda taken her to London."

"I've known men like that," he said.

"Inheriting the title surprised him," continued the inn-keeper. "I heard he wanted to turn it down—he was vicar to a parish in Shropshire at the time." He grinned. "I 'spect his parishioners were glad to lose him. He disapproves most everything."

But the only additional fact that emerged from half an hour of gossip was that everyone believed the daughter was dead. The innkeeper knew no details, nor did he care. Sir Quentin's arrogance meant he had few friends.

A footman opened the door. Max proffered his card. "May I see Sir Quentin?"

"He's ill."

"This is urgent. I will be as brief as possible."

The footman frowned. "Perhaps Mr. Godfrey will speak with you."

"And he is—?"

"Sir Quentin's son."

"Excellent."

Luck was still with him, he reflected as he awaited the footman's return. Sir Quentin would be difficult to convince, but his heir might be more amenable.

The hall was paneled in centuries-old linenfold. A portrait frowned down upon visitors, depicting a long-faced man whose face was creased into a permanent scowl. If this was Sir Quentin, he was in for a difficult day.

"This way, my lord," said the footman.

They twisted through several passageways until they reached a study. The man behind the desk raised his head, then broke into a smile.

"Maxwell Longford. What the devil are you doing here?"

The smile clicked a name into place. "Richard Godfrey. We met at a house party—" He frowned. "Seven years ago."

"At which you neglected to mention your title."

"I was avoiding any ties to my father at the time," he admitted. "But I appreciated your views on crop rotation and plan to implement some of them on an estate I recently acquired."

They discussed agriculture for several minutes.

"But this is not why you called," said Richard at last, refilling their glasses. "You will have to do business with me. Father is quite ill."

"Unless he is unconscious, I must see him." He paused. There was no easy way to introduce the topic. "It concerns your sister."

"I have no sister, or haven't for many years. Katy died when I was a child." His eyes betrayed no anger, only faint regret and surprise at the subject.

"Do you recall her death?"

"I was away at school at the time. Father wrote that she had died, but gave no details. He despised answering questions—parents tell children what they need to know, thus questions betray an unacceptable curiosity—so I grieved in private."

"Your father lied." He met the shocked gaze with his own. "An unscrupulous libertine seduced and abandoned her. When Sir Quentin learned that she was with child, he threw her out and disowned her."

"My God!" His face was white.

Max relaxed. While Richard was clearly shocked, his face revealed no condemnation. "Having nowhere else to go, she walked to Sussex, to the estate of the man's father."

Richard's hands gripped the desk.

"The father forced his son to do the right thing, though the results were less than ideal. Marriage legitimized the child, but he turned his frustration on his wife, beating her several times. Fortunately, he drowned shortly after a daughter was born."

Richard's cry of horror reassured him.

"She raised the child alone. Her father-in-law did what he could to help her, but his younger son hated her."

"Why did she never tell us?" He sounded bewildered.

Max's voice softened. "She wrote home twice, but received no response. Sir Quentin knew where she was."

"What do you want?"

"Her father-in-law died ten years ago, leaving her at the mercy of the son. With only her daughter left to support her, she has become increasingly melancholy. She is now suffering an inflammation of the lungs, but I fear she has lost the will to live. I am hoping that a kind word from the family she still mourns might help her. When delirious, she cries for someone named Dickie."

Richard blanched, a sob escaping his throat.

"Will you recognize her?" Max asked.

"Of course. But what is your interest in this?"

"They lease a house from me, and I am courting the daughter. She will be devastated if her mother dies."

Richard paced to the window and back, then emptied his glass and poured another. His hand shook. "My head is reeling," he admitted when Max noted the tremor. "In minutes you have resurrected my sister, revealed a niece I did not know existed, then hinted that the very sister I thought dead may soon become so. It is too much."

"I understand, but I have little time. Your own forgiveness—which is how she will consider your recognition—will help, but it will not be enough. I must convince your father to pardon her. She has carried the burden of his condemnation for too long."

"And a deep burden it must be. He doubtless consigned her to hell for all eternity—a horrid end, for she was always very religious. Being a vicar gave his utterances a power unshared by others. When we were children, he considered himself the voice of God. Katy believed him. Even after we moved here, she accepted his edicts as coming straight from the lips of the Almighty. If Mother had lived, it might have been different, but she died bringing me into the world. Any influence she might have exerted on Father died with her."

"May I see him?"

Richard nodded, leading him upstairs. "I've no idea what mood he is in today. His illness is advanced, with no cure possible. Some days he rails at the world. At other times he welcomes death, or frets about the family's fate once he is no longer here to lead us. Occasionally he ignores us altogether."

"I will manage. I am known for stubborn persistence."

"It should be an interesting confrontation, then, though I won't see it. He's not pleased with me at the moment. You will have better luck alone."

"Thank you."

"But he may do something stupid—like try to stand," Richard warned. "He is capable of unbelievable strength when in the throes of delusion. I will be in the hall if you need me."

Sir Quentin's appearance shocked Max. Only the faintest resemblance remained to the portrait in the hall. He looked at least a hundred, with parchment skin so thin it was nearly transparent. His problem was obviously a wasting disease, for most of the flesh had disappeared, leaving only a skin-covered skeleton.

"Who are you?" His voice quavered, but it was stronger than Max had expected. "Have you come at last to lead me into heaven?"

"No." The question surprised him, but it suggested an approach that might prove effective. He quickly revised his plans, pitching his voice for maximum resonance. "I am here to enumerate your sins, Quentin Godfrey. Your time on earth is nearly gone. This is your last chance to repent if you wish to gain the admission you seek."

"What sins? I have lived my life as a servant of God."

"You have lived your life as a usurper of God's authority." He wasn't sure where the words came from, but they seemed right.

"What?"

"Your daughter, Catherine. You sinned greatly against her."

"She was a whore of Babylon, a Jezebel sent to tempt mankind. Such a one is unfit to live in a godly household."

"She was an innocent girl, seduced by a cruel lecher because you failed to protect her."

Sir Quentin screamed in protest, but his face had paled.

Max raised his palm in the direction of the door to prevent Richard from entering. "You failed her thrice, Quentin Godfrey," he intoned. "You failed to teach her to recognize danger. You failed to provide chaperons to protect her from predators. And once she'd been ravished, you failed to offer compassion, taking it upon yourself to judge her."

"She was a whore!"

"She was a child, an innocent victim of a man she would never have met if you had done your duty. A loving father would have helped her, just as a loving God instructed. You claim to be a man of God, yet you ignore His very words. What of the good Samaritan? What of Mary Magdalene, who was forgiven and accepted by Christ Himself?"

He cringed.

"You are the sinner, Quentin Godfrey. You are arrogant, holding yourself above all others. You are vengeful, striking out at anyone who fails to accept your opinion of yourself. And you are a fraud, choosing to follow only those Scriptures that support your own desires. But God sees all. And He holds the real power. He *can* judge. And he *can* condemn."

"Am I to spend eternity in hell?"

Max remained silent for a long, tense moment. "You usurped a power that was not yours, consigning your daughter to hell." He softened his tone. "But it is not too late to repent."

"H-how?"

"You will write to her. Today. She has suffered greatly because of your harsh and unjust treatment, yet she still reveres you. She needs your forgiveness. Even more, she needs your apology. She, too, lies on a deathbed. Let her go with a peaceful heart. Then examine your soul for other transgressions and do what you can to atone."

Sir Quentin nodded. "Paper."

"Your son will bring it." Max left the room. "Take him paper and pen, but do not tell him who I am. He might change his mind if he realizes I am not an emissary from heaven."

Richard shook his head in amazement. "I would never have thought something like that would work. What made you think of it?"

"I didn't. It just happened." He pushed the question aside, uneasy with the answers shimmering in his head. "Will you come with me?"

Richard glanced toward the bedchamber.

Max shook his head. "You must choose. I am more concerned with your sister, but I doubt he'll die just yet. He has a great deal to do before he quits this earth."

"My man can pack while he writes."

"Excellent. It is early enough that we can reach Redrock today."

Chapter Sixteen

Hope stood at the window, her eyes barely registering the gardens spread below her bedchamber. She'd caught Agnes poking about in the stables yesterday—Rockhurst's coachman and groom were the only ones there at the moment, making it easy to enter unseen.

"Liar!" Agnes had screeched, pointing to Rockhurst's carriage. "Where have you hidden Merimont?"

"Go home, Agnes," she'd ordered. "You are being a goose. That isn't even Merimont's crest. I'm storing it for the owner."

It had taken half an hour to oust her, but the situation was growing serious. The longer she put Agnes off, the more determined the girl became. And the Porters did nothing to halt the girl's antics. Did they hope to snare a future marquess?

At least she no longer had to lie about Merimont's whereabouts. He had departed several days ago, shocking her by acceding to her frantic plea that he leave. She'd wallowed in relief for nearly a day, though she'd been irritated that he'd left without a word. Even Rockhurst did not know where he was.

By the second day, fear had replaced relief. Wilkins remained, as did much of Merimont's luggage, so he could not have gone far. Had he suffered an accident in a remote area of the estate? He'd planned a tour as soon as he could slip away without drawing Agnes's attention. Perhaps her uncle had abducted him as part of a new plot. Or Dornbras might have discovered his ruse and struck back.

Fearing that he was hurt or in trouble had upset her so much that it had taken hours to realize how silly she was. Though Wilkins remained, his curricle did not. He could not have taken it into the fields. So he had left willingly, but planned to return.

That was when guilt had set in. She had overreacted. Yes, he'd tried to force her into marriage, but she could hardly blame him for adhering to the rules of his class. She had no proof that he was scheming for Redrock, and he honestly believed that he had wronged her.

In retrospect, she should have considered her response more closely. There was no hope of keeping his presence quiet, and she knew many who would build the news into scandal. If her mother had been well, there would have been no problem, but everyone knew that she had been bedridden for weeks. So failing to wed would tarnish both their reputations, leaving him under a cloud of suspicion and giving him a grievance.

Yet accepting him would give him a different grievance. No man wished to be saddled with an unwanted wife as her father and uncle had been. He would be frustrated, and she would be at his mercy.

"But would Max attack me?" she murmured, reviewing everything she knew of him.

He put his credit on the line every time he helped courtesans escape their masters. It was a different situation, but it showed that he cared little for society's opinion—which made his claims suspect. Why would he care about his reputation this time?

But it was your reputation he sought to protect, protested the voice in her head.

True. He might not care on his own account, but he disliked harming others—which fit with what she'd learned of him from Missy.

Max helped courtesans escape because he despised the men who had forced them into the position. He had begun his crusade after one of his father's tenants was abducted and sold to a brothel. He'd found her quite by accident two years later and brought her home. Her descriptions had angered him enough that he had sworn to help others who wanted to escape.

And he was not the only man who helped those in need. Missy had been quite candid about gentlemen before leaving for Plymouth—another of Max's rescues. They came in all varieties—good to evil, gentle to vicious. Rank, fortune, reputation—nothing could predict how a man would behave. Her discourse had convinced Hope that arrogance did not always translate into violence, as her mother had claimed.

Thus her own observations had to be valid. She'd watched Max's eyes when he learned of Missy's injuries and when he mentioned Jeanette's black eye. His fury had been genuine, but not aimed at the women. Could such a man condone violence in himself?

He had been out of control at their last meeting, she admitted, shocked. His anger had pulsed through the room, inciting her own until the air was almost thick enough to see. Yet instead of attacking, he had kissed her . . .

Her body flushed with the same exhilarating heat as when he'd held her. She paced to the fireplace and back, finding it impossible to remain motionless under the onslaught. Every touch, every sound, every sensation had lodged so thoroughly in her mind that she could relive the encounter all too easily—and had done so too often.

Squeezing her eyes tightly closed, she tried to banish the memories, but it did no good. She missed him. He had already inserted himself so deeply into her affairs that the house seemed lonely without him. He could brighten the bleakest day with a smile, or warm any room merely by entering. Talking to him lightened her heart more than talking to Rockhurst or even her mother.

Other memories surfaced, belying her insistence that he was an arrogant, unfeeling cad. He'd taken on jobs that even those of lesser breeding considered menial, because the work needed doing and there was no staff. But beyond his willingness to help was an ability to laugh at himself. Images paraded through her mind— Max scraping porridge from the hearth, Max swearing quite creatively at a chicken he was trying to pluck, Max grinning up from the puddle of soapy water he'd unexpectedly sat in. . . .

Damn his blue eyes for twinkling when most men

would be shouting the house down for having to suffer such indignity. He'd seduced her far more than she'd realized. For all her determination to avoid danger, she'd become yet another frustrated spinster who fell in love with the first man who paid her heed.

The admission was the last straw for her composure. She curled into a chair, hugging her knees to control her shaking.

Fool.

This complicated the situation immensely. She had nearly decided to accept his offer. He would be hurt no matter what she did, but the public pain of destroying her reputation had seemed worse than the private pain of accepting a wife he didn't want. Now she couldn't consider it. A marriage neither of them wanted could work after a fashion. They could negotiate duties and responsibilities that would keep them individually occupied much of the time.

But a marriage in which one loved and the other did not would be too painful. She would rather face censure than see pity in his eyes when he learned of her folly—which he would; it was not something she could hide in a moment of intimacy.

He would never return her feelings. She lacked the assets that high-ranking gentlemen needed. Red hair drew attention but could never appear elegant. Her breeding was respectable, but several ranks below his. Her accomplishments were limited to mediocre keyboard and worse voice. She had no experience in society and little tolerance for idle chatter. And her naïveté could never satisfy a rake.

So Max would be better off without her. He would survive the tempest—men rarely suffered the way women did—especially when people learned that he had offered. She would be lonely without him, but time would heal that particular wound. And it was better to be alone than live with a man who could never care.

In the meantime, he must never learn of her folly. She must remain aloof when he returned, giving him no opportunity to touch her. When he renewed his offer, she must refuse, calmly but with enough conviction that he would accept her decision.

Hope set her mending aside as a carriage drew up to the door. It was probably Rockhurst returning from Oakhampton—he had escorted Mrs. Tweed to replenish supplies. Rose was with her mother, and Wilkins had just gone down to the kitchen. She would have to open the door herself, for she'd kept the house securely locked since the day Max had arrived.

But it wasn't Rockhurst. Max was striding up the steps, another gentleman in tow.

"More friends?" she hissed, off balance from a surge of joy at the sight of his blue eyes and beguiling smile. She stifled all emotion, clinging to her decision to remain aloof.

"May I present your uncle, Mr. Richard Godfrey? Miss Hope Ashburton," he added to his guest.

Her knees weakened.

"This must be a shock," said Richard gently. "If I had known of your existence, I would have visited long ago, but I was away at school when Katy left home. Father informed me that she was dead. I heard differently only this morning."

"Perhaps we should adjourn to the drawing room." Max grasped her elbow and steered her in that direction. His touch burned through his glove and into her skin, but she could not pull away. Without his support, she would sprawl on her face.

Wilkins hurried into the hall. "Refreshments, Reeves," ordered Max.

Hope fought to regain her composure. Seeing an uncle she had never heard of was bad enough, but Max's touch was playing havoc with her senses. For now, he would attribute her reaction to shock. She had to control herself before he suspected the true cause.

Her new uncle remained silent until a tray arrived and she poured tea. "Is Katy well enough to see me?" he asked.

She frowned. "I do not know. She is so weak that even pleasant shocks might kill her."

"Has she suffered a relapse?" asked Max, looking anxious.

"No, but neither has she improved."

His eyes captured hers, sending heat into her face. "Then perhaps she needs to know that you are not her only family," he murmured for her ears only. He'd joined her on the couch. "Remember her anguish the night I fetched Dr. Jenkins."

She stared, recalling those cries. *Dickie . . . where are you . . . Dickieee.* In a rush of relief, she made the connection. Richard. She had feared that her father had not been her mother's only seducer. Now she knew better. Max must have tracked down this unknown uncle to improve her mother's spirits. Tremors attacked her fingers, forcing her to set her cup aside.

"Let us see if she is awake."

Max's eyes warmed as he took her arm. "Relax," he whispered. "He will not distress her."

How had he known her fears? But that was a question for later. His closeness again threatened her composure. She stiffened her back. Only ignoring him could protect her dignity. It was all she had left.

"Wait here," she instructed when they reached her mother's door.

The draperies were drawn, keeping the room dim. But her mother was awake. "Hope?"

"I am here." She sent Rose downstairs, then took one frail hand in her own. "You have a visitor, Mama. He would like to speak with you if you feel strong enough."

"I cannot imagine who would call." Her head twisted away to stare at the fireplace, but Hope knew that the motion hid fear.

"He claims to be your brother," she said gently.

"Dickie?" She lurched back to stare at Hope.

"Katy?" asked a voice from the doorway. "May I enter your fairy bower?"

"Praise God. It really is you." Tears drenched her face.

"Katy." He reached the bed in two strides, pulling his sister into his arms. "He told me you were dead, Katy.

I never knew, never questioned . . ." His own tears flowed freely.

Hope slipped from the room, her eyes so wet she ran into Max without seeing him. Only his arm prevented a fall.

"He cares," she said in wonder.

"He has always cared," Max said, squeezing her once before releasing her. "But he was a child, away at school, and could only believe what his father told him."

"How could any man be so cruel?" The action surpassed even Uncle Edward's persecution.

"Sir Quentin banished Catherine, but didn't trust the family to accept his decision—they all adored her—so he told everyone that she'd died. Richard suffered for her absence. They had been closer than most siblings, for they had no mother, only a cold, demanding father who enjoyed wielding power. Sir Quentin even prohibited them from mingling with others of their own class lest they be contaminated by sin. And he kept them busy with chores and Bible study, allowing them no pleasures. It is no wonder that she slipped away whenever possible to enjoy a few minutes of freedom."

"Naïve and unprotected," she agreed. "She would have offered no challenge to my father."

"I pointed that out to your grandfather."

She tripped, jamming her hip against the corner of a table as she tried to recover. "You spoke with him?"

"I suspect that his sins were tormenting him even before I met him. I can guarantee that he is pondering them now. And he is trying to atone."

"Why the sudden change of heart?" she demanded coldly.

"He is dying, and he knows it. He will not last out the year."

She shrugged, not caring about the fate of a man who deserved worse than her long-standing contempt.

"He is trying to make amends," he said, pulling her around to face him. "You may not care about him—I would be surprised if you did—but think about your mother. The burden of his curse has weighed on her shoulders since before you were born. Despite his many faults, he is her father. His word carries much weight with her.''

''He cursed her?''

He nodded. ''When he threw her out. She was very religious. He had been unyielding as a vicar and remained devout even after acceding to the baronetcy. So when he consigned her soul to hell, what could she do?''

''No wonder she accepted Uncle Edward's hatred.''

''A just punishment for an unforgivable sin is how her father would have described it.'' His voice sounded sad. ''But no more. Richard is delivering Sir Quentin's letter absolving her of guilt and begging her forgiveness for his stubborn pride.''

''How did you manage that?'' She backed out of reach, staring. ''I do not believe that such a man is capable of repentance.''

''Astute of you. I played on his fear of meeting his Maker. And I had the help of an emissary from beyond.'' His eyes twinkled.

''You must tell me about that some time. But now I must prepare a room—the one next to Mother's would be best. Thank you, my lord,'' she added formally, striving to put the necessary distance between them. ''Mother will relate her own appreciation when she is strong enough to receive you.''

An hour later, Hope was again mending in the drawing room. Rockhurst had returned and was upstairs with Max. She'd sent Wilkins to pluck two more chickens and was trying to decide whether she dared feed this new uncle in the servants' hall, when he paused in the doorway as if hesitant to join her.

''Come in, sir,'' she said, setting aside her work. He looked forlorn.

''I have so many questions,'' he murmured, taking a seat. ''Will you answer some of them? I feared to press Katy, for she is so weak.''

''If I can, but I know few answers myself. Mother never talked of her family. I did not even know the name.''

"Merimont told me the basics, but I would know more of Ashburton's purpose. Why does he despise her?"

"No one knows, though Mother and I have discussed it often enough. For some reason, he blames her for Father's death, though it seems odd. Father drank himself into a stupor, then tumbled into a river and drowned. She was not even there at the time. Edward adored his brother, but it's been twenty-six years, and the loss was more than offset when the title and family fortune came to him. Why would it still matter?"

"It sounds as though he has changed little since school."

"Did you know him?"

"Not well. He was three years ahead of me. But his intelligence has always been questionable, and he is the stubborn sort who rarely repudiates an idea once it lodges in his head."

Further discourse was interrupted when the front door crashed open. Hope cursed. She'd neglected to relock it after letting Max and Richard in. Rockhurst had returned through the kitchen.

Ashburton stormed into the room, halting when he spied Hope's visitor. "What the devil are you doing here, Godfrey?"

"Calling on my sister."

He laughed. "Forget the jests. The reason is obvious. The counterfeit Puritans are finally displaying their true colors. Are you calling on my father's whore or is little Hope accepting patrons these days? I knew she would give in sooner or later." He swaggered across the room and reached for her.

"Leave," she ordered, putting a chair between them. "You are trespassing."

"Did your mother teach you all her tricks?" He leered.

Richard's fist lashed out, connecting solidly with Edward's nose.

"You'll show respect for my family or meet me at dawn." His voice was cold enough to freeze hell. A second blow sent Edward to the floor.

"Family?" Edward shook his head, gingerly fingering his nose.

"Family. You knew Arnold better than that. He would attack anything wearing skirts. My sister had the misfortune to encounter him when she was alone. He forced himself on her, then left. When our father threw her out, she had nowhere to go but to yours. But marriage merely compounded her problems. Like you, he preyed on the weak, beating her until she nearly died."

"You lie." He struggled to his knees, his eyes burning with rage. "Father's servants knew she'd been one of his whores. When she turned up pregnant, he believed her claim that he'd fathered the brat, so he forced her on Arnold. But he couldn't stay away from the bitch, having his way with her again and again until it finally killed him."

Richard landed a kick in Edward's gut, knocking him back to the floor. "Name your seconds, Ashburton. Even you can't be stupid enough to believe such filth. Anyone with half an eye can see that Katy is a gently bred lady. Your father had never seen her before she showed up looking for Arnold. Your brother was a fool. But beyond that, he was a selfish man who took whatever he wanted with no thought to the consequences. Katy has done nothing to harm you."

"She tricked—"

"Trouble?" asked Max from the doorway. He glanced at Edward, still sprawled on the floor. "I thought Miss Ashburton told you to leave her alone. Redrock is no longer yours."

"I knew it!" Ashburton surged to his feet, one hand clutching his stomach. "I knew the great libertine couldn't resist so delectable a morsel."

Hope gasped, her eyes flitting from one man to the next as she registered the fury and violence in their faces.

"He arrived with me," said Richard coldly, shoving Edward into a chair. "You haven't changed a whit since school, have you, Ashburton? Again I must pound the truth into that wooden head of yours."

"If you touch me again, I'll ruin you."

Max shook his head. "Impossible. If you make this public, you will be ruined. The truth is there for anyone who looks—witnesses to Catherine Godfrey's innocence, witnesses to Arnold's long history of seduction, witnesses to his brutality against his wife, at least one witness to his death, and the damning evidence of your father's will."

Edward growled.

Hope gripped the back of the chair, reeling from his words.

Max turned to face her. "You were wrong, Hope. Your grandfather planned for every contingency. The tuition was already paid—and forfeited when you failed to attend. Provision was made for a Season and a dowry. Your uncle lied to the solicitor, claiming that ill health prevented a come-out. Then he moved the Ashburton business to a new solicitor who knew better than to ask questions." He turned back to Edward. "Your father's solicitor was shocked to hear that Hope did not fall prey to consumption. And he was furious to learn that her mother had not remarried after Hope's death eight years ago."

Edward swore. "How could he expect me to sponsor a whore's brat into society? You should be thanking me for protecting us all."

"As usual, you choose the hard way to learn your lessons," growled Richard, grabbing Edward's cravat and pulling him to his feet. "You are as stupid and stubborn as you were thirty years ago."

"I will explain it to him," Max said, jerking Edward toward the door. "By the time we finish our discussion, he will understand his mistakes."

Hope started to object, but Max frowned her into silence. His eyes promised that all would be well. When she spotted Rockhurst hovering in the hall, she understood.

Her head spun. She was more naïve than she'd believed. Not once had she thought to confirm Uncle Edward's claims. She had assumed that someone would let them know if they had been mentioned in her grandfather's will. When they heard nothing, she'd put the matter aside. By the time she realized the depth of Edward's hatred, she had forgotten all about it.

Max had gone to a great deal of trouble, and done it quite efficiently, she realized with a start. Was it possible that he had been as affected by that kiss as she?

"Forgive me, my dear," said Richard, making her jump. "I cannot imagine what you have endured all these years. Ashburton makes rocks seem intelligent and mules appear cooperative."

"It could have been worse," she said on a sigh. "He rarely called on us. Most of his schemes merely reduced our income." At least until this last one. It was obvious that he had meant to ruin her. Only his stupidity had saved her, for he'd accepted the worst rumors about Max as true, failing to see that the man was honorable.

"You are fortunate, then. He has done worse. It was his attack on one of my classmates that precipitated our last confrontation."

"That sounds like an interesting story."

"But not for your ears." He sighed. "I owe you so many apologies, I hardly know where to begin. Losing my temper in your drawing room belies my standing as a gentleman. And I should have questioned Father's claims long ago, particularly when he refused to erect a stone upon her grave, declaring it an unworthy conceit. That was the last time I asked about her illness," he added sadly.

"It was not your fault," she assured him. "You were hardly more than a child yourself."

"Thank you. You have grown to be a lovely lady and a credit to Katy. I look forward to knowing you better, but for the moment, I feel a need for rest. Do not expect me down for dinner," he added. "I promised Katy to eat with her. She hopes to be well enough to come home within the week."

"Home?" Her hand suddenly shook.

"Father is dying. She must make peace with him now, or he will be forever beyond her reach. You will join us, of course."

Fury prevented a response, but he did not notice. By the time she suppressed the initial wave, he was gone.

Idiot!

She should have known. Merimont might be easing her mother's melancholy, but his motives were strictly selfish. Reuniting her with a long-estranged family provided the perfect way to break the lease. He'd taken her refusal to heart—undoubtedly with a great deal of relief—so he'd found another place for them to live, not caring that removing them from Redrock eliminated every shilling of their income and placed them at the mercy of men they barely knew.

She swore. He would not succeed with such subterfuge. She would decline Uncle Richard's invitation, with regrets. Her mother would understand. As for Lord Merimont, he would have to take himself elsewhere.

Chapter Seventeen

$\mathbf{M}$ax and Blake shoved Ashburton's battered body into his carriage and watched him disappear down the drive. It had taken longer than he'd expected, but in the end, Ashburton had repented his mistakes.

What a family! Hope's grandfather had ordered Arnold home to explain why he'd beaten Catherine, leading to an argument that had been overheard by most of the staff. Arnold had claimed innocence, offering his own version of events: The birth had been full term, proving Catherine a liar. She was a whore who'd hoped to improve her lot by gulling an old fool. He had no idea who had sired the babe, nor did he care.

The servant sent to fetch Edward home from his grand tour had repeated Arnold's claims and had also revealed the old man's taste for a certain brothel in London. Edward had taken the hints to heart. By the time he'd reached England, he not only believed that Hope was his half sister, but he thought Arnold's death had been a plot to rid Catherine of an inconvenient husband whose only purpose had been to legitimize her brat. Only the fact that Hope was a girl had kept Edward in the succession. His father's claims had meant nothing because they were calculated to hide the man's culpability in elevating his mistress into the aristocracy. And those frequent visits to Redrock proved that she remained his mistress.

But Edward had finally accepted the truth.

Max glanced through the documents in his hand. One was a signed confession. Dornbras's only contribution had been an inadvertent portrayal of Max as a gullible fool and unbridled libertine. Ashburton expected Max to seduce Hope. He then planned to lock both women in a brothel and be done with them.

The papers also included a letter to Ashburton's solicitor ordering the release of all obligations under his father's will—Hope and her mother were not the only beneficiaries who had been ignored—an apology to his father's solicitor, and two drafts on his bank. The one for forty thousand guineas was made out to Catherine Ashburton, repaying the money stolen from her through mismanagement of Redrock House. The other was to Hope for the ten-thousand-guinea dowry that should have become hers when she'd remained unwed at age five-and-twenty. Ashburton would never bother them again. Max had vowed to release the confession if one word against Hope or her mother ever appeared in public.

"Good work," said Blake, flexing his fingers.

"Thanks to Gentleman Jackson." He turned toward the door. "I'm going to wash up, then I must talk to Hope."

"Good luck. I have no idea what she'll do. She's hardly spoken to me since you left, but I suspect she has been strengthening her defenses."

He grimaced, though he hoped Blake was wrong. At least today's events must make her think. The expression on her face when she'd left Richard with her mother had warmed his heart, and she'd looked almost worshipful when he'd revealed the terms of her grandfather's will. Restoring her mother's legacy and evicting Ashburton from her life should complete his rehabilitation.

Or so he prayed. He recalled the cool aloofness she'd donned more than once and the rigid formality of her thanks. She'd surprised him too often to assume anything.

Wilkins had managed only one pitcher of warm water, but Max cleaned up well enough. He was heading downstairs to look for Hope when the knocker sounded.

"What now?" He muttered, jerking open the door. Had Ashburton come back for another round?

"Father!" He stared. Montcalm stared back. The man hadn't even sent his groom to demand admittance.

"Did your staff quit rather than put up with your antics?" Montcalm snapped.

"How did you know where I was?"

"Ashburton claims you are making an ass of yourself again."

"And you believed him?" He fought down his fury. "Come in. We'll talk in the office."

He was shutting the door when Hope appeared. His heart sank when he met her eyes to see only fury, and a bleakness he did not comprehend.

"So he was right," snapped Montcalm. "You've set up your latest doxy here."

She bristled. "Another of Uncle's brainless friends, I presume. Throw him out, Merimont. I'm through being insulted in my own home."

"That would be difficult, Miss Ashburton. This is my father."

"Miss Ashburton?" Montcalm's tone could freeze water. "My God, Max. This is your worst escapade yet. You've ruined the girl."

Hope stiffened. "No wonder Merimont is so addlepated," she said coldly. "You are as bad as my uncle—trusting chronic liars, drawing conclusions based on little or no evidence, then expecting others to accept your idiotic notions."

"I have eyes, girl," said Montcalm.

"But no more sense than a stone." She glared at Max. "Send him to the White Heron. Then do me a favor and join him. You obviously deserve each other."

Before Max could figure out why she was so angry, she whirled toward the kitchen stairs. Henry hurried in as she disappeared.

"Tell Mrs. Tweed to make up the blue room for my father," he ordered the lad, naming the bedchamber between his and Blake's. He would consider Hope's outburst later. First he had to deal with Montcalm.

Walking to the office gave him a moment to catch his breath. He took Hope's chair behind the desk and motioned his father to sit. It felt odd to have their positions reversed, but he welcomed the advantage it gave him.

Montcalm's lips thinned. "So you won Redrock in a wild card game."

"It came into my possession while I was playing cards, but my hand was not the winner."

Montcalm frowned.

"Ashburton gave me the estate, though I didn't realize that until later." He explained. "Like you, he believed exaggerated stories and assumed that I would destroy his brother's widow and her daughter. He now knows better and won't be bothering them again."

"What about your friends and the ruin you brought on that innocent child?" His fury filled the room.

"Lies. Anything Ashburton said was either twisted or downright false—as he will confirm if you ask him. He is on his way to Sussex as we speak."

"What?"

"He has been plotting this for at least a year, though I was no part of his plan in the beginning. Your rush to make our recent spat public convinced him that I would make a convenient tool, so he set the plan in motion. Once he caught me in his snare, he must have decided to use you as well. He could count on you to repeat his charges to all and sundry, thus spreading Miss Ashburton's supposed ruin to every level of society." His stomach churned, fearing that his own efforts were for naught, for Ashburton had said nothing about involving Montcalm. What else had the man left out of his confession?

"He miscalculated," said Montcalm. "I did not want to believe that my own son could be so venal, so I came here to discover the truth for myself."

"And promptly insulted an innocent lady with charges that would demand satisfaction if you weren't my own blood."

"I will apologize in due time if the situation warrants it," he said stiffly.

"How pompous. Why not investigate first and save the insults until you know they are justified?" He reined in his temper, reminding himself that side issues too often clouded their arguments. That was how they had gone wrong the last time. "Ashburton has seen the error of his ways," he said in a calmer tone. "Blake and I poured him into his coach an hour ago."

Montcalm's eyes gleamed, but the humor rapidly disappeared. "He claimed you are hosting an orgy with the most disreputable rakes in England."

Max shook his head. "Several gentlemen and ladies of the evening left London the same time Blake did, though only Blake is here," he replied carefully. He could not lie, but neither could he reveal everything. "The only member of the group I would consider disreputable was Dornbras."

"I thought him your closest friend."

"Hardly, but your tirades sometimes prompt exaggerations."

Montcalm met his gaze and nodded.

Max felt a great weight shift from his shoulders. Their relationship had changed in that brief glance. It was the first time he had admitted fault to his father's face and the first time Montcalm had accepted a claim without argument. No longer were they meeting as parent and child, but as two adults.

"Blake is here, as I mentioned. Most of the girls were headed elsewhere, though Blake took one to Plymouth. She wanted to start a new life, so I paid her fare to America."

"Why?"

"She has no family to protect her from reprisals here." He shrugged.

Montcalm started to speak, but closed his mouth.

Max returned to the original subject. "Ashburton showed up here a week later. When informed that I wasn't here, he was furious, though Miss Ashburton managed to push him out of the house."

"Wait a minute. I thought you owned Redrock."

"I do, but Mrs. Ashburton and her daughter lease the house and park."

"Where were you?"

"Mrs. Ashburton was ill. Though I had considerable business with the steward, it would not have been proper to stay here while she was bedridden. The daughter had no other chaperon."

"And now?"

"Mrs. Ashburton's brother, Richard Godfrey, has arrived."

"Godfrey . . . Where do I know that name?"

"Sir Quentin Godfrey's heir. With him in residence and with Mrs. Ashburton's improvement, Blake and I can properly stay here, which makes it more convenient to work with my steward on next year's planting schedule."

As hoped, that diverted Montcalm from anything else Ashburton might have written. Max could only pray the man had not included others in his scheme, though Montcalm's support would quash any rumors.

They passed an hour in friendly argument over agricultural theories. For the first time, Montcalm listened, giving Max's ideas the respect they deserved even when he disagreed. By the time Max showed him to his room, their relationship had changed. More lighthearted than he had ever been before, he went in search of Hope.

Hope angrily sieved onions and milk-coddled bread into a pot of chicken stock to make a soup, then added yet another chicken to the roasting spit. She'd sent Wilkins to the stream with a fishing line, but had no guarantee that he'd catch anything.

Cursing Max for at least the thousandth time in the last hour, she hung her largest rack above the fire. Somehow she would have to fill a dozen pots if she hoped to satisfy all the mouths that would be waiting for dinner. How dared the man descend on her without warning, an army of lords and retainers in tow, when he knew she had no staff? She had planned a simple dinner for herself, Rockhurst, her mother, and seven servants. Ten people. Now she must add her uncle, Merimont, his father, and eleven more servants, all of them males incapable of helping with the work.

Let Max deal with it, whispered a voice. *You feed your people and let him manage his.*

It was tempting—especially since she knew he'd make a hash of things if he tried—but she couldn't do it. If she willingly turned over responsibility for the house, he

might use it against her. Finding her uncle was proof of
his intentions. And his father would add his influence to
overturn the lease.

She buried her pain under a new round of curses.

Rose had heard him laughing with Montcalm, so whatever rift they'd suffered must be healed. Heat rose in
her cheeks as she recalled her own outburst to the man.
Her only excuse was that she'd still been reeling from
her recognition of Merimont's perfidy. But how could
she face him after being so rude?

She couldn't. At least not yet. She would put him in
the dining room with Max and Rockhurst. Henry could
serve three, especially if Wilkins agreed to help. Uncle
Richard was eating with her mother. She would eat in
the kitchen, leaving Mrs. Tweed to preside over a proper
servants' hall. There might be complaints over the food,
but no one could fault either her hospitality or her
propriety.

Setting several pots of water to boil, she chopped
enough turnips to fill one. After tossing carrots into another, she cut up some broccoli.

Max walked in as she was basting the beef loin and
chickens. "Richard says that you and your mother will
be going home with him in a week or so."

"You won't be rid of us that easily," she snapped,
giving the third spit a quarter turn before pulling out
her one fish. There was no sign of Wilkins with more,
so she would have to filet and braise this one for the
three gentlemen in the dining room. Uncle Richard must
do without a fish course tonight.

"What are you talking about?" he demanded,
rounding the table to her side. She nearly sliced her
thumb with the boning knife, but pretended she was unaware of his nearness.

"As if you didn't know, you manipulative sneak," she
said stonily. "Did you think I was too stupid to see
through your scheme? Such a magnanimous gesture—
find the long-lost family. Of course, we would have to
visit them. How could we not? And the moment we
leave, you will claim abandonment and cancel the lease.

Who would dare rule against the great Marquess of Montcalm when he backs you?"

"My God!"

"You needn't sound so shocked. You know the terms as well as I do. Grandfather made sure he could recover control if we no longer needed Redrock, but the wording means we must remain here to protect our interest. Mother needs to see her father, but I'm going nowhere."

Max stared at her in shock. How could he have missed that interpretation of the abandonment clause—though he had to admit that Ashburton would have reacted just like that had he been smart enough to think of it.

Fury clawed at his chest. And pain. Her suspicions overrode all else. And his father's assumption that she was ruined would have supported her fears. If his own father believed him capable of dishonor, why would she think him any better?

He bit back a groan. If she believed he could be that devious, how would she react to the settlement he'd wrested from Ashburton? For the first time, the bruises on his knuckles stabbed pain up his arms.

"Damn you!" he growled, knocking a ladle to the floor as he lunged for the paper lying on the corner of the table. Ignoring the butcher's order on one side, he turned it over, scrawling hard enough that the pen split, spattering ink across a mound of chopped broccoli. "I'm sick of leases. And I'm sick of your never-ending distrust. The estate is yours. House. Tenants. Everything." He shoved the paper into her hands. "Free and clear. Lock, stock, and barrel. Visit China. Set up housekeeping in America if you want. No one can touch it."

A voice whispered that he would be sorry, but he ignored it. If she turned him down, he could never live here anyway.

"Wha—" She was staring at the paper as if it might rear up and bite her.

"Are you happy now? Your house is safe. Your mother is recovering. And your uncle won't ever bother you again."

She burst into tears.

He cursed, then pulled her head against his shoulder. "Don't cry, love."

She cried even harder.

With another oath, he scooped her up and carried her to a chair where he could cradle her in his lap, holding her close until her tears ceased.

"Let's start from the beginning," he said, handing her a handkerchief. "Finding your mother's family had nothing to do with the lease. You were making yourself sick fretting over her illness, and she was sunk so deep in melancholy that I feared she would die. The estrangement from her family clearly distressed her, so I hoped her father's forgiveness might bring her round."

"You did it to make her better?"

"Nothing else was working. Even that new cure Dr. Jenkins tried didn't raise her spirits."

"But you hardly know her."

"I did it for you."

She stared, but her eyes no longer held shock. They were so warm he could barely breathe. "Why?" Her voice sounded hoarse.

"I love you, Hope. I would do anything for you."

Her eyes widened.

"Let's see if I can do better this time, love—though I doubt it is possible to bungle things any worse than I did last time."

"True." But her smile lifted his last fears.

"This has nothing to do with leases or compromises or society's expectations," he said, rubbing the side of her neck with his thumb before tugging on a lock of fiery hair. "And it has nothing to do with plots or reprisals or any of our relatives. I love you, Hope. You bring sunshine to the stormiest day. You are loyal to those you love and caring of anyone in need. So care for me, please? I need you to keep me from growing haughty and grumpy like my father. I need you to make life worth living. I love you, Hope. Marry me." He dipped his head closer, brushing her lips with a light kiss.

At least he meant it to be light. But her response shattered his control. She leaned into him, opening her mouth her arms twining around his neck. It wasn't surprise this time, or shock, or even curiosity. She was as ravenous as he.

Groaning, he pulled her closer.

Hope reeled under his passion. The shocks had piled one atop another all afternoon, destroying her fears, her promises, even her control. It was too much—Uncle Richard, Uncle Edward, her mother's happiness, her own suspicions, the safety she felt in Max's arms. She could not have pulled away if her life had depended on it.

Not that she wanted to. The last doubts fled, never to return. He was everything her instincts had claimed, and more. The earth-shattering gift of Redrock proved it. As did his care for people in need. She should have listened earlier.

But he'd given her another chance.

She basked in his kiss, savoring the heat, the excitement, the promise of a future beyond her comprehension. It was more than she had dreamed possible. More than imagination had conjured after their last kiss. His shoulders were powerful, his hair silky. Fire raged through her body, making her breasts so sensitive she nearly cried out in pain.

His hand brushed one tip, eliciting a moan that would have embarrassed her under any other circumstance.

"Hope," he groaned, pulling back slightly. "Marry me, love. I need you."

"Yes." But even as the word escaped her lips, she stiffened.

"You aren't sure." She could hear the pain in his voice. "I should not have pressured you."

"Yes . . . no . . ." She cursed under her breath. "I am making a hash of this, too. Let me try again," she begged, twisting so she could capture his face between her hands and look directly into his eyes. "My dearest lord, I spent twenty-six years believing that all gentlemen were alike."

"Max. At least give me that much."

"Max. You have taught me so much, Max. The most important lesson was that gentlemen come in all varieties and must be judged as individuals. You may enjoy many of the things I was taught to despise, but beneath it all, you are an honorable man. And a kind man. I realized after you left that I loved you. What you have done for Mother can only make me love you more. My reaction just now was shock at accepting so easily something I had never believed possible. I would be proud to be your wife, Max. I cannot think of a better husband."

"Thank God. My sweet Hope. You truly are the hope of my future." He pulled her into another kiss. "And you are better in person than in any dream, love. You've no idea how many of mine you've invaded."

"No more than you've invaded of mine, I'd wager," she murmured, tracing his jaw as she kissed him again. "I haven't slept well since you arrived."

"Good." He nibbled an ear.

Sizzling filled the room. "Oh, Lord! I forgot dinner." Hope jumped up to turn the spits and stir the soup.

"It is just as well that it reminded you. It was time to stop," he said with a sigh. "I'll not take you until our wedding night."

"Which had better be soon." She had learned enough about passion in the last five minutes to be irritated at his declaration.

"As soon as we can arrange it, though it will be weeks at best. My father will probably insist on holding it at Widicomb Abbey."

"Speaking of your father, why is he here?"

He slid his arms around her waist from behind. "Another of Ashburton's schemes. But it failed. We mended a few fences, and I believe I've found a new friend."

"Wonderful." She kissed him on the nose when he leaned over her shoulder.

"What's for dinner?"

"Not much. You doubled the mouths I have to feed, you horrible man. I don't know how I can come up with a meal that will satisfy a marquess, two earls, and a baronet's heir, let alone all the stable hands and valets."

"We will be easy to please, I promise. And I can help—if you will trust me. I'm sure I can do better this time."

"I will trust you with anything, Max. Even dinner."

He was as good as his word. He stirred. He basted. He turned spits and carved meats.

Hope laughed helplessly as Henry carried a dish of very odd-shaped chicken parts into the servants' hall, which would be presided over by the Marquess of Montcalm this evening.

"I will trust you with anything but dinner, Max," she emended, taking in the syllabub spattered against the back door, the drippings running from fireplace to table, the broken crockery, and the blanket of flour coating his waistcoat and pantaloons. "How do you manage to live from morning to night without killing yourself?"

"I've never been clumsy before," he swore from his position on the floor, where he'd collapsed after the flour incident. "I am the epitome of grace in a ballroom."

"Never mind, Max. I love you anyway. But we need to find a cook tomorrow. And at least two maids."

"Plus a butler, two footmen, and a housekeeper," he finished, grinning as he sprang to his feet and swept her into his arms. "They should arrive by noon, unless the agency is quite off its usual efficiency. They were scheduled to leave London the morning after I did."

She tried to frown at his high-handedness, but his eyes were too full of laughter to care. "Wonderful. Let's eat, and then we can visit Mother. I think she can handle one more shock today."

Dusting him off, she headed for the servants' hall.

Max firmly shut the drawing room door, then pulled Hope into a heated embrace. "I thought I'd never find you alone," he grumbled. "I stumble over people every time I turn around."

"I warned you that Redrock is too small for house parties." She laughed as she traced the line of his ear.

"So you did. We will have to expand it."

The new staff had arrived, relieving Hope of the housework she had shouldered for so long. Richard was sitting with her mother. A real cook presided over the kitchen, assisted by three helpers. Blake and Montcalm had ridden out to supervise the demolition of the dower house.

"Expansion . . ." She grinned. "Does that mean we will stay here?"

"For a time. You need to remain near your mother."

"I'm glad you understand." To prove she trusted him, she had given back Redrock. Her mother would return here after visiting Sir Quentin. "So what do you have in mind?"

He released her to pull a sketch from his pocket, spreading it on a table. "I thought we could add a wing on the west end—which would leave your mother's rooms intact."

The door burst open. "You're back!" shouted Agnes, hurtling across the room with her arms extended. "How could you remain away so long, my darling? You knew we were planning a dinner party just for you."

Max stepped behind the couch as Hope grabbed one of Agnes's hands.

"How nice to see you, Agnes," she said calmly, ignoring the girl's appalling entrance. "It's been nearly three days."

"I could not remain away when I heard Merimont had returned."

"How quickly news spreads. You must have called to wish us happy on the occasion of our betrothal." She drew Agnes to the couch. Max had retreated to the far side of the room. She nearly laughed as he slipped behind a chair next to the door, allowing an easy escape if Agnes pounced again.

"Betrothal?" Agnes squeaked. "But you can't!"

"Of course we can. The first banns will be called tomorrow," said Max. "We will wed a fortnight later. Hope's mother should be fully recovered by then."

"How can you do this after all we've meant to each other?" demanded Agnes, the whites of her eyes showing. "You vowed to save me. Papa will force me on Squire Foley. I know he will."

"These fantasies must stop, Miss Porter," snapped Max. "We mean nothing to each other. I doubt we were even introduced. Lady Marchbanks will be appalled to discover that she allowed a forward hoyden into her drawing room."

Agnes broke into tears.

"You are making a cake of yourself," Hope said sternly. "And you haven't the slightest idea what Max is like. He prefers the country, you know. We will be living here, for he is a farmer at heart."

"But everyone says—"

"Gossip rarely conveys truth," Max declared.

Hope nodded. "If you do not wish to accept Squire Foley, then use your trip to Bath to find someone more suitable."

It took her a quarter hour to push Agnes outside, but Max finally closed the door behind her. This time he locked it.

"Alone at last, my love." He pulled her close.

"Poor Max. Are all girls so silly?"

"Like men, they come in many varieties, though I must admit that Agnes is worse than most. But enough of her."

"Ah, yes. The new wing."

"First we should discuss Dornbras." He pulled out a letter, joining her on the couch. "This just arrived from the runner I hired. Dornbras is a procurer for several London brothels."

"Dear Lord, no!"

His eyes had darkened, revealing his pain at having unwittingly supported the very man he had long opposed. "He abducts country girls," he said with a sigh. "That may have been what he wanted from you that morning. Perhaps he thought my friendship would protect him if the truth ever emerged."

"It is more likely that he knew of your crusade but expected that flattery would prevent you from unmasking him."

"Another blunder."

"No, Max." She caught his gaze, willing him to put the past behind him. "You are not responsible for his actions, and you have already done more than your share to repair the damage. What did your runner find?"

He drew her close to his side, resting his head atop hers. "Dornbras abducted his latest victim last week. The runner could not accost him until he'd delivered her in London, but Dornbras is now in custody, and the girl has come to no harm."

"Good. Has he enough evidence for transportation?"

"More than enough. Dornbras made a huge mistake this time. The girl's father is only a vicar, but her grandfather is a duke. He's demanding a life sentence. We'll not be troubled by Dornbras again."

"Thank God." She twisted to look him in the eye, relieved that his guilt was already fading. "So what are your plans for the house?"

"First I need to clear a very bad taste from my mouth." He lifted her into his lap, running his fingers through her hair as his mouth swooped down for a kiss.

"How will I last two more weeks?" he groaned several minutes later.

"You are the most stubborn man in England, love," she said, stroking his hair. "You will keep your vow if it kills you."

"It might just do that." His eyes blazed. "What did I do to deserve you, Hope? You have made me the happiest man on earth."

"And you have taught me to trust, my love." She smiled. "It's only two weeks . . ."

Her emphasis on the word *trust* made him sigh. He was already counting the hours. But he was stubborn. A gentleman's word was sacred. "Now about the new wing . . ."